E.L. BATES

Magic Most Deadly

Contents

Acknowledgement

Ten years ago, I published my debut novel, a fantasy-mystery titled Magic Most Deadly. As the series progressed and my skills as a writer improved, I gradually became convinced of the need to update that book both to bring it more in line with the rest of the series, and to tighten and polish the writing itself. This book, the second (and heavily revised) edition of Magic Most Deadly, is the result of that conviction, and it couldn't have happened without help.

First thanks, as always, have to go to my long-suffering husband and children, who have endured many late and hurried meals, much distraction on my part during conversations, and a general state of chaos as I've tried to juggle work, writing, and school. Life with a writer can be hard sometimes, and I'm so thankful for the grace and love you three show me!

Thanks are also due to my husband for his Latin skills, without which the spells in this and all the Whitney & Davies books would be much shoddier.

I could never bring one of my books to life without my editor A.M. Offenwanger, who both gets the way my brain works and knows how to translate it to the rest of the world (and calls me out every single time I write something that I think is "good enough" and forces me to rewrite it until it is "as good as it can be"). Thank you so much, dear friend!

Thanks also go to my Tumblr friends who have cheered me

on every step of the way during this rewrite. I know most of you have a horror of your handles being widely known, so I won't name you all here, but know that I am so grateful for your encouragement, every one of you.

Special thanks to Kelsi Johnson for her incredible artwork of Maia and Len, now featured on bookmarks and stickers for the series!

Amanda McCrina designed the cover for the first edition of Magic Most Deadly, as well as every cover for Whitney & Davies since, and she was my first call when I started the rewrite, to see if she would be willing to do a new cover. It exceeded expectations! I'm always blown away by her skills. Thank you for sticking with me on this ten-year adventure, Amanda!

Finally, thank you to all the readers who have followed Len and Maia's adventures over the last ten years, and who have come back to this story to read and be enchanted by the beginning all over again. I hope this new version helps you fall in love with them even more—it did me.

1

The Beginning

"Sit down, Davies," Harrison said irritably.

Lennox Davies did not take the irritation to heart. Harrison Eastwood had been his mentor since Len was a youngster, and only once in his entire career had Len heard him sound anything less than short-tempered.

Professionally, that was. When not engaged in their particular line of work, Harrison was amiable and easy-going. Even after all these years, Len wasn't sure which was the mask and which the real man. Harrison's wife Joanna might know, but even though she and Len were cousins, she would never betray a secret of her husband's to him or anyone.

"What is it now, sir?" Len strove to keep his weariness from bleeding through his tone. He'd hoped for a few weeks off after the last job, to give him a chance to go north to Scotland and see his sister and her husband, or even just to enjoy some leisure in London, but he'd received word from Harrison yesterday that they needed him to take on another case.

"The Corbin affair has sprung to new life," Harrison said.

Len's weariness vanished. This was more than business as

usual. The Corbin affair had affected both him and Harrison on a deeply personal level.

"After all this time?" That affair had happened five years ago, in 1916, the heart of the war.

"MacDonald caught wind of him in France last month, and we've been tracking him down ever since. It seems he's going to be in Hertfordshire next week, and it's likely he'll be meeting with a buyer for the papers. We're not sure if the buyer is English, using them for their own personal gain, or a German seeking revenge, but either way—well, you know as well as I do that we cannot let those papers out of Corbin's hands."

"They should never have been in his hands in the first place," Len said, his own hands clenching involuntarily.

The lines in Harrison's face deepened. "We cannot afford to dwell on the past, my boy. What's done is done. All we can do now is try to ensure no one else is hurt through Corbin's actions."

Len took a few calming breaths. "What do you want me to do?"

"Daniel Foy's estate, Little Oaks, is in that part of the world, and his wife is hosting a house party next week. We think that Corbin's buyer may be a guest. Even if not, it would be a good base for you to use to snoop around. I've already had Joanna wangle you an invitation from Foy for the party. I want you to go down there and find Corbin, intercept the exchange, discover the identity of the buyer, and, as should go without saying, recover and destroy those papers."

Len raised an eyebrow. "And what will I do the second night?"

"It's no joking matter, Davies!" Harrison barked.

Len stifled a sigh. So much for lightening the atmosphere

with a bit of levity. "Of course not, sir."

"You'll take Becket with you, of course. He can investigate the servants while you hobnob with the lofty."

Len would have taken his valet regardless, but he wished Harrison hadn't made it an order. He trusted Becket, of course. The two had been working together for years, and Becket was excellent backup. But ever since 1916, Len had been uncomfortable with feeling responsible for other people's lives. He'd started trying to keep Becket out of dangerous situations as much as possible, preferring to work alone, where the only life at risk was his. Here, though … he had to admit that without any clue as to who Corbin's buyer might be, it was going to require someone downstairs as well as up to keep a proper eye out.

"Yes sir."

"You know the role you have to play as a guest, of course."

Of course. The wealthy, idle, man-about-town, without much of a brain in his head and no way to use it if he had one. That was Len's mask, and with each year that passed he was more concerned that the mask would one day become the man.

"Of course, sah," he said in an airy tone. "A house party will be just the ticket, don't you know. A good way to rest from all the frightful fuss and bother of life in town. Sometimes a fella just wants a bucolic country retreat, what? Shouldn't be surprised if I settle down on m'own estate one of these days—though then I'd have to be responsible for tenants and rents and drains and whatnot. Ghastly!" He gave an artistic shudder.

"You'll do." Harrison stood up from behind his desk, indicating the end of the interview. "And Len, I needn't tell you how important this is. Not only to bring closure for you and me, but for all of us. If Corbin sells those papers to the wrong person, the truth about magic could be revealed to the entire world, and the result would be a catastrophe worse than the war. For the sake of all magicians, not just in England but everywhere, *get those papers back.*"

"You have my word," Len said.

He left Harrison's office, automatically using his favorite chameleon spell to obscure him from any prying or curious eyes that might see and remember him. Not that there was anything too peculiar about Len choosing to visit his cousin's husband at his place of business, but the less the world saw of Harrison and Len together outside of family gatherings, the better.

He dropped the spell once he was several streets away, and stretched his long legs in a walk more suited to the open and free countryside than the crowded streets of East London. He barely noticed the people scrambling to get out of his way as he strode masterfully along.

He'd waited five years for this chance. Five years to finish the job he'd started and others had bungled. Five years to avenge Alec's death. Nothing was going to interfere with his mission this time.

A bitter smile crossed Len's lips. "Little Oaks, here I come."

2

Daughter of Stars

Maia Whitney pasted a smile on her face and hoped her exhaustion didn't leak onto her face or into her voice as she greeted her hostess for the evening with an appropriately light laugh.

"Julia darling! Did you receive my note about the party?"

"Yes, and I am extremely cross with you," Julia Foy answered with a scowl that sat oddly on a face made for laughter and merriment.

They were quite the contrast, Maia and Julia. Maia was tall and sturdily built, with chestnut hair cropped into a long bob, a wide mouth and square chin, and eyes that shone either blue or green depending on her mood. Julia was a petite and vivacious blonde, with her hair cut into a bob as short and stylish as that of Irene Castle in *The Amateur Wife*, a film Julia had told Maia she had seen and adored when she and Dan were over in the States the previous winter. Julia's eyes were brown, and she had a sparkle that lit her entire being, while Maia, though she hated to admit it, had never sparkled in her entire life. No one would have guessed, looking at them, that Julia was the elder,

5

being twenty-four years old to Maia's twenty-one.

The two women had worked together as nurses for the Voluntary Aid Detachment during the war and had, despite their differences (or perhaps because of them), become good friends. Maia was delighted when Julia came to visit her at Stanbury after the war, and even more when she had proceeded to meet, fall in love with, and marry the Whitneys' closest neighbor, Daniel Foy. Maia had been bridesmaid at their wedding, and the two had remained good friends ever since—no matter how "cross" Julia was with Maia now.

"Your note said that you cannot be a house guest after all," Julia said, "because your aunt is coming for an unexpected visit, but darling, that's absurd. If she has come unannounced it's too ridiculous of her to expect all the family to be at home, and anyway, surely she is there to see your mother and father, not you and your sisters. Besides, why should you have to stay home if Ellie and Merry can still come?"

"Merry's lectures on the Brotherhood of Man and the Degradation of Servitude have succeeded in inspiring our last two maids to pack their bags and become shop girls instead of housemaids," Maia said, letting her eyes stray to where her youngest sister was entrusting her small blue Austin Twenty automobile to one of the footmen.

"Oh no, not again," Julia said.

"Yes, and our housekeeper was so incensed at losing yet another batch of housemaids that she quit as well, which leaves only our cook," Maia said. "We cannot possibly get in new servants by tomorrow, so someone has to make sure that the guest room is ready and Mrs. Humphrey has everything she needs for meals."

Maia was aware that Julia knew better than to suggest Mrs.

Whitney take on that responsibility—a brief acquaintance with Maia's mother had shown her that Mrs. Whitney would make more of a mess of things than she would help.

"I suppose it's unreasonable to expect your sisters to help so that all of you could come, even if it would mean being later," she said with a sigh instead.

Maia raised her eyebrows. "Given that Merry's idea of helping is to chase away all our servants, and Ellie has inherited Mother's deep and abiding love of creating drama where none need exist … to be honest, I'd rather do it myself, even if it does mean giving up the house party." She struggled to keep the calm smile from slipping off her face.

Maia had long ago accepted that her role in her charming but chaotic family was to be the sensible one, the one who kept her head and kept things functioning despite her mother's drama, her father's tendency to disappear into his own world of books and daydreams, Ellie's self-centered view of life, and Merry's passion for lost causes. That didn't mean she enjoyed it. Especially lately. She'd had a difficult time slipping back into that role after her two years at the front (she had lied about her age when signing up in 1916, and they had been so desperate for volunteers they'd accepted her without question), and now, almost three years after the end of the war, she was still restless.

Surely there was something more she could do with her life, something of value, something that wasn't quite so mind-numbingly boring as soothing her sisters' tantrums and making her parents' lives easy. But was it selfish of her to wish to escape? Maia had seen enough selfishness from her family members that she had a horror of anything even close to that for herself.

Even this house party at Julia and Dan's—it had promised a brief but delightful escape from the mundanity of her everyday life, a chance to enjoy being taken care of instead of taking care of others, an opportunity to mingle with people outside her usual scope, who perhaps would not automatically dismiss her as "reliable but dull Maia Whitney." No, it had not been easy to give that up when they received the telegram from Aunt Amelia announcing her descent on them for the next day. But if she didn't stay home, who would?

"I was relying on you, you know," Julia said, slipping her arm through Maia's and walking with her along the terrace rather than going in through the double front doors along with Ellie and Merry, who had given perfunctory waves of greeting to their hostess but hadn't bothered coming over to say hello. "So many people, some of them friends or neighbors I invited and some Daniel's acquaintances from town … I don't know how I'm going to entertain them all, and I was certain you would be able to help me. I don't know if I can forgive you for only coming to dinner tonight instead!" She laughed.

A flare of anger spiked deep inside of Maia, surprising her in its intensity. For a moment, it was so strong her vision almost greyed out, leaving a silvery haze at the corners of her eyes. She blinked several times, trying to dislodge it. Despite the fact that it was a balmy day, almost too warm for September, a cold breeze came out of nowhere, causing both ladies to shiver. The coldness calmed Maia's tumultuous emotions somewhat, though the bitterness remained.

So Julia hadn't wanted Maia here for her company, but only for her help! Even to Julia, she was "good old reliable Maia," not "my friend with whom I enjoy spending time." Oh, Maia supposed she was a fool to ever hope for anything more, but so be it: she was a fool. If only there were something—someplace—*someone* who would value her for who she was, not for her abilities to make other people's lives easier!

In that moment, she was almost glad of Aunt Amelia's unexpected arrival. If all Maia was wanted for was her usefulness, she would be better off home at Stanbury. And at least with Merry and Ellie here at Little Oaks, she would be spared some of her usual family turmoil.

Maia relaxed further and her smile became almost genuine as she reflected that for once, Julia was helping her, by taking her sisters off her hands for the weekend, rather than Maia helping Julia.

The last vestiges of the silver haze vanished from her vision, and with that gone the air temperature returned to normal as well. Odd—but then, who could predict English weather?

"I suppose we'd best go in to dinner," Julia said, rubbing her bare arms with a puzzled frown. "If you can't help me for the entire weekend, you can at least support me through the evening!"

* * *

Dinner was an informal affair, as most of the staff were given over to preparations for the dance that was to follow. Julia cheerfully broke with convention by having her guests seated according to a whim of her own, rather than the typical man-woman-man-woman set up, and also made it clear she expected conversation to be general rather than limited to one's own dinner partners.

Maia found herself seated between Tim Spencer, a nice boy she'd known since he was in short trousers, and an unknown woman with dull blonde hair and lines of discontent worn into her face.

"Hullo, Maia," Tim said cheerfully.

"Hullo, Tim," she replied. "Is Laura here with you?"

"Oh yes, though I assume she's found Merry by now and the two are busy despising the rest of us as useless weight on society. Search me why either of them come to events like these if all they're going to do is criticize."

Laura was seventeen, a year younger than Tim and the same age as Merry, and the two girls had discovered politics at much the same time and were sorely trying their families' patience with their radical ways. Maia hoped that Laura had less success than Merry in inspiring the Spencer servants to give up their so-called menial employment for something nobler and more suited for an equal society.

It wasn't that Maia didn't approve of the idea of an equal society, it was simply that she found it terribly impractical to try to live with.

"Oh well, how would we know they disapprove of us if they didn't attend and spend the entire time criticizing?" she said now with a laugh.

Her neighbor on the other side sniffed. "Young women these days are given far too much freedom. When I was a girl, we respected our elders, spoke when we were spoken to, and knew our place."

Maia looked at her again. She didn't seem much more than thirty, which meant that she would have been a girl in the nineties. Victorian morals and modes were still in play then—how ghastly. As irritating as Merry's crazes and Ellie's dramatics were, and as horrible as the war had been, at least no one was expecting girls to sit at home anymore with hands folded and eyes demurely lowered.

"Young people always have their passions," Maia said. "I suppose politics are relatively harmless."

"Politics are no fit topic for young ladies!" her neighbor insisted. "And they are far from harmless. It's politics that start wars, you know. The wrong political ideas in the wrong hands …"

Tim coughed, and Maia held back a sigh. It was true that politics had the potential to be dangerous, but surely not in England—and in any case, this was hardly the time or the place for this sort of discussion. No wonder Julia had wanted her here!

It was an odd crowd, now that she took a moment to look around the table. There were the usual County young folk: Tim and Laura Spencer; Paul and Rob Danvers, the vicar's sons; Maia herself and Merry and Ellie. Then there were the Honorable Frederick Winters and his sister Hermione, daring as usual in her masculine attire of impeccably tailored trousers and dinner jacket. They were friends of Julia's family, Maia recalled from the last time they had paid a visit to Little Oaks. The rest must have been Dan's acquaintances from town: the woman seated on Maia's right; a faded, indeterminate-looking man around the same age sitting across from her; a gentleman with a narrow, pointed face and over-bright brown eyes next to Ellie; and another gentleman sitting directly across from Maia, a tall, well-built man perhaps a few years older than herself, with dark hair, blue eyes that crinkled at the corners, and a determined chin.

None of them seemed likely to get along well with the others, aside from Freddie Winters and maybe the gentleman across the table. He spoke up now, having apparently been following their conversation rather than participating in his own—no wonder, with Merry on one side ignoring him in favor of lecturing Paul Danvers on the snobbery of public schools, and the Honorable Hermione on the other looking impatiently at the clock as she waited for the meal to end and the dance to begin (though by all accounts it wasn't the dancing that Miss Winters fancied, but the games of chance that generally accompanied it).

"I've always believed it was the desire for power that started wars," the dark-haired man said, "and politics merely serves as the excuse."

His voice was deep and rich, rumbling up from his chest and easily cutting through the higher-pitched tones around him.

Maia's neighbor tossed her head and sniffed again, but made no reply. The gentleman caught Maia's eye and smiled at her in a conspiratorial manner. She couldn't help but smile back, wondering just who he was as she did. He was old enough to have fought in the war—was his opinion of it influenced by his own experience? She would have liked to ask him more about what he meant about power and politics, but there was no time now. Much to the relief of the Honorable Hermione and the delight of Ellie and others, Julia announced that it was time for them to leave the table and prepare for the dance, as the first guests were about to arrive.

Maia grimaced and lightly rubbed her temples. She was quite good at dancing, and enjoyed it when she had the chance, but somehow men never seemed to want her for a partner. She wasn't sure if it was because she was too tall or if she simply did not look like someone who would dance well, but whatever the reason, dances were often frustrating for her, always wanting to participate and rarely being able to.

Besides that, people were bound to be smoking, and of late, Maia had found that the smell of cigarette smoke made her terribly ill. It was noticeable enough that even her mother had said something the last time Maia had fled, green-faced, from Ellie's attempt at sophistication with a cigarette in a long jade holder.

"Really, Maia, one wouldn't expect you to be so finicky!" she'd said. "You needn't make everything about you. Your sister can smoke the occasional cigarette without you having to make an exhibition of yourself. Honestly, you remind me more and more of my sister Amelia."

As this was the same Amelia who had unexpectedly announced her visit one day before her arrival, Maia now found that comparison even more insulting than she had at the time.

Whatever the cause, Maia was not looking forward to spending the evening in a room full of people smoking, especially when it was unlikely she'd even be able to dance much to make up for it. Her headache had returned, and with it those same silver flickers at the edge of her vision. She ought to see an oculist, she supposed. She'd had these sort of headaches before, when she was around fourteen, but then the war began and she'd had so much else to occupy her attention that she had not had the time to do anything about them, and eventually they went away on their own. She hadn't even thought about them in years, until they started coming back a month or so ago.

Julia appeared at her side as they all left the dining room for Little Oaks' well-designed ballroom.

"Maia darling, I want you to meet someone," she said, looping her arm through Maia's. To Maia's disappointment, the "someone" was not the deep-voiced gentleman who had sat across the table from her, but rather the gentleman with the pointed face and reddish hair, who reminded her of a fox.

"Sir Bertram Grimes, my dear friend, Maia Whitney. Maia was supposed to be a guest at the house party this weekend, Sir Bertram, and I was counting on her to provide you with intellectual conversation, but family duty calls and she'll only be here for the evening, so you must make the most of her time. Maia, Sir Bertram owns several factories and has the most modern outlook on how to operate them—I can't understand half of what he says, but I know you'll be interested."

With that, she vanished, leaving Maia and Sir Bertram to size each other up.

"Are you interested in factories and modern working methods, Miss Whitney?" Sir Bertram asked.

"Not especially," she answered with caution, not wanting to offend but also unwilling to pretend an interest where none existed. "My younger sister Merope might be, though. She has quite strong opinions on the poor conditions for today's workers."

"Ah," Sir Bertram said. His eyes gleamed. "Yet you must have some opinions on the matter, or Mrs. Foy would not have introduced us. Unless she had other motivations?" He glanced down at Maia's left hand, where no ring shone on any finger.

Maia stiffened. Was he implying that this was some matchmaking scheme? Odious little man! How appallingly vulgar! Heat rushed into her cheeks, through anger rather than embarrassment, and it took an act of severe self-control to keep her hands from clenching into fists.

"I don't believe I quite understand you," she said, her tone icy. "Excuse me, Sir Bertram."

She stalked away into the ballroom, hearing a contemptuous

snort behind her from the odious fox-man. What on earth had possessed Daniel to invite him to the house party this weekend?

Under ordinary circumstances, Maia appreciated the ballroom at Little Oaks. It had been dark and dingy when Julia first married Dan, but since then, the couple had improved it vastly. The walls were papered in a soft green with thin gold vertical stripes, and the same gold was picked up in the trim along the tops of the walls and the windows. French windows lined one side, opening onto the terrace in good weather and covered with warm brown curtains in poor. The floor was polished parquet, chandeliers and wall fixtures brought electric light into the room, and overall it was an example of marvelous good taste and wise expenditure.

Tonight, filled as it already was with a band and gyrating bodies on the parquet floor, Maia was nearly repulsed by it. Already disappointed by the way the evening was going and irritated at Sir Bertram's insinuations, she was in no mood to find enjoyment in the sight of other people behaving like fools. She brushed past a potted fern, noting in passing how withered and brown it seemed—odd, that, as the staff would surely have not placed a dying fern in the ballroom at all, much less so close to the entryway—and tried to squeeze her way around the edges of the crowd to reach the French doors, where she could escape into the fresh air and breathe freely before making her excuses to Julia and going home.

"Maia! I've barely had a chance to say one word to you all evening. How are you, m'dear?"

Maia had to stop and smile at her host, Julia's husband and her neighbor. They hadn't grown up together, the way the Whitneys, Spencers, and Danvers' had.. Though Little Oaks had been in the Foy family for several generations, it had belonged to Dan's uncle. But that elder Mr. Foy's son, a grave man some ten years older than Maia, had been killed at Mons in 1914, and when his father had died of old age and heartbreak only two years later, Dan was left the unexpected heir.

Dan had had his own troubles in the war, having lost his right leg on the battlefield. He'd been fitted with a false leg and got about on that admirably, with only the slightest hint of a limp, but it did eliminate many of the activities that other men his age enjoyed, dancing being one of them. He still rode, but only for pleasure, not for hunting, and more active games such as football, cricket, and tennis were also no longer available to him. Luckily he enjoyed reading, and he and Julia went on long walks through the Chiltern Hills together, but Maia knew it couldn't have been easy for him.

Yet with all that, Daniel Foy remained pleasant, uncomplaining, and one of the kindest men Maia had ever met. Even in her current black mood, she couldn't be irritable with him.

"I'm a little overwhelmed with all these people," she answered him honestly. "Where does Julia find them all?"

Dan raised one shoulder in an amused shrug. "The Good Lord above only knows."

Maia wanted to say something about the guests he had brought to the house, but she decided that would be rude, and swallowed her words.

"Would you like a drink, old thing? I believe Julia has champers circulating, or I can get you a sherry if you prefer." Dan's face creased in a smile. "I heard Ellie complaining earlier about the lack of any new and exciting cocktails, but somehow I don't think you'd be bothered by that."

Maia laughed with him. "No, indeed not. And I apologize

for my sister's rudeness."

Dan waved a hand. "Good heavens, don't think of it! Ellie is just a little thoughtless sometimes, that's all. We're all of us afflicted with that in our youth. Age and experience beats it out of us soon enough." A momentary shadow darkened his eyes, and Maia felt a sympathetic chill.

The war had aged so many of them far too early.

A couple whirled past, the lady holding a cigarette with noxious smoke pouring from its tip. Nausea rose up in Maia's throat, and even Dan's nose wrinkled.

"I think I'll pass on that drink," Maia choked out. "I find myself in dire need of fresh air."

Without waiting for Dan to answer for fear that if she stayed there one more moment she would embarrass herself and everyone else horribly by being sick, Maia fled for the French doors, not even noticing the way the crowd parted smoothly around her without a single person so much as brushing her skirt. Her entire being was concentrated on getting outside.

As it was such a warm evening, the doors were unlatched and partially open. Maia slipped through onto the terrace, where she breathed deeply for what felt like the first time since arriving at Little Oaks.

The lawn, gray in the moonlight, rolled down gracefully to the edge of the woods that separated Little Oaks from Stanbury, the Whitney home. The path between the two properties had been barely used in the years before Dan and Julia were married, but was now well-trodden from the frequent visits Julia and Maia made to each other. Maia looked longingly in that direction, but supposed she really ought not to flee before saying goodbye to Julia and Dan and getting a footman to fetch her coat. Not that she needed a coat on a night such as this, even though she was, daringly enough for her, wearing a sleeveless evening dress. Still, it wouldn't do to leave her wrap behind; this time of year, one never knew when the weather might turn, and she wouldn't want to have to come back here tomorrow for it.

No, the best thing to do would be to sit here on the terrace until she felt she could bear to go back inside with all the crush of people, bid her hosts farewell, ask Mrs. Blackwood, the housekeeper, to send a footman for her coat, and then leave.

Maia suited action to thought, and she seated herself at one of the small wrought-iron tables scattered along the terrace, deliberately choosing one out of way of the windows, so she couldn't be seen from inside. She leaned back and tilted her head to look at the moon, shining silver in the dark sky. There was something comforting about its cool color and calm distance from the troubles and worries of earth. What wouldn't she give for a chance to fly up there in the night sky and escape her mundane life, with its endless duties and responsibilities that had so little to show for it!

"Excuse me, I hope you don't mind, but I brought you some sherry," said the beautifully rich, deep voice of the gentleman from across the table.

Maia wrenched her gaze back to earth with a start. "Oh!" she said inanely as the man set two glasses of lemonade down on the table and seated himself across from her.

"Terribly rude to presume like this when we haven't even been introduced, but I saw you leave just as I was looking for a way to escape the crush, and so I snatched two glasses from a passing tray and followed in your wake." He smiled. "I'll leave if you prefer solitude."

Maia was flustered over the thought that this man—any

man—had not only noticed her, but had chosen to follow her rather than enjoy the company of others. "I—no, thank you, you're very kind."

The horrible thought that perhaps he *was* only being kind, that he'd followed her out of pity—or worse, that Julia had asked him to come after her—crossed her mind. She tried to push it away, but it stayed a tickle in the back of her thoughts, causing her to stiffen up despite herself. Her companion didn't seem to notice.

"A beautiful night like this seems a shame to waste on being indoors, don't you think? I can't imagine why everyone isn't out here enjoying it."

"Just as well," Maia said despite her discomfort. "Then the crowd would be out here and we'd have to go back inside." Oh horrors—she'd said *we*, as though they were together! How awful! He would think she was throwing herself at him.

The gentleman didn't seem discomposed by her statement. Quite the opposite, as he tossed his head back and laughed heartily. "A fair point!" he said. "We'll leave them to their music and their dancing and be the only sensible ones in the entire bunch."

Sensible again. Maia winced. It wasn't that she wanted to be insensible, but she was tired of that always being the only way anyone ever described her. At least this man included himself in that description.

"I used to dream of flying up to the moon," he said now, looking upward. "On a night like tonight it almost seems possible."

"I was just thinking how lovely it would be to go soaring through the night sky," Maia blurted. Worse and worse— now it sounded like she was echoing him like a sycophant.

Whatever was wrong with her tonight? She wasn't usually this gauche. As pleasant as this gentleman was, if she was going to embarrass herself every time she spoke to him she almost wished he would go away.

"Were you really? How splendid!" he said heartily. "Tell me, if you could pick, would you choose to visit the moon or a star?"

"You mean, if stars weren't really distant suns?" Maia said.

He waved an impatient hand. "Yes, yes, let's not bother about technicalities. Imagine that a star is a shining planetary body and you could set foot on it without burning up. Which would you visit?"

"A star," Maia said without hesitation. She'd never thought about it before, but she knew it without a doubt.

"Jolly good! Which one?"

Now she did hesitate—it sounded so pretentious.

"Go on," he said, leaning forward. "I'll tell if you do."

Maia gave in. She'd already made an idiot of herself several times in front of this man, what would one more hurt? Besides, this was the maddest conversation she'd ever had with a stranger, and she was rather enjoying the Alice in Wonderland feel of it.

"I'd visit my star, of course. My namesake." She couldn't help smiling at his confused expression. "My father is a classical scholar, and he named my sisters and me for the Pleiades. I'm Maia, and my sisters are Electra and Merope. I think Papa was always a little disappointed that there weren't seven of us to complete the set."

"I like that," the gentleman said, his eyes looking over her face and then gazing back up at the night sky. "You're a daughter of the stars."

Nobody had *ever* said anything like that about Maia before. She couldn't decide if she should be flattered or suspicious of such an extravagant compliment.

"And which would you travel to, the moon or a star?" she asked, to hide her confusion.

"The moon," he said. "Although I wish I had as good a reason to visit the stars as you do. But there's something about the moon … it's so far off, but not as far as the stars, and the way it waxes and wanes in a pattern no matter what other sort of madness is happening in the world … The moon was a good friend to me during the war. Madmen are said to be moonstruck, but I think the moon kept me sane." He stopped and brought his eyes back to her. "D'you know, I don't think I've ever told anyone that before."

"Oh," Maia said.

He smiled again, and this time there was real warmth in the smile rather than mere politeness. "You told me your name—at least your first name, and I met Miss Electra earlier and if she's your sister I know your family name is Whitney—but I haven't told you mine yet, even though you've been listening to me chattering on about all sorts of nonsense. I'm Lennox Davies. My friends call me Len."

"How do you do," Maia said automatically, then felt, once again, like a fool. What an absurd thing to say after the conversation they'd been having!

But once again Mr. Davies didn't seem bothered by her stupidity. "I am very well indeed, Miss Whitney. Very well indeed."

3

Death in the Dark

Len realized the smile on his face was real, not the practiced smirk of the fool-about-town he was supposed to act. He'd slipped out of character in the conversation as well—the questions were supposed to be silly, but something about Miss Whitney had struck a spark, and he'd found himself enjoying the back and forth too much. Dash it, he had only come out here because he thought there was a strong chance the papers were going to be exchanged tonight, and more likely outside than in, and bringing her a drink had made a good excuse for following her out. He'd expected her to say yes, she had come out here to be alone—she had that look about her—but she'd been too gracious, and the next thing he knew they were having a real conversation.

He wasn't supposed to be a real person to anyone when he was on a job. What was he thinking?

Miss Whitney did look smashing in the moonlight. Her frock looked black out here, but he knew from earlier that it was a rich red frock that brought out the red in her otherwise brown hair. The simple style looked elegant on her tall, stately frame.

He couldn't tell the color of her eyes, but he liked the wisdom and the patience behind them, not something one usually found in a woman of that age. Yet she wasn't anywhere near stuffy or dull, either. He'd seen the humor in her at dinner, and she'd shown it again now.

In fact, if he was honest—which he always tried to be with himself, at least, since he couldn't be with anyone else—he had been paying more attention to her in the ballroom than he had been to the rest of the crowd, and following her out had been a pleasure more than an excuse. He would have to be careful. This was no time to lose his head over a woman, no matter how engaging her smile or how well-spoken she was or how enchanting he found her laugh.

He tore his gaze away from her face in time to see a shadow slip out through one of the other windows opening onto the terrace a short distance behind Miss Whitney. He couldn't make out details from this distance in the poor light, aside from the fact that it was a man, and of about average height and build. There was no woman with him, or Len might have suspected a tryst. As it was, he suspected this was the buyer of the papers, leaving for the meeting.

Len needed to follow him, but having engaged Miss Whitney in conversation he couldn't very well bolt after the fellow without a word of explanation.

"I do beg your pardon, Miss Whitney, but I am suddenly finding myself in need of stretching my legs. Dashed long auto ride here this afternoon, y'see, and then sitting all through the meal. I think I'll take a turn around the garden."

Miss Whitney rose when he did. "I suppose I ought to return inside," she said, not-quite-sighing. Len had the mad impulse to ask her to walk with him, as she was clearly much too proper to invite herself—but of course he couldn't, since he wasn't actually walking around the garden, but following a sneaking villain, who even now was crossing the lawn and heading toward the woods.

Len must have been too obvious in watching the fellow, or else missed his proper cue to respond to Miss Whitney's statement, for she frowned and followed his line of sight to where the man was furtively skirting the edge of the lawn.

She looked at Len, looked back at the man, and looked at Len again, her brain clearly trying to work out what was going on.

Len hastened into an explanation that he hoped would satisfy. "You caught me, Miss Whitney. I saw this fellow creep out in a furtive way, and I think he might be stealing something from the Foys, or up to something unsavory. I don't want to accuse him without proof, though, especially since there's a chance he's just a waiter sneaking out to meet his sweetheart, don't you know, so I thought I might follow him and see what he's up to before deciding on a course of action."

To his surprise, a flash of something like excitement crossed Miss Whitney's face. "Right!" she said. "Let's go."

"What—not you," Len said, casting another agonized glance. The man was entering the fringe of the woods now. If he didn't hurry, he'd lose him. "It could be dangerous."

"I know these woods better than you, better than probably anyone else here, including Dan," Maia said. "I can help you follow him without needing to use the trail, so that we can stay hidden. Besides, there's no way I would let someone possibly steal from Julia and Dan and not try to stop them. If you don't let me come with you, I'll come alone."

There was no more time to argue, and Len couldn't very well use a spell on a non-magician to stop her, although really he wasn't supposed to use spells even on other magicians, as that sort of thing was frowned upon by the High Council. Still, sometimes in his work he had to do the ungentlemanly thing.

Not in this case, though. There was no yielding in the laws against letting non-magicians find out about magic.

"Very well," he said, giving in. He would just have to figure out a way to keep her from learning what was really going on while at the same time stopping the exchange of the papers. A dashed nuisance, but what could he do?

This was what came of letting oneself be distracted by a delightful woman.

Len stalked off the terrace, trusting Miss Whitney to keep up, only to find her moving briskly ahead of him.

"I say, hold up, if the fellow is watching from the trees he'll see us!" he hissed, catching up to her.

"Not if it looks like we're going elsewhere," she said, veering from the path. "This will make it seem like we're going to the glasshouse, but there's a break in the treeline before we get there that will let us walk parallel to the path. If we're quick enough, we can walk beside this man instead of following him, and we won't have to worry about being seen." She cast a quick glance at his feet. "So long as we can move quietly, that is."

Len wasn't about to tell her that there had been more than once that his life had depended on his ability to move quietly, and since he was still here, obviously it had worked, but his pride was ruffled.

Still, her plan was a good one, and enough to make him almost glad she had insisted on joining him. Had he been alone he could have used the chameleon spell to go unnoticed behind this chap, but this allowed him to save his strength for a bigger spell, should it be necessary to prevent the exchange of the papers.

How he was going to use any spell without Miss Whitney noticing was another matter, but he would face that challenge when and if it arose.

Against all reason, Len's spirits lifted. Dire as the situation was, nothing made him feel more alive than using his wits and keeping on his toes, ready to jump one way or the other depending on the situation, everything on the line and no one to save his skin should he fail. This was what kept him in the job through the bleak times. This was why he could never quit to live the life of a leisured English gentleman, return to the family estate and settle down to raise a family and keep the Davies line going for another generation. No feeling in the world was better than this.

They had reached the gap in the trees by this point. It was narrow, but Miss Whitney turned sideways and slipped through without so much as a flutter of her skirt catching on the rough bark of the oak tree. Len hunched his shoulders, sucked in his stomach, and followed suit. He felt his back scrape against the tree a little, but considering how much broader he was than Miss Whitney, he wasn't too terribly ashamed.

"Stay close," she muttered, avoiding the hissing sibilants that would have come with a whisper. Dash it all, if only she were a magician, what an agent she would make! She had all the right instincts.

Len followed hard on her heels, admiring how quietly she stepped, never once cracking so much as a twig. He hoped she was as impressed with his ability to move silently. There were patches of moonlight filtering through the trees here and there, but for the most part it was instinct and training that kept him from tripping over roots or rocks or walking into branches.

They had gone about a hundred feet into the woods, in a particularly dense part with practically no light coming through the trees at all, when he heard the voices. Len stopped at once, resting a hand on Miss Whitney's shoulder to stop her as well, though from the way she froze it seemed unnecessary—she must have heard them too.

The trees and the darkness hid the speakers from Len and Miss Whitney, but the words carried clearly through the air.

"Do you have them?"

The voice was exactly that hissing whisper that Miss Whitney had avoided so adroitly. It carried admirably on the still night, but was unfortunately stripped of anything that might identify the speaker. Len cursed silently and wished for a spell to help him see in the dark. Such things were considered highly dangerous—casting a spell on oneself was not as bad as casting a spell on another person, but still carried high risk—but he would have done it if he'd been a stronger magician. With his skills, though, he could only get halfway through before losing strength, and that would be a disaster.

He was back to trusting his wits and straining his ears. Ignoring Miss Whitney for the moment, he moved in the direction of the voice, stopping before he crossed the line of trees next to the path. He stayed in the deepest shadows, pressed tightly against a tree so that he couldn't be seen. Unfortunately, that limited his ability to see as well—he could make out the outlines of three people, but nothing more. Still, at least now he was close enough to do *something* when the time came.

A presence at his elbow told him Miss Whitney had moved forward with him. He wished she'd stayed behind, but that would have been too much to hope for. She had already proven she was not the type to stay safe when dangerous deeds needed to be done. It was an admirable trait, but at the moment, one he wished she didn't have.

"Of course I have them," another voice answered the first. This was louder than the whisper, clearly male, and clearly nervous. "Do you have the money?"

That had to be Corbin. Selling the papers for money! Len clenched his fists. Alec—and Jamie—had paid for those papers with their lives, and Corbin would trade them for filthy lucre. He would wring the fellow's neck—once the papers were secure. Until then, he would muster his patience.

"And who is this?" the whisperer hissed. "I thought we agreed no witnesses?"

"My valet," Corbin said sullenly. "I'm not so stupid as to come alone. I know your reputation. He's here to make sure you don't kill me and take them without paying."

"And how will he do that?"

"He has a pistol aimed at you." Now Corbin sounded smug. "If you don't follow through, he'll shoot you."

Len's entire body stiffened. Firearms! This had gotten much more dangerous, especially for the silent woman at his side. He knew a spell to ruin the inner works of any gun, but how to cast it without Miss Whitney noticing?

"How clever of you," the whisperer hissed. "But how do I know that you don't intend to take my money and then have your man shoot me rather than give me the papers?"

"You'll have to trust me," Corbin said.

Len held back a snort. He held the intention of the gun-ruining spell firmly in his mind. Luckily it was too dark for Miss Whitney to clearly see his motions for casting the spell, but she might sense his movement. He would have to shape the incantation with his mouth and made the motions subtly with his hands, and hope that it was enough to work without Miss Whitney noticing anything odd. Breathing slowly and steadily, he opened his mouth to begin.

"Trust you? I think not," the whisperer said. "And unfortunately for you, I have excellent night vision. I know exactly where your man is standing."

"What does that matt—" Corbin began, when there was a loud "pop" and a brief flash of light followed instantly by a soft sigh, a crackle of branches, and a thump as the third outline crumpled to the ground.

Len went cold. He knew those sounds. The threads of the spell were lost as he frantically went over his options of how to salvage this mess and protect Miss Whitney who, the Lord be thanked, hadn't moved a muscle since this entire thing started.

"What—Carter!" Corbin shouted.

"He is dead," the whisperer said, and the lack of any emotion in that voice would have chilled Len's blood if he hadn't already been cold as ice. "You fool! You brought along a man to protect you who couldn't see his target in the dark—or when his target was aiming a weapon at him in return. Now, give me those papers."

"You killed him," Corbin said, sounding stunned. "You killed my man."

"I'll kill you too if you don't give me those papers."

There was a softer "thump" as Corbin presumably tossed the case containing the papers at the whisperer.

"My thanks," the hiss came. "Here is your reward."

Len braced himself for another shot, but the noise this time was a jingle, as of coins in a pocket. There was another brief flash of light, as Corbin risked a torch in order to see what the whisperer had thrown to him. The light was aimed down, preventing Len from making out any details of the two remaining men, but he saw the glint of metal and heard the clinking of coins.

"What is this? This is just a few… Thirty silver shillings! That wasn't what we agreed upon! Cheat! Cheat and murderer!"

"The proper payment for those who betray their own," the whisperer said. "At least you have your life. I suggest you leave now, before I change my mind."

Corbin swore horribly, but his fear was greater than his outrage, for eventually he turned, torched aimed at the ground before him, and crashed down the path away from Little Oaks. Len tensed his muscles. Now was the time—he would cast the spell to destroy the whisperer's gun, spring out upon him, and wrest the papers from him. He began to mutter the incantation under his breath.

"Who's there?"

In addition to excellent night vision, the whisperer appeared to have uncanny hearing. Len closed his mouth abruptly. For himself, he would risk getting shot, but he couldn't run the chance of Miss Whitney being injured or killed. Despite Harrison's warning of how important these papers were, despite his own burning desire to see Alec's death avenged, despite his years of training, Len could not see another innocent life taken because of these papers—and because of his ineptitude.

The whisperer would return to Little Oaks. He had no

reason to believe himself suspected. Len could track him down and regain the papers there.

He kept his mouth closed and his hands by his side, and stayed firmly behind his tree while the whisperer moved closer to the edge of the path, almost certainly looking for whoever or whatever had made the noise. Len wished he weren't wearing a white shirt under his dinner jacket, but the tree protected him from even the whisperer's excellent night vision, as after a few moments of scuffling about the whisperer, apparently satisfied, moved back up the path toward Little Oaks. They heard his footsteps retreating through the trees.

Still Len waited, and Miss Whitney with him, in case it was a trick, but at last, when the night creatures started up their usual chorus again, he breathed out and dared move.

"I say, Miss Whitney," he said. "Are you all right?"

His mind still stunned by the events that had just occurred, he struggled to focus his attention on his companion, especially as she too seemed to have taken refuge behind a tree when the whispering murderer had looked for them. Len squinted, and it suddenly appeared as though a faint silver glow outlined Miss Whitney's body. The moon must have come out from behind a cloud—but no, that didn't make sense, either, as it had never gone behind one. What was this?

He shook his head. Whatever the cause, the faint light allowed him to see that at least Miss Whitney was still upright, albeit hanging on to a beech tree as though for dear life.

"I am not sure that I can move," she said, her voice remarkably steady. "My body decided to stop obeying me the instant that one man fired—fired the—the gun."

Len tried for a light tone. "Dashed good thing it decided to take charge by freezing, then."

"Yes, it would have been rather inconvenient if it had decided to break into a foxtrot, wouldn't it?" Miss Whitney's giggle sounded dangerously close to a sob. Len recognized the signs of incipient hysteria, in part because he'd seen it in many people before now, men and women, and in part because he was feeling more than a little on edge himself.

"I say, Miss Whitney, this won't do. Awfully sorry and all that, but we simply must pull ourselves together long enough to get back to the house." He took off his jacket and draped it around her shoulders, hoping the warmth would help to steady her.

She sobered. "You're right. We must get help. That poor man! I should check … he might still be alive. If I can stop the bleeding while you get help …"

Len didn't think there was any hope, but she was right, they should check. Not that he had any intention of leaving a lady with a dying man while he trotted off to fetch help! He wasn't sure he even *could* get help. Where did his duty lie now? He had to recover those papers—would a dead body complicate or aid his mission?

"I don't think it's right for you to have to go near," he said. "I can check him while you go find Foy and bring him here."

"Nonsense," she said, and she gave herself a shake and then moved past him, ducking under the low-hanging branches of the hemlock bordering the path. "I was a nurse for over two years during the war, Mr. Davies. I've seen dead and dying men plenty of times before now."

With no argument against that, Len closed his mouth and once again followed her.

On the path, the moonlight was clearer, and he could see the crumpled body of the shot man in a sad heap on the ground.

Miss Whitney dropped to her knees beside him, regardless of any potential damage to her dress, and felt for a heartbeat before pulling back.

"Shot cleanly through the heart," she said, sorrow lacing her words. "The poor man never had a chance."

Len wordlessly handed her his handkerchief so she could wipe her stained fingers. She did so, and then gently placed the handkerchief over the man's face.

"What now?" she asked, rising to her feet. "One of us should go fetch the police. I don't mind staying with the—the body, but I also know the police sergeant and might have an easier time persuading him this is not some drunken sport Dan and Julia's rowdier guests are indulging in."

"No police!" Len blurted. The last thing he needed were some clod-hopper local policemen trampling all over and getting in his way.

He couldn't make out details of Miss Whitney's facial expression, but from the surprise in her voice he imagined her eyebrows had raised exactly as Len's sister's governess's used to do when Pippa misbehaved. "Whyever not?"

Lennox Davies had been an agent for Magical Intelligence since he was eighteen, and apprenticed to an agent for three years before that. Never before in his career had he found himself wholly at a loss for a plausible story. He was a mediocre magician, but a gifted storyteller, which went a long way toward making up for his lack of magical prowess.

Now, however, faced with a situation the likes of which he'd never been in before, his mind went entirely blank.

"Well, Mr. Davies?"

When no plausible lie presents itself, try the truth—it might just work. Or at least a version of the truth.

"Those papers that the men were here to exchange … they contain important government secrets."

"Oh *really*, Mr. Davies."

"I know it sounds absurd, but it is true—secrets that date back to the war, to alliances and promises that should never have been made, much less recorded, only it was seen as necessary then for the survival of Britain and France. They were stolen, and one of our people—"

"'Our' people?" she interrupted.

"Yes," said Len, without elaborating. "One of our people got wind that they were going to be sold at this house party, which is why I am here. I was meant to stop the sale and retrieve the papers. We did not expect murder to be done over it."

"You are serious, aren't you?" Miss Whitney asked.

"Deadly serious," Len assured her.

She was silent for a few moments, apparently mulling this over. Len needed to return to Little Oaks, to see if he could discover the identity of the murderer or at least determine who had been gone from the dance and who hadn't so he could narrow down his list of suspects, but he could give Miss Whitney a brief period of time to take all this in.

"I don't know why, but I believe you," she said at last. "Perhaps because I can't think of anything else that fits the events that have happened here this evening." She paused a moment more, then said briskly. "Very well. You are saying, I take it, that you work for the British government, but in such a secretive capacity that you dare not even involve the police?"

"Exactly," Len said flatly, astonished at how well and practically she was taking this. He had anticipated a demand for more information, one that he would have to refuse, and a long and drawn-out argument. He wasn't quite sure if he could trust her seeming reasonableness.

"So you don't want the police involved because you don't want to have to explain all of this to them, and you'd rather retrieve the papers quietly," she mulled, an edge to her voice.

Len hurried to explain as much as he was able. "It isn't that I don't want this poor chap to receive justice, but rather that I can't afford to be mixed up in this as a witness. It is important that I be able to stay in the shadows so as to be able to move freely and discover who took the papers, and then get them back. If we tell the police what we heard, they're going to start asking questions about just what was so important one man would kill for, and you and I might be called at the inquest, and I might even be a suspect, though likely not you if you know the police, and …"

"I understand," Miss Whitney said, cutting him off. Her voice was warmer now. "And even if we tell them we simply found his body, we'd have to explain why we were in the woods, and many of those same difficulties might arise."

Len could think of one good reason why a man and a woman would sneak off away from a party into the woods, but he didn't want to even *hint* at that to Miss Whitney.

"Very well," she said after thinking more. "You must return to Little Oaks, and I'll continue home, and when I get back I'll telephone the police that I found a dead body in the woods."

"Home?" Len asked. "What do you mean?"

"Oh, of course, you wouldn't know—I'm not an overnight guest at the house party, I live just over the hill, at Stanbury Manor. I was at Little Oaks for dinner and the dance, and my sisters are staying, but I had to go home in order to prepare for a guest who will be arriving tomorrow." Len heard a rueful tone enter her voice. "So it will be perfectly plausible that I was coming home alone through the shortcut in the woods when I stumbled over the body."

"Oh, but I say, really—Miss Whitney, I can't let you simply walk home alone after this!"

Miss Whitney's laugh, when not tinged with hysteria, was as clear and crystalline as Len would have imagined for a star's namesake. "I'm afraid there's no way around it, not if we want to keep your name out of the situation while still ensuring that this poor fellow is given a proper burial and investigation. And I don't think you need worry about the police interfering with your own investigation—if anything, if they catch the murderer it ought to be easier for you to recover those papers."

That was a fair point, though he rather doubted any local police force had sufficient wits to catch whoever was responsible for this. Still, if they were sniffing around after a murderer, no one would pay much attention to Len snooping for papers, and he could always claim he was trying to help the police by finding clues if anyone did notice his actions.

Really, if it weren't for the fact that he'd have to let Miss Whitney bear the responsibility for this, it was the best solution one could hope for.

"Very well," he said reluctantly. "Though I still feel a heel for letting you do this."

"Nonsense, it's only common sense," she said briskly. She started to remove his jacket to return to him.

"Keep it," he said. "It's a pleasant night, but it will still be chilly walking home. I say—" he had a flash of brilliance. "We'll say that I met you in the garden at the dance and you said you were not feeling quite the thing and wanted to go home, but didn't want to have to fetch your coat, so I lent you mine. That way it will seem perfectly reasonable for me to come to your house—Stanbury Manor, you said?—tomorrow to bring you your coat and retrieve mine. I know you said you have a guest coming, but I won't take up much of your time, and that way you can tell me how things went with the police."

"Excellent!" Miss Whitney said. "And now, I suppose, we ought to be going." She glanced down. "It seems wrong to leave him here … but there's nothing else to be done, is there?"

"Nothing right now," Len agreed, his voice sober. "But we'll see to it he doesn't go unavenged."

Now, why did he say "we?" Really, the best thing to do was let her go, ring the police, and then stay out of each other's way at least until Len's own task was done. But somehow, he couldn't bring himself to do that. Miss Whitney was a dashed good sport, and even though he couldn't let her in on all his secrets, the way she had responded to the first one made him wish he could. They would make a good team.

Harrison would be furious about all this, but Len's ability to adapt to swiftly-changing circumstances was another of his assets in the field. If Harrison didn't like it, *he* could try coming back and being a field agent again. Otherwise, he would simply have to trust Len's judgment.

"Good," Miss Whitney replied. "Well then—good night, Mr. Davies."

"Good night, Miss Whitney," Len replied, feeling suddenly bereft as she carefully picked her way past him and on down the path. He kept watching even as the gloom swallowed her up, until even the sound of her footsteps faded into the night.

He heaved a sigh, turning back in the direction of Little Oaks. Miss Whitney would perform her task admirably, he was certain, and in the meantime, he had his own work to do. It was time he got to it.

4

A Stunning Truth

This was not the worst walk Maia had ever taken, but it was by no means her best, either. Despite her airy words to Mr. Davies, she could not feel entirely comfortable as she hurried along the path as quickly as she could without tripping and falling or spraining an ankle. She'd never thought of herself as over-burdened with imagination, rather the opposite, but her fancy had no trouble whatsoever in peopling the woods with murderers and thieves lurking behind every tree, ready to pop out and steal her life too, just like that poor man lying back there on the path.

Maia shivered. Not even the lingering warmth left behind in Mr. Davies' jacket was enough to chase away the chill that shook her. She'd thought she had left that kind of violence behind when she came home to England from France in 1918. She never expected to find it practically on her doorstep. Indignation rose up in her throat. How dare those brutes bring their treachery and their murder to Stanbury? Stanbury, manor and village alike, may be dull, but they were safe. She wouldn't stand for this, this, *desecration*.

Her anger carried her the rest of the way home, where she pushed open the creaky kitchen garden gate only wide enough to slip through the gap, in hopes of not being overheard by her mother, and then up the winding path, around the corner, and into the house through the kitchen door.

Mrs. Humphrey had already gone to bed, but Maia had spent enough time in this kitchen over her life to know exactly where everything was kept for a cup of tea. The kettle was always kept filled on the stove, ready to be heated as soon as the fire was built up, and the tea leaves were close at hand. Within a few minutes Maia had stirred the fire back to life, and before long her hands were wrapped around a steaming cup of tea, with three heaping spoonfuls of sugar added. She loathed sugar in her tea, but her nursing experience had taught her what to do for shock.

The first sip was disgusting, the second no better, but by the time Maia had half the cup down the tension was starting to loosen from her muscles. She set the cup down and moved to the telephone closet, thankful for the first time that her father considered the telephone an "infernal machine" and insisted on it being installed as far away from the rest of the house as possible. Most of the time having to place phone calls while standing in the back entryway was a terrible nuisance, but tonight it meant Maia did not have to fret over being overheard as she 'phoned the police station.

"Hello, is this Sergeant Andrews? Oh, Constable Maddox. Hullo, Alan, this is Maia Whitney. I'm terribly sorry to bother you so late, but … well, this is going to sound odd, but I found a dead body in the woods between Little Oaks and Stanbury. What? Yes, I said a dead body. No, I haven't had any cocktails tonight! On the path between the two properties, closer to

Little Oaks than to Stanbury but I couldn't tell you exactly where. I left the dance early to come home to get a good night's sleep before my aunt arrives tomorrow, and I practically tripped over the body of a man. I checked to make sure he was dead, and then I came home as soon as I could so as to call you. It looked to me as though he'd been shot, but of course you'll be better able to tell. What's that? Oh. No, it never even occurred to me to go back to Little Oaks for help, or call you from there. Goodness, I don't know, I suppose because I didn't want to disturb the dance. Besides, there was nothing any of them could do. He was already dead. It seemed to me the best thing to do was inform you discreetly rather than make a fuss.

"Oh … yes, I suppose I could come and show you where, but can't you go look for yourself? I'd really rather not have to view it again. Oh I see. No, I understand. Yes, policy and procedure." Maia sighed. "I'll meet you at the edge of our property."

At least she had enough time to change into something more practical. Still, more than anything else she wanted to crawl into bed and sleep for what remained of the night, but she understood that Alan Maddox couldn't simply take her word for it but rather needed her to accompany him to prove this wasn't a hoax. Not that he mistrusted her, but it was policy. Maia wished it had been Ray Andrews on duty tonight. Not only was Ray a sergeant rather than a constable, and therefore able to use his discretion more when it came to such matters, he had always been a little less set on doing things by the book than Alan when they were all younger, a little more willing to bend the rules.

Maia quickly swilled down the rest of her tea, changed out of her flimsy red frock, stained slippers, and ruined stockings into a much more practical tweed skirt, knitted jumper, thick walking shoes and warm stockings, and folded Mr. Davies' jacket neatly, setting it on the table next to her bed. Then she went back outside to meet Alan Maddox to take him to the dead body.

By now, she felt neither fear nor indignation, but rather weariness combined with a slight nausea over the ugliness of it all. Violent death was always ugly, but murder … that was enough to make anyone ill.

Alan awaited her at the entrance to the woods, a torch in hand. He touched his free hand to his helmet.

"Hullo, Maia—Miss Whitney, I mean."

"Goodness Alan, we've known each other too long for you to start 'Miss Whitney'-ing me," Maia said briskly.

His face looked sheepish even in the moonlight. The Maddoxes were a good few steps below the Whitneys socially. Mrs. Whitney had attempted once to ban Maia from playing with the village children, but Maia had put her foot down, and even at age six had been strong-willed enough to win that battle against her mother. Still, it had been many years since Maia, Alan, Ray Andrews, and a few of the other local youngsters had paddled in the Stanbury stream and climbed trees in the Stanbury woods.

Some of those youngsters now lay buried in France. Alan had only been eligible to join up in the last year of the war, and had come through without any visible wounds—but Maia had seen the haunted look in his eyes after they both returned, and recognized it as the sign of someone who had experienced things no one should ever have to endure.

"Let's go find your body, Miss—Maia," he said now.

Maia shuddered. "Not my body," she pleaded. "I didn't ask

to practically trip over it on my way home!"

"Sorry," he said.

After that, there didn't seem to be anything else to say until they had tramped along for about half a mile and reached the spot where Maia had parted from Mr. Davies, leaving behind a dead body and many unanswered questions.

No body lay there now. The path was empty.

"I don't understand," Maia said blankly. "It—he—it was right here."

To his eternal credit, Alan didn't dismiss her as mad.

"Could he have been injured, not dead? Maybe it wasn't as bad as you thought, and he was able to go back to Little Oaks after you left."

"I checked the body," she said. "There was no heartbeat."

Alan didn't argue with her. He knew she'd been a VAD; it wasn't likely she'd make a mistake about that.

"Perhaps someone else from Little Oaks came along after you went through and took the body back to the house?" he suggested next. "If they weren't as experienced as you, and thought he still had a chance?"

"But then surely they would have rung the station," Maia said slowly. And surely Mr. Davies would have prevented that—though obviously she couldn't tell Alan that.

"Unless they rang through after I'd already left to meet you," Alan said.

It was possible, but unlikely. But what other option made sense?

"I appreciate you not hinting that I was hallucinating, Alan," Maia said.

Alan had been scuffling about, shining the torch at various places on the ground and inspecting the nearby trees. "I'm certain you weren't," he said, and Maia was surprised by a new grimness in his voice.

"What do you mean?"

He pointed along the beam from the torch to some discoloration on the dirt. "That's blood. You don't mistake that color, not if you've seen it as often as I did in 'eighteen. And look there." He flashed the light to something white stuck on a holly bush. "That's a man's handkerchief—and it looks like there's blood on that as well."

Maia's heart jumped. She'd forgotten entirely that she'd placed Mr. Davies' handkerchief over the dead man's face. Oh dear—what if it was monogrammed with his initials? He would be dragged into this case after all unless she could think of a convincing story—ah. Of course. His jacket.

"Of course," she said, allowing her voice to sound surprised. "I'd forgotten—it must have been the shock. There was a gentleman at the dance who lent me his jacket for coming home because I didn't want to have to go through the crowd for my own coat. When I checked the—the body for a heartbeat, my fingers got bloody, and I used the handkerchief I found in his jacket to clean them off. And then—this sounds foolish, but I mustn't have been thinking clearly—I put the handkerchief over the—his—face."

"Ah," Alan said.

Maia wasn't sure what to make of that monosyllable.

He sighed. "I'll see you home, Miss Maia, and then I'd best fetch the sergeant and inform him of all this. He'll likely want to visit Little Oaks and ask if anyone there knows anything about this, and if not, we'll have to start searching the woods."

"I feel as though I ought to apologize for the trouble," Maia said.

"As you said, you didn't ask to trip over the body," Alan answered. "It isn't your fault."

Perhaps not, but whether it was because she had been the one to report it, or because she still felt guilty over hiding some of the truth from her childhood friend, or because the Whitney family had been the unofficial squires of the village of Stanbury for generations and they still felt a sense of feudal care for the place and its inhabitants, Maia couldn't shake her guilt.

She would only be in the way of an official police investigation, and despite everything that had happened this night, she did still have to prepare for Aunt Amelia's arrival tomorrow (or today—it was well past midnight now). All the same, Maia vowed then and there that she would find the man responsible for all of this, and see to it that he faced justice.

For now, home, a brief nap, and facing the responsibilities of the oncoming day.

* * *

Eight o'clock came far too early, but Maia was up and dressed by the time her alarm rang. She hadn't expected to sleep at all, but in the end exhaustion had overtaken her, and she'd fallen asleep as soon as she'd crawled into her bed after her second return home.

She bundled up her dance frock, stockings, and shoes and shoved them into the back of her wardrobe. Fortunately there was no need to fret about an over-zealous housemaid discovering them and wondering why they'd been hidden and just what were the stains on them, since Merry had chased away all their housemaids as well as their housekeeper. Then she determinedly put all thoughts of murder and treachery out of her mind and descended the stairs to enter the kitchen and greet their faithful Mrs. Humphrey, whom not even Merry's political persuasions nor Ellie's tantrums could ever induce to leave.

"You had quite the night, Miss Maia," said the cook, nodding a morning greeting from the counter where she was kneading bread. "I heard you come in practically as the birds began singing this morning! I half expected to be bringing you a tray at eleven."

"Not with Aunt Amelia expected to arrive at that time!" Maia said with a laugh. "We've far too much to do. Mercy, I wish Mrs. Jarvis hadn't left."

"Miss Merope will outgrow her notions in time, and then perhaps we'll be able to keep the help around here for longer than a few months. She has a silver tongue, that one. Now then, let me get you some tea and a bite to eat, Miss Maia, and then you'll be able to face the day."

With one of Mrs. Humphrey's substantial breakfasts in her, Maia did feel far more able to tackle the tasks awaiting her. Clean and prepare the guest room, make sure the rest of the house was in perfect condition, and above all, prevent Mother from interfering with Maia's arrangements. It kept her busy enough that she had little time or energy to spare for wondering what was happening at Little Oaks, if Ray and Alan had found the body, what Mr. Davies was doing and when he would come to the house ostensibly to exchange her wrap for his jacket, and in reality to exchange information. The thoughts were never far from her mind, but she was able to subdue them in favor of the work that needed to be done.

By eleven Maia was finished with her tasks and had changed

from her working clothes into one of her favorite afternoon frocks, a soft fern-colored crepe de chine dress a couple years old and therefore with a waistline too high for fashion, but with delicate embroidery around the square neck and the bottom of the slim skirt, and an overall air of dainty elegance. Maia didn't wear much green—it was Ellie's favorite color and she didn't take kindly to her sisters sharing in it—but because this frock's style was outmoded Ellie no longer fussed when Maia wore it.

Maia had just applied a touch of powder to the tip of her nose when Mrs. Whitney announced in a voice that could be heard throughout the house,

"She has arrived!"

Maia ran down the wide main stairs, coming out the front door to join her parents on the graveled path as a shining black touring car purred to a stop and a short, stout woman entangled in yards of motoring veil heaved herself out of the driver's seat. She dusted off her gloves and impatiently pushed the veil out of her face, and Maia saw her Aunt Amelia for the first time she could remember.

Where Mrs. Whitney was tall and statuesque, Aunt Amelia was round and plump. Her blue eyes were the exact shade and shape as Merry's, bright and inquisitive as a bird's. Overall she reminded Maia irresistibly of a pouter pigeon, with her generous bosom, her strutting walk, and her manner of tilting her head in inquiry.

"Ha!" were her first words. "This mausoleum hasn't changed a bit."

"Welcome to our home, Amelia," Mrs. Whitney said repressively. "We are always glad to have you dignify us with a visit."

"No you aren't," Aunt Amelia contradicted. "That's why I

waited so long to come, and why I didn't tell you I was coming any sooner. Didn't want to give you a chance to wiggle out of it." She pulled off her hat as she approached, revealing grey hair pulled up in an untidy pompadour. "Hullo, Robert. I see you've forgotten who I am already."

"Nonsense, Millie," Mr. Whitney said, smiling affably as he dropped a kiss on her cheek. "One could never forget you."

She nodded. "You mean that as a jibe, I know—but I take it as a compliment! Well," ignoring her sister's outstretched arms and coming to a stop in front of Maia, "and which one are you?"

"Maia," she said, bending down for her own kiss. "I'm very pleased to meet you, Aunt."

"You've met me before, but you were a wee thing at the time, so I don't expect you to remember. Young people these days are so flighty, couldn't remember their own names if they didn't have 'em dinned in their ears all the time. So, where are the other two? Too lazy to come greet their aunt, eh?"

"They had prior plans they could not change," Mrs. Whitney said. "If you had given us more warning—"

"Then you all would have had prior plans," Aunt Amelia said with a wicked grin. "I know you, Lettie! Well, I suppose Maia here is the only one with sense, anyway. She looks like it."

Maia couldn't hide her own grin. Aunt Amelia was nothing like what she'd expected. She was far, far better. Merry and Ellie would be sorry they missed her arrival.

"Won't you come inside, Aunt?" she asked.

"Oh yes, you must be tired from your long journey," echoed Mrs. Whitney. "Really, Mille, I don't know why you didn't take the train, or hire a driver. I'm sure you must want to rest before dinner."

"Nonsense! Driving always leaves me feeling marvelously energized. You should try it, Lettie, or make Robert learn. It might wake him up once in a while. Rest is the last thing I want. You two shoo, now. Young Maia can show me the gardens. Robert, you may bring my bags inside, since it seems you are without servants yet again. Did you drive them away with your dramatics and tantrums, Lettie?"

Maia had to turn her head away and pretend to cough into her sleeve to hide her giggles.

"Servants are so faithless these days," Mrs. Whitney said, striving for dignity.

"Mine aren't," Aunt Amelia said. "Pay 'em enough and treat 'em like real people, and they'll stay with you through thick and thin. Well, what are we all still standing here for? Come along, Maia!"

Mr. Whitney did, in fact, lift Aunt Amelia's bags from the boot of her car to carry inside. Mrs. Whitney, unable to indulge her love for the dramatic in front of a sister who simply would not cooperate, sniffed and retreated inside behind him, leaving Maia and her aunt alone together.

"You wanted to see the gardens?" Maia asked, suddenly nervous. Why was Aunt Amelia staring at her so intently? Could she somehow see Maia's adventures from last night in her face? She seemed capable of practically anything, including clairvoyance.

"Not particularly, but I want to talk to you, and the gardens are the only place where Lettie can't eavesdrop," Aunt Amelia said, placing her hat on her head and jabbing a couple of pins through it. "That maze your father was trying to create when I was here last—did he have any success with it?"

"Oh yes, Father's maze is quite the showpiece of the county,"

Maia said. "It isn't really difficult to navigate, once you have the trick of it."

"Right. Follow me, then."

Maia wondered how her aunt was going to find her way when she'd never been through the maze before, but Aunt Amelia strutted past all the other gardens and shrubs right to the entrance of the maze, and charged inside without pausing once.

"Keep up!" she barked over her shoulder.

Maia's lips quivered in amused wonder, but she followed obediently. The only time Aunt Amelia hesitated was when she came to the first of the "guardian statues" Mrs. Whitney had insisted on placing at every major junction in the maze. The first any visitor would see was Juno, modeled after Mrs. Whitney herself. The nobly patient and weary expression on the marble face would have been a dead giveaway, even without the imposing shape and perfectly sculpted pompadour.

Aunt Amelia snorted. "Typical."

"Mother insisted on doing one of each of us," Maia offered. She didn't particularly want her aunt thinking all of them were so vain. "Father, of course, is Jove."

Aunt Amelia laughed, and Maia agreed. Her quiet, gentle, scholarly father was not exactly what one pictured when one thought of the king of the gods.

"Ellie is Venus, Merry is Diana, and I am Athena." The only thing Maia liked about her statue was the little marble owl perched on the goddess's shoulder. The sculptor had given it a whimsically wise expression, and Maia always felt sure it was about to whisper a witticism in Athena's ear.

"Beauty, the Hunt, and Wisdom." Aunt Amelia resembled an owl herself as she tilted her head and fixed Maia with a sharp eye. "How accurate are those representations?"

"Not very at all," Maia confessed cheerfully. "Merry is the beauty of the family, even though most people are tricked by Ellie's charm into thinking she is. And Merry hates hunting, thinks it is cruel."

"And are you wise?"

"Nowhere near as much as I would like to be," Maia said with a little sigh.

Aunt Amelia nodded her head once, a quick tilt downward and then back up. "Good," was all she said, but Maia felt she had passed some test.

Oddly, she did not feel reassured.

After that, Aunt Amelia only glanced at the other statues, though she chuckled for a good five minutes after passing Mr. Whitney as Jove.

Once they were in the heart of the maze, seated side by side in the fanum Mrs. Whitney had ordered built there, Maia ventured a question.

"What was it you wanted to talk about, Aunt?" What was such a great secret that nobody could be allowed to overhear? Maia thought again of her nocturnal adventure and shivered.

"Before I answer that, I have some questions for you," Aunt Amelia said. "First: do you smoke?"

"No," Maia answered, flushing a little.

"Why not?"

Amusement started slipping away. Maia did not want to have to satisfy her aunt's curiosity. Still, courtesy demanded she answer.

"The smell makes me nauseous."

"Excellent," Aunt Amelia said, startling Maia.

Excellent?

"How's your vision been lately?" was the next unexpected question. "Been seeing odd colors? Around your hands, perhaps?"

Now Maia was almost frightened. Her headaches and the silver flickers—were those some sign of an inherited illness her mother had never told her about? How else could Aunt Amelia know about them?

"Not my hands," she said slowly. "But yes, I have found lately that sometimes I see shimmers of silver out of the corners of my eyes. Sometimes even an entire haze."

Aunt Amelia clapped her hands. "I knew it!"

"Knew what? Aunt, what does this mean?"

Without once taking her eyes from Maia's face, Aunt Amelia said, "Magic."

Maia blinked.

"Sorry," she said. "Could you say that again?"

Aunt Amelia snorted. "Magic, girl, *magic*. Is your hearing affected as well?"

First Maia thought perhaps "magic" was a euphemism for something else: charm, spunk, or elegance.

Then, tentatively, she wondered if her aunt was just a little mad.

"Are you … quite well, Aunt?"

Aunt Amelia sat imperturbably on the uncomfortable marble bench with bees droning around the flowers on her hat; a short, stout woman apparently unaware she had said anything unusual.

"Yes, yes," she said, waving an impatient hand. "I know, I know what you're thinking! You're thinking I'm barmy, bonkers, off my head and whatever else the words are you young people use these days. I am not mad. Magic is real, girl, get that through your head. It exists, it's real, and some few people in this world have the ability to use it. I am one, and so are you."

"I!" Even if magic were real, which Maia couldn't accept for one second, she certainly was not able to use it. Good heavens, if she could perform magic, she wouldn't have spent her time cleaning this morning—she would have used a spell. And she certainly wouldn't have stood passively by last night while a man was murdered in cold blood practically under her very nose! No indeed, she would have done something about *that*.

Although now that she thought of it, she recalled that the silver haze her aunt had just reminded her of had been peculiarly strong during that entire incident, the first time it had obscured Maia's vision without the accompanying headache. And if she concentrated hard enough, she thought she could remember that Mr. Davies had had some sort of bronze glow about his hands during all that. Was that—could that possibly be—was seeing colored shimmers under stress a sign of …

No, of course not. Absolute rubbish. Aunt Amelia was either playing some joke on her, or else truly was mad, despite her protests.

Aunt Amelia watched her with shrewd eyes. "I can see I am going to have to prove it to you. Very well. Watch closely, so you can be sure there is no trickery involved."

She tugged off her pearl-grey gloves and laid them neatly on the bench beside her. Then she held out her left hand, palm up. Squinting a little in the bright sunlight, she muttered a few words (they sounded like Latin) under her breath. Before Maia's startled eyes, there was a gentle "pop" and out of nowhere a flame burst to life, hovering like a small star above

Aunt Amelia's bare hand.

Maia yelped. "What? How? I don't—!"

"Touch it," Aunt Amelia said.

Maia drew back, both fascinated and repulsed by this unnatural flame. It had to be a trick—of course it was—but how?

"Touch it!" her aunt insisted.

Almost against her will, Maia reached out a cautious finger to the flame.

"Ouch!"

She pulled back. A blister was already forming on her fingertip. The flame was real.

"*Finiatur,*" Aunt Amelia said, closing her hand into a fist. The flame vanished. "Now, I am no healer, but even I can take care of that blister for you," she said. "We generally don't encourage magicians to use their craft directly against other people, but there are exceptions made when it comes to healing, though of course one must be careful even then."

"Of course," Maia agreed in a daze.

Aunt Amelia held her left hand palm up under Maia's burned finger and placed her right hand palm down over it, her hand hovering close to the burned skin but not quite touching.

"*Restitue,*" she said.

As Maia stared in fascination, the blister shrank into itself and then vanished entirely, leaving her finger whole and unblemished, as it had been before.

"Now do you believe?" Aunt Amelia demanded.

"I—I—"

Maia's head whirled. For a moment, instead of sitting in the heart of an English country garden featuring the traditional trimmed shrubs and impeccable rosebushes, she was hovering on the edge of a black night sky peppered with blazing suns and burning stars. It ought to have frightened her, but somehow she felt more alive than she had in ages.

She had a sudden flash of memory of one horrible day in France—the front lines had shifted while the nurses were tending their patients, and there was a frantic scramble to get all of the wounded soldiers, the doctors, and the nurses onto transport and away from the shelling. It had been mad, terrible, and terrifying, fleeing at the last moment, knowing that if the transport they were riding on was too slow they could all be killed, trying desperately to keep the wounded soldiers alive through it all—and yet underneath all of that, there was a type of exhilaration, a sense that life was too precious and fulfilling to be taken lightly, a deep thankfulness and even joy in being alive even to experience such horrible things.

This was not horrible—it was bizarre, strange beyond belief, utterly impossible, but not horrible—but Maia felt that same sort of deep wonder and joy beneath all her bewilderment and disbelief. *This is mad*, her brain whispered. *But isn't it wonderful?* her soul whispered back.

Maia's life since returning from the war had been endless petty duties, settling back into a role that never quite fit comfortably, always wondering if there could be something else out there that would make life worth living again.

Now it seemed there was.

"I think I must believe," she said at last.

"Good," her aunt said with satisfaction. "Now we can get somewhere."

5

The Body in the Shrubbery

N o rest for the wicked. After returning to Little Oaks, Len had spent the rest of the evening trying to discreetly discover who had been gone around the same time he had and who had witnesses for being there the entire time. At the end of his efforts, all he could say for certain was that Freddie had not left, as many young ladies clearly remembered dancing with him all through the party, practically without pause.

That left young Spencer, both of the vicar's sons, Sir Bertram Grimes, and Saunders as possible suspects among the house party guests alone. That didn't even begin to cover the people who were there only for the dance.

Len was inclined to think the murderer must have been a gentleman in social standing, though clearly not in behavior, simply by the way he spoke and carried himself, so he didn't think he needed to worry about adding the servants to his suspect list, though as potential witnesses they were invaluable—they saw everything and were rarely noticed by others. He'd set Becket to learning all he could from them, which wasn't much, given the work they all had clearing things up after the dance and seeing to their masters and mistresses.

By four in the morning Len had enough, and he finally crawled into bed to get what little sleep he could for what remained of the night. He was awakened about two hours later by a housemaid's shrill scream.

Screams, in Len's experience, usually meant immediate danger and the need for a quick escape. He shot upright, leapt out of bed, snatched up his dressing gown and jammed his feet into his slippers, and was halfway down the hall before his brain caught up with him and he realized this particular scream was not likely to indicate enemies were after him.

Little Oaks didn't have a guest wing, as so many great houses did, but rather the entire back side of the first floor was given over to spare bedrooms. Len's was on the far right as one faced the house, the side closest to the gardens, with a window that looked out over lawn toward the woods that separated Little Oaks from Stanbury Manor, home of Miss Whitney. Next to his room was a shared bathroom, and then another bedroom, this one occupied by Freddie Winters. Judging by the lack of alarmed or irritated heads poking out of the other bedroom doors, including Freddie's, Len came to the brilliant conclusion that the housemaid's scream must have been uttered directly beneath his open window, which was why he heard it when no one else had.

Therefore it behooved him to make his way down to the ground floor and thence to the gardens, to see whether her scream had been caused by an overeager visiting valet trying to steal an early morning kiss, or something rather more serious.

And wouldn't he feel like a fool if it was the former!

He arrived in the garden at the same time as Julia, Dan, and the formidable housekeeper Mrs. Blackwood, all in various stages of dress and irritation.

But all other considerations were driven out of their minds when they saw what had caused the housemaid, still standing frozen in terror with a bucket of water clutched tightly in her hands, to scream.

A dead body, sprawled facedown between the rosebushes.

In addition to the shock and horror the others were, presumably, experiencing, Len also felt a deep sense of incredulity. Even without seeing the face he could tell this was the same dead body he had left in the woods not seven hours previously, to be reported by Miss Whitney to the police. How, then, had it ended up here? And when?

And, dash it all, *why?*

Most importantly of all, what was he supposed to do about it?

Upon seeing her employers, a guest, and the housekeeper, the maid dropped the bucket and began to sob. Len stifled a curse and jumped back as the water spilled and seeped toward the toes of his slippers.

As though it were a signal, the clang of the bucket released everyone's tongues and movements.

Mrs. Blackwood said, "Hush, girl! What will the gentry think?"

Julia, a trifle pale but otherwise in good control of herself, said, "Daniel darling, am I going mad, or is that a corpse in our roses?"

Foy rubbed his chin and said, "God bless my soul!"

Len remembered his role and said, "I say, Foy, what's all this?"

Foy looked at Len across Julia's head, and as the two men's

eyes met Len saw that the other had a shrewd idea that Len's image was just that—an image—and perhaps even that Len had better knowledge of the corpse than anyone else there.

Harrison must not have been as subtle as he thought in wangling this invitation for Len.

"Julia dearest," Foy said gently, "go inside with Mrs. Blackwood and—what's your name, my dear? Sarah?—and Sarah, please. Mrs. Blackwood, could you kindly see to it that Sarah and Mrs. Foy—and yourself, of course—have a cup of tea to help recover their nerves?" As Julia opened her mouth, presumably to protest that her nerves were fine, he added in an undertone, "I need you to keep the rest of the staff out of here until we know what's happening, my love, as well as any other early rising guests." Julia closed her mouth and nodded. "And ring the police to tell them we've found their missing body," he finished.

Len's head swiveled from the corpse to Foy. "I'm sorry, did you say the police's missing body?" he demanded.

Foy waited until the ladies had retreated toward the house, Mrs. Blackwood leading the way, her back stiff with outrage, Julia with a comforting arm around the still-weeping maid. Then he said,

"Yes, it's rather curious. Late last night, after most of the non-staying guests had left and the rest of you had toddled off to bed, we received a telephone call from the local police asking if we had an injured or dead man stashed away somewhere. It seemed someone had reported a body in the woods but when the police arrived nothing was there, and they thought perhaps it—or rather he—might have made its—his—way to Little Oaks as the closest residence. At the time, of course, the question seemed nonsensical, but now it looks as though there was something in it after all."

"How peculiar," Len said, feeling the inadequacy of the word. What the devil was going on?

"Isn't it just," Foy said, looking Len squarely in the eyes. He coughed and added, "I had best pop inside in case the police want to speak to me over the 'phone. It's a terrible imposition, I know, but since you're already here, would you mind keeping an eye on things to make sure nobody interferes with the body? I don't know much about how these things work, but I believe the police tend to get squiffy if people trample all over the scene of a crime. Even if the crime didn't take place exactly here," he added. "Unless moving a body from one spot to another is a crime. In any case, I don't know anything about it and I don't want to."

Len understood the unspoken message clearly. Foy was willing to give him space to do whatever his job entailed, but did not want to be involved more closely in any of it.

Fair enough—Len preferred it that way.

"Right-oh," he said. "I'll see to it the jolly old body doesn't get up and wander away yet again before the police arrive. Dash it, you'd think the fellow didn't want to be found, vanishing like that and popping up here! You can count on me, old chap."

A half smile twisted Foy's lips. "I'm sure I can."

Then he, too, retreated back into the house, leaving Len alone for a few precious minutes before the police would arrive. It was early enough that it wasn't likely any other guests would come wandering out, but he would still have to be careful in case of curious servants coming to see the sight.

No time to waste, then.

He couldn't go closer to the body without leaving footprints in the soft loam around the flowers—there was no spell to lighten a man enough so that he would leave no sign of his passing, and while Len knew a spell to smooth the dirt after he was finished, that would eliminate any other useful prints that were there as well. No sense in making things simpler for whoever had brought the body here.

No matter—he'd already seen the body last night, and he had no need to re-examine it. What he wanted now was a chance to look around before the police arrived. Footprints, yes, but other signs that they might not notice. And most especially, signs of magic.

Magicians could see the residue of their own magic, but no one else's. Whenever Len cast a spell, it left a faint bronze glow around his hands. When he was first learning to use his magic and hadn't yet developed the ability to concentrate it in specific spells projected through his hands, he would sometimes look down to see his entire body coated in a bronze shimmer. It would be dashed useful if he could use a spell now to identify and follow someone else's magic, but no such thing existed.

What he could do, however, was cast a general spell to identify if magic had been used at all in the area. Like called to like, and magic always reacted to itself. *If* it was a magician who had brought the body here, and *if* that magician had cast a spell while here, Len would be able tell. If the person had cast a spell in the woods, then Len was out of luck, but he would at least start with the most obvious search and then go from there.

He cleared his throat, gathered his concentration, and said, "*Similis ad similem.*"

Invisible to anyone else, but clear to his eyes, bronze light left his open palms and curled around the garden, whisking across shrubs and skimming above the ground, continually on the hunt for something like itself. Len had about given up hope after a few minutes of fruitless searching and was on the verge of canceling the spell when the light pulsed once, flashing immediately above the ground near the body.

Something at last!

Len walked around the garden bed, being careful to stay on the graveled path or the grass as he did. He bent down to see if he could identify what sort of a spell his hunter had found. The ground looked empty and innocent enough to his eyes. He passed a hand over the spot, careful not to touch the dirt, and felt something odd in the air, a sort of stickiness as though he'd touched a cobweb. He grinned. This spell, he knew—it was the one he'd been thinking of but saw no point in using.

First to end his hunter spell. Len curled his free hand closed. "*Finiatur*."

The bronze light vanished. Len then passed his hand three more times through the stickiness, then wrapped it all up in a fist and pulled both physically and magically. This was no spell, just a brute force use of magic. It was frowned upon in English circles, but he had learned it from a chap in the Middle East and found dashed useful in some out-of-the-way spots.

The force of his pull wrenched the other magician's spell loose, and it broke apart, showing two footprints as plain as day. Len shook his head. Sloppy! Far better to have scuffed the ground and then used the spell to hide the scuff marks rather than relying on magic alone to cover the prints.

Well now, what did this tell him? Whoever had brought the corpse here was a magician, that much was clear. Was it the murderer, Corbin, or another magician?

Harrison believed that Corbin was selling the papers to a non-magician. There weren't many people in the world who knew about magic without being able to use it themselves. Part of that was due to the nature of magic, as it tended to slip from people's memories when they weren't exposed to it regularly, and part of it was due to the deliberate choices of magicians for generations to hide themselves from the rest of the world to avoid either persecution or the temptation to power that came from having an ability others did not. There were some non-magicians, though, especially since the war, who had inklings of the truth and were always searching for proof. The papers that Corbin stole contained that proof, written down so no one could forget it, and if a non-magician got a hold of them and chose to reveal them to the world … that was the end of magic as it was now known, and would throw the world into another catastrophe the likes of which would make the war seem a mere triviality.

If Harrison was right, then, it wasn't the murderer that had brought the corpse here. Which made sense—if the murderer was a guest at Little Oaks, he wouldn't want to advertise his involvement by bringing the body closer to where he was staying.

That left either Corbin or an unknown magician. Len discarded the unknown magician theory—it was possible, but unlikely, especially given how secret this entire affair had been kept. But Corbin—he was furiously angry at the murderer, both for killing his valet and for cheating him out of the price they'd agreed upon for the papers. If he knew, or guessed, that the murderer was a guest at Little Oaks, he could have returned to the scene after Len and Miss Whitney had left it and brought the body here in an attempt to draw the police's attention to this spot and the guests. And this sort of shoddy spell-work was exactly what Len would expect of a magic-user who had never progressed beyond the apprentice stage.

Very well, then, the working hypothesis was that Corbin had returned sometime after Len and Miss Whitney had departed, and brought the body here in order to throw suspicion on the murderer. The question that followed, then, was: how did this information help Len identify the murderer?

Reluctantly, he had to admit he had no idea how to answer that one.

No more time to think about it, either, as the police came rattling up the drive and stopped in a spray of gravel. Len cast a quick glance around the scene to ensure there weren't any other clues he'd missed, and braced himself to perform the "good-natured blithering idiot" role that was his greatest defense from ever being identified as an MI agent, or even a person of any sort of intelligence at all.

* * *

Len didn't have a chance to slip away from Little Oaks until after the cold luncheon that Julia had managed to persuade her staff to put together despite the events of the morning. After he'd been questioned by the police, Len had secured himself a spot where he could witness the reactions of each of the guests to the information that their enjoyable weekend house party had been interrupted by the discovery of a murder victim in their hosts' rose garden, and they were all going to have to be questioned as to whether or not they knew anything about it.

Freddie Winters looked on it as a bit of a joke, with the well-bred amiability Len would have expected of him. His sister Hermione was outraged and threatened to leave at once, though Len suspected that was more due to the fact that she had lost badly at cards the previous night than a genuine distress over the dead body and police presence. Freddie talked her down.

The Danvers lads, nice chaps that they were and vicar's sons to boot, seemed genuinely distressed by the news, and offered to help in any way possible. Len supposed one or both of them *could* be an accomplished liar and a secret murderer and treasonous snake, but it didn't seem likely.

Mrs. Saunders had swooned and Mr. Saunders seemed highly nervous. That was about what Len would have expected from people of their class, though, so it wasn't necessarily suspicious, though it didn't leave them above suspicion, either.

Both Miss Laura Spencer and Miss Merry Whitney burst into a diatribe against police brutality and the way in which the laws of England favored the upper classes while the working class were always overlooked. The rants were similar enough to each other than Len cynically wondered if they'd been rehearsed ahead of time and held in reserve if ever the young ladies had a chance to use them. If it hadn't clearly been a *man* he had seen leaving Little Oaks for the woods the previous night, he might have suspected the ladies—if they despised their own class for holding themselves above others, how much more would they hate magicians for having something no one else could possess?—but neither of them seemed capable of murder, however irritating they might be.

Timothy Spencer seemed concerned and wary, but that could possibly be the natural reaction of a barrister's son who was more aware of the legal difficulties that could arise from this sort of situation than the others were, as opposed to fear of being discovered as a murderer. Besides—while it was not at all professional to dismiss someone from his suspect list because of a feeling, Len's instincts told him young Spencer could not possibly have been the cold-blooded killer he'd heard the night before.

Sir Bertram Grimes did not react much at all, merely raising his eyebrows and proceeding to the breakfast room after expressing his willingness to aid the police in any way they deemed necessary. Not enough to speak for or against him—a hard-headed businessman like him wouldn't be likely to give himself away if he were the murderer, and if he weren't, he'd probably consider it a matter of pride to take anything in his stride.

Miss Electra Whitney screamed and attempted to swoon into Len's arms when Julia told her the news. Luckily Len had started to move out of the way even before her figure began to gracefully droop in his direction, and she'd had to catch herself on the balusters of the stairs instead.

"How horrible!" she cried, fanning herself vigorously. "Will *Scotland Yard* be called out? Shall we all have to be *fingerprinted?* Oh, I just know I shall faint when those awful policemen question me! Mr. Davies, you'll be *sure* to come with me and protect me, won't you?"

She made so much noise that the police sergeant and Foy came out of Foy's study, where they'd been closeted, to see what all the fuss was about.

"Ah," said the sergeant. "I should have known it would be you, Miss Ellie."

Miss Electra stood up straight, her faintness forgotten, and glared at him. "If you're in charge of the case, Ray Andrews, we'll all be stuck here forever waiting on you to solve it!"

He grinned up at her. "Not to fret, Miss Ellie, the Chief Constable will soon decide if this is the sort of case a lowly sergeant like myself is capable of solving or if we need to reach out for more help. I'm sure you'll be able to persuade anyone else who has to question you of your utter innocence and delicacy of mind."

The constable, who had trailed out behind them, turned beet red and coughed frantically into his sleeve.

Miss Electra came the rest of the way down the stairs in a huff. "Well … good," she said inadequately. Before entering the breakfast room, she turned and offered what she clearly believed to be a Parthian shot. "And at least I don't look like a caterpillar crawled onto my upper lip and died there!"

It was Len's turn to have to turn a laugh into a cough. It was true that Sergeant Andrews sported a truly impressive mustache, but it was the mental image of Miss Electra with a luxuriant, bushy growth of hair above her upper lip that had him wanting to howl with laughter.

Sergeant Andrews maintained his cheerful grin even after Miss Electra's parting words. "Sorry about that, sir," he said to Foy, half-including Len in the apology. "It's hard for some people to have respect for you when you were their escort to their first dance, at which they humiliated themselves by drinking too much champagne and then being sick in the bushes outside, after which they decided they never wanted to see you again."

Len's only surprise from that revelation was that Miss Electra would have deigned to lower herself to attend a village dance with someone who was so obviously middle class as Sergeant Andrews.

The sergeant seemed to have guessed his thoughts, for he added, "It was during the war. I think she only agreed to go with me because of my uniform."

All of which cast a fascinating side light on the personalities involved, but did not help Len particularly much.

He'd had his own interview with Sergeant Andrews and Constable Maddox after breakfast, during which he stuck to the story he and Miss Whitney had created, and devoutly hoped she had done the same. To his relief, she must have, because neither of them looked particularly suspicious, although the sergeant gave him a bad moment when he said,

"It's a pity it didn't occur to you to escort Miss Whitney home, Mr. Davies, rather than simply lending her your coat. If there had been two of you to find the body, one of you could have stayed with it while the other came to tell us."

Len met his sharp gaze with a bland smile. "Yes, it is, isn't it? As a matter of fact, I did offer—seemed a bit caddish to just let her go off like that, don't you know, but the lady refused. Said something about preferring to be alone. I still didn't like it, but one can't just go about forcing one's company on a lady once she's made it clear she doesn't like one, can one?"

The constable snorted. "That sounds like Miss Maia," he said.

"That's enough, Maddox," Sergeant Andrews said sharply, "and that's Miss Whitney to you."

"But sir, she told me to call her—"

"I don't care what she told you, you'll show her proper respect."

"Seems more respectful to me to use the name she asked me to," Constable Maddox grumbled under his breath, but he didn't argue any more.

Sergeant Andrews appeared to believe Len's story, for he didn't press him for any more details. Instead, he asked several questions about how well Len knew Foy, and if he had seen him anywhere around during the time between Miss Whitney's leaving and the departure of the other guests.

Was he suspecting Foy? What rubbish! Though, come to think of it, Foy did have a better opportunity than anyone else to arrange to meet Corbin here, and he could have planned the house party at the same time in order to hide his tracks.

But no, Foy was a magician, and what's more, a decent fellow. Plus he only had one leg, and Len was certain he would have heard the slight drag that the false leg made if it had been Foy in the woods last night.

So he said firmly, "As a matter of fact, I did see him frequently. He was being a good host, y'know—making sure everyone was comfortable, chatting with those who weren't dancing, all that sort of thing. No, I don't think he would have had time at all to have got to the woods and back."

"I suppose not," Sergeant Andrews said, sounding almost disappointed. "Very well, thank you, Mr. Davies. We'll let you know if we have any more questions."

Len was itching to ask if they'd noticed the footprints he'd uncovered for them, but that would have drawn more attention to his powers of observation than he wanted, so he held his tongue and went about his business.

He first consulted with Becket (the servants were all astonished, frightened, or excited, depending on their temperament, but none of them had any insight on the affair, or showed any indication that their master or mistress might be a cold-blooded killer), and then spent the rest of the morning mingling with the others guests while joining in their outrage tinged with excitement over it all. After all, while he was on the lookout for anything that might give away the killer's identity, he had to be equally cautious that he was not at the same time giving away his own identity.

Thus it was that he did not feel free to keep his appointment with Miss Whitney until after luncheon.

Despite the murder, the vanishing of the papers, and the general mess, not to mention how angry Harrison was going to be when Len got around to reporting all this to him (Harrison would likely have knocked Miss Whitney out to keep her safe, stolen the papers back, and fled the county with no explanation, but dash it, Len was still a gentleman), Len found himself whistling as he walked along the path through the woods, where there were now no signs of any dastardly deeds. He wasn't sure if it was the fresh air, the escape from the inanities of the other guests at Little Oaks, or the anticipation of seeing Miss Whitney again that caused his light-heartedness, but he wasn't terribly inclined to question it too closely. Moments like these came rarely in his life; he would savor them when he could.

He rounded a final curve in the path and stepped out of the woods. Stanbury Manor lay before him, the path carrying on past the building, winding up the chalk hills in the north like a white snake against a green backdrop. A little spark of delight lit in him when his eyes fell on Miss Whitney standing by the gate to her family's house, looking like the spirit of the woods herself in a soft green dress—though a dryad would likely not have worn the very fetching little hat she had tugged down over her head.

She saw him and began walking in his direction. Len blinked. What was that—that *haze* around her? A silvery glow … it reminded him of his own magical aura, except silver instead of bronze. But Miss Whitney was not a magician, nor could he have seen her aura if she were! Had someone cast a spell over her? He doubted even Corbin would do such a thing, and besides, he'd never heard of or seen a spell that left this sort of residue behind. But what could it be if not magic?

On an impulse, Len called up his own magic, letting it flow out through his arms and hands and hover formlessly around him.

To his utter shock, Miss Whitney stopped walking, her eyes widening as they followed the bronze glow.

"By Jove," Len breathed. "You can see it. And I can see yours. That means …"

"You're a magician as well!" Miss Whitney said, her mouth breaking into a wide smile. "Oh, how delightful!"

"But—but—" Len stammered.

"I only found out this morning, from my aunt," she said. "I still have a hard time believing it. Oh, but you must have known as soon as you saw me, if magicians can recognize each other by this light?" Then she frowned. "Although I haven't seen my aunt's light. And she had to ask me about mine …"

"Miss Whitney—I am astonished," Len forced out. "I had no idea—you say you only found out now? From your aunt, who is also a magician?"

"Yes, she told me that this," she waved a hand, leaving a faint silver tracing behind in the air, "is a sign of my—my magic, which I still find strange to say, and that as I learn more control it won't—won't *leak* as much."

Len's brain scrambled to catch up. It wasn't unheard of for some magicians to develop their powers late. For most of them the magic sprang up during adolescence, but for others it was delayed. It also wasn't unheard of for magic to skip around in families, or even show up in a line where it had never been before—Len had inherited his from his mother, and she from her father, and so on and so forth for many generations, but despite what some snobs in the Circle thought, bloodline didn't matter much to magic.

But nobody that he'd ever heard of was able to see another person's magic—and now he could see Miss Whitney's and she his.

He couldn't understand it at all.

"I am delighted that you have come into your magical heritage," he said at last, shelving these problems. "Though I wish it could have come at a time less fraught with difficulty."

Miss Whitney inclined her head. "Thank you. I must say it is all quite strange to me. I feel as though a part of me has known it all along, and another part of me still can't believe it is real. I confess, I'd almost forgotten about the murder until I saw your coat in my wardrobe after lunch and remembered. Here it is, by the way. I brought it out with me when I left the house to wait for you."

Len couldn't blame her for losing track of the murder. Learning that one was a magician would do that to a person. He took his coat back and exchanged it for her long wrap.

"Mrs. Blackwood tells me this is yours," he said.

Maia nodded and folded it over her arm. "Tell me, have they found the body yet?"

Len told her the story of the morning at Little Oaks. Maia listened with commendable patience and attentiveness.

"Mr. Davies—my aunt has told me of the restriction against letting non-magicians learn of magic. Tell me, had I not been there last night, could you have used magic to stop the murder?"

Len wanted to assure her she'd done nothing wrong, but looking at her clear eyes—mostly blue, he noticed, but with hints of green through them—he found he couldn't lie to her.

"I don't know if I could have stopped the murder," he said. "It happened so unexpectedly. But I could have stopped the murderer from getting away with the papers, yes."

"I see." Miss Whitney was silent for a moment. "I thought I was helping," she said. "But I made things worse, didn't I?"

"Not to sound like a prig, but we can't ever foresee all the possible consequences of our actions," Len answered. "All we can ever do at the time is make the best decisions we are able. Sometimes they are the right ones and sometimes they aren't. That doesn't mean we weren't right to try."

"Thank you," she said. "But I still feel some responsibility. Tell me, will I be in your way again if I try to help you identify the murderer and recover the papers?"

He should have said yes, but the thought of having a partner, even if she didn't know exactly what was going on, was intoxicating. Oh, Becket did his best, but he was far too diffident and reserved to be the kind of companion Len wished for.

"What about your guest? Your aunt?"

Miss Whitney's smile now was rueful. "She will be cross. She has offered to take me on as her apprentice, but I'd already told her I have to think about it. It would mean moving to London to live with her, and I'm not sure I ought to leave my family just for the sake of something that only benefits me, especially when I can't even tell them about it."

From what Len had seen of her sisters, if it was him he would have run away from the family at the earliest opportunity, but there, everyone was different.

"At any rate," Miss Whitney continued, "I don't feel right about rushing into something new while leaving this unfinished. I know Julia would be happy to have me come join the house party—if she wished for my support before all this, she surely would want it even more now that the police have found a body in her roses. My aunt will simply have to accept that I can't make any decision about pursuing magic until I've seen this through—so long as I won't be in the way."

"You would be more than welcome," Len told her with utter sincerity. "But do think about it—a magical apprenticeship is not something to lightly discard. No one would think less of you for leaving this business to those who can't escape it in order to learn how to use your gift."

"I would," she said simply.

Len believed her. Rather than continue to try to persuade her, he changed the subject.

"Your aunt must be a master magician if she's able to take you on as her apprentice. And you said she lives in London? I'm sure I know who she is, there aren't many magicians in town that I'm not acquainted with at least by name. I don't recall any Whitneys, though …"

"Oh, her name isn't Whitney, she's my mother's sister, not my father's," Miss Whitney said. "Her name is Rawlings. Amelia Rawlings."

Len clamped his teeth together to keep his jaw from dropping.

Amelia Rawlings? Here? *Now?* Surely it couldn't be a coincidence. He would have to tell Harrison right away. This changed everything.

And Miss Maia Whitney was her niece, and in position to become her next apprentice.

Had Len been wrong about her, and about this entire situation, from the very beginning?

He was very much afraid he might have been.

6

Magic, Murder, and Mayhem

To say that Aunt Amelia was unhappy with Maia's decision to put any talk of a magical career on hold until after the house party and the murder situation had been cleared up would have been an understatement. They were back in the garden, to Mrs. Whitney's confusion—Aunt Amelia had never expressed an interest in country gardens before, rather the opposite, but it was the best place to have a conversation without being overheard.

"You are being offered the chance of a lifetime, girl, and you would put it off because you wish to play detective?" Aunt Amelia spluttered. "Leave detecting to the police, or those nitwits who call themselves Domestic Protection if magic is involved, or Magical Intelligence—ha, a misnomer if I ever I heard one—if it involves something beyond minor magical infractions. You have the chance for something bigger! As my niece and my apprentice, you would have every door in England's magical community opened to you, every opportunity available for you! You could do and be anything, anything at all. There's no nonsense about appropriate roles for females versus males when it comes to magic, or about class divisions. Why, I was governor of Dorset—the magical population of Dorset, you understand—until I joined the Circle."

Maia was determined not to be tempted away from her duty, but her curiosity was piqued. "The Circle?"

"We magicians hold to a very strict order, one which has been in place ever since the Romans ruled Britain. Other nations, of course, have different structures. Most of Europe, at least before the War, followed our order. The Asians are very mysterious about their magicians, the Russians confusing, and the Americans, of course, have no kind of structure at all." She sniffed.

Maia turned her head to hide a smile. She had met a few Americans during the War, and found they didn't match the stereotypes at all. For their part, they were always amazed at how different the English were from their preconceived ideas of them.

The lecture continued. "So. We have a High Council of Magicians, commonly called the Circle. In that council there are several smaller divisions, each dedicated to a different aspect of magic. Each magician in the British Isles falls under the direct governance of one or more of those divisions. The Circle has its representatives in each county to whom the magicians in that area must report. A magician need not work for the Circle—one may practice magic independently, if one wishes—but everyone must report to the government, and follow its laws. And above all, every magician must take an oath to never reveal the secrets of magic to anyone outside our circles."

Maia could only imagine how the King and Parliament

would react to hearing there was an entirely separate body of government operating in the British Isles. Magicians had good reason to keep themselves secret!

"And what do magicians do? What's all this magic used for?" If they had to keep themselves secret, what good was magic anyway?

"Oh, my dear. So many things! Some are craftsmen, using their magic to make beautiful things. Some put their magic into the land, improving crops. Some use it to protect Britain, maintaining her borders and defenses. Many go about completely ordinary lives, using their magic in small ways to make those lives better. And some, as I said, use their magic to govern other magic-users, make sure all obey our laws and do not use magic to harm anyone or anything."

"What role do you play, Aunt Amelia?" She couldn't imagine her aunt as anything but an important member of the High Council.

Aunt Amelia smiled complacently and craned her neck a little in the sunshine. Had she been a cat, Maia was sure she would have purred. "I am a member of the Foreign Affairs division of the Circle. Before that, I was Governor of Dorset. Miserable job, that, trying to keep track of all the petty magicians in the place. I was quite happy when I was promoted to the Foreign Office."

"And apprentices? How do we—they—fit in?"

"Any magician who has passed a certain level of testing can take on an apprentice. As with any craft, after the apprentice passes the basic tests, he or she becomes a journeyman, permitted to work magic alone. After a few more years one may attempt another test to become a qualified magician. Some few take it yet further, submit an independent project to become masters, and qualified to take on apprentices of their own."

It did sound tempting—oh, it did! A chance to develop an inherent skill, a chance to do something more with her life than sit at home and make things smooth for her family, a chance to find meaningful work and like-minded friends. In that moment, Maia wanted it more than anything she'd ever desired.

But could she accept it, knowing she was abandoning a mess she had contributed to making? Even if Mr. Davies had turned oddly silent and stuffy at the end of their conversation, he *had* said her help would be useful. And her excuse for helping him, that Julia needed her assistance, had more than a smattering of truth in it as well. Maia didn't like always having to be the reliable friend—but she was, and she could no more abandon a friend in need than she could turn on her own self.

Besides, if she was being completely honest, she wanted to know who the murderer was, and she wanted to have a hand in bringing him to justice. He had shattered the peace of her world here in Stanbury, taken a life on the very edge of her family's property, and she had the right as well as the responsibility to see him punished for that.

And her curiosity would never be satisfied about his identity or those missing papers unless she helped solve the puzzle, because she couldn't believe that Mr. Davies would be allowed to tell her government secrets without her being more closely involved in the hunt.

"I do want to do this, Aunt," she said. The bed of purple asters next to the uncomfortable marble bench nodded in the gentle breeze. A little ways off stood the absurd statue of Maia as Athena. Maia imagined she could see the stone owl scowling at her for her unwise choice—but what else could she do?

"I sense a "but" coming," Aunt Amelia said tartly.

Maia kept her eyes on the asters, taking comfort in their serene color and dauntless carriage. "But I cannot turn my back on my duty here. I would hope that I could help Mr. Davies solve the murder of that poor man Carter and then be able to take you up on your generous offer to take me on as an apprentice, but I understand if you are not able to do so."

Aunt Amelia stiffened. "Did you say Davies? That's who you are working with on this?"

"Yes," Maia answered with caution.

"And Carter? Carter is the name of the man who was killed last night? You are certain?"

Maia recalled too late that she was only supposed to have stumbled across the body after the fact, which would preclude her knowing the man's name—but she wasn't going to lie about it now. She would have to trust that Aunt Amelia, who was so insistent on magic being secret, would be able to respect Maia keeping a secret about how she knew the man's name.

"Yes."

Aunt Amelia stood up abruptly and began to pace. Maia's brow creased with confusion as she watched.

"I begin to see," the older woman muttered.

"I am glad you do, because I do not!" Maia said tartly. Just why were both her aunt and Mr. Davies behaving so oddly upon learning of the other's involvement in things? What exactly was between them? And why did the name Carter mean something to her aunt? Had she known the dead man?

"I am afraid I have some unexpected business to attend to," Aunt Amelia announced, turning back to face Maia. "So you may go play at being a detective with Mr. Davies at this house party if you wish. Once my business is over, if you still wish to apprentice yourself to me, I will take you on, and we will see just what sort of a magician we can make of you."

Despite her confusion and her irritation at secrets and mysteries that deliberately excluded her, a gush of joy sprang up in Maia's heart at her aunt's promise. "Thank you!" she exclaimed, coming to her feet and taking her aunt's hands in her own in an unusual show of affection. "I cannot thank you enough!"

Aunt Amelia sniffed and extracted her hands. "Well, well," she said, absently patting Maia's shoulder. "What else is family for?"

* * *

Julia practically fell upon Maia's neck and wept tears of thanksgiving when Maia arrived at Little Oaks' French doors later that afternoon bearing a small valise.

"I knew you wouldn't abandon me at the time like this!" she cried. "Oh, Maia, it's been dreadful!"

Maia handed her bag to one of the footmen lurking in the background. "My other bag will be coming shortly," she told him. She had one piece of luggage she wouldn't want the maids seeing as they unpacked for her, but that was stowed safely on her person, and she intended to keep it there until this was all over. She hoped it would not be required, but she would not take any chances.

Bag disposed of, she looped her arm through Julia's and steered her into the breakfast parlor, requesting a pot of tea for two over her shoulder as she did.

"Do tell me about it," she said sympathetically, sitting down at the small table by the window.

Julia collapsed into the opposite chair. "Well, that stupid girl screamed and screamed this morning when she found the body—though thankfully Mr. Davies is the only one she awoke—and then all the servants have been upset ever since. She sat there in the kitchen and told her story over and over again to anyone who would listen, and it got more dramatic with each telling, until half of our maids were ready to flee home in terror of being killed in their beds, and all of our menservants were preparing to hunt down the perpetrator— or so they claim, though I suspect all of them would be just as terrified as the maids if not more so if actually confronted with even a petty burglar."

She paused while the tea was brought to them by a still-nervous housemaid, supervised by Mrs. Blackwood herself, prim and disapproving in her black dress.

"I'd be lost if it weren't for Blackie here," Julia said, smiling up at the housekeeper. "She finally sent that silly girl home for the day, or else the servants would still be listening to her story."

"Not to fret, Mrs. Foy, I've told them all what I expect of staff in a house such as this," Mrs. Blackwood said, nodding at the housemaid, who bit her lip and carefully poured the tea. "The guests' servants are another matter, but even there I was able to make it clear I didn't hold with gossip. We'll soon have things back to normal."

She exited the room, back stiff with dignity, the housemaid trailing after.

"Blackie is an angel," Julia said fervently, "And you are another. The servants may be under control, but the guests are another matter. Of course we couldn't hide this from them, and now none of them know what to do with themselves, and I don't know what to do with them. It seems callous to go on with our planned activities when a man's body has just been taken out of the garden, but it's silly to sit around inside and act as though our nearest and dearest of friends has been killed. None of us even knew the man! And nothing has been helped by your sister's foolishness."

Maia took a sip of tea. "Which one?" she asked in resignation.

"Ellie, of course. Merry simply grumbles about class differences while she and Laura attempt to make the servants feel they are being unjustly treated, but given that the police have been exquisitely polite to all the staff it's hard for her complaints to make much impact. But Ellie goes from attempting to flirt with Mr. Davies or Sir Bertram or Freddie, whoever happens to be convenient at the time, in the most outrageous way, to insulting poor Sergeant Andrews, who after all is just doing his job, to behaving just as badly as the maids, shrieking in terror that we'll all be murdered in our beds. I am sorry, Maia, but that girl is a menace. She ought not to be allowed out without a keeper!"

And it was Maia who was her keeper. That old resentment stirred in her, but the silver haze that suddenly blurred her vision distracted her.

She was no longer bound to staying at Stanbury and playing nursemaid to Ellie for the rest of her life. She had a new purpose now, a new goal. Let Mother and Father find a way to keep her under control. As soon as this murder was solved, Maia would be gone.

It was an intoxicating thought. The haze faded, though Maia could still see a slight glow around her fingertips.

"I'm here now," she said briskly. "What do you want me to do?"

"Tell Ellie to act her age," Julia said bluntly. "And if possible, get Merry to stop attempting to antagonize everyone. I am sorry to have to say that after this, I don't want to ever invite them to the house again. I could manage the servants with Blackie's help and attempt to keep the other guests amused if your sisters—mostly Ellie—weren't going out of their way to make this as painful as possible."

Maia stifled a sigh. This was not particularly helpful for investigating the murder, plus experience had taught her that her sisters would resent her interference and do their best to make her miserable for attempting to put a check on their behavior, but nonetheless it had to be done.

"Where are they now?" she asked, finishing her tea and setting her cup down decisively. If she had to speak to them, better sooner rather than later. She could always look for Ray Andrews afterward to apologize to him for Ellie's behavior and then also discreetly inquire as to how the investigation was coming.

"Merry has cornered Sir Bertram in the library and has been lecturing him on fair labor practices," Julia said. "Last I knew, Ellie was in the billiard room pouting because Mr. Davies said he couldn't teach her how to play."

Ellie had learned to play billiards at age fourteen. This was one of her blatant attempts at flirting that Julia had mentioned. Poor Mr. Davies! Regardless of what was happening between him and Aunt Amelia, he didn't deserve this.

"Very well, I'll start with Merry and then tackle Ellie," Maia said.

"You *are* an angel," Julia said fervently. "I'll try to persuade the others that it isn't inappropriate to play tennis outside, so long as we avoid the rose garden."

Maia knew the library at Little Oaks well—she wasn't much for reading, as there always seemed to be too much to do to allow time to sit around with a book unless one was ill, but the peaceful atmosphere within was one that drew her whenever socializing with Julia's other guests became too much of a strain. Even now, on an unpleasant task, she felt some weight drop off her shoulders as soon as she crossed the threshold and saw the lights gleaming on the spines of the leather-bound books lined up with precision on the polished wooden shelves.

As she passed between two rows of shelves in pursuit of the low murmur of voices she heard at the other end of the room, a title embossed in gold on a red leather book jumped out at her.

Spells and Incantations for Beginners, it read. Maia blinked.

Suddenly, all the books on that shelf began to glow as though lit from within.

Useful Household Magic. A History of Magic in the British Isles. Wizard or Magician? How to Tell the Untrained from the Trained.

These were all magic books! How had she never noticed them before? And what did it mean?

There must have been some spell on them to make them unnoticeable to those without magic or whose magic hadn't shown up yet, and that was why she could see them now and not before. But for that to be the case ... either Dan was a magician or his uncle or cousin had been. Maia was inclined to guess that it was Dan, but she admitted that without knowing more about how magic worked she couldn't say for certain. It was astonishing news either way.

Her fingers itched to pick up one or all of the books so that she could start learning more about what it meant to have magic running through one's veins, but once again, duty had to come before enjoyment. Promising herself she would return later and investigate the shelf more fully, Maia forced her way onward.

She had been distracted enough by the magic books that she had only half-noticed that the murmuring voices had stopped … until she rounded the corner of the shelves and saw Merry standing far too close to Sir Bertram, gazing up at him in utter adoration while he let his eyes roam boldly over her. Even as Maia watched, he lifted Merry's hand to his lips and pressed a passionate kiss to the backs of her fingers.

"Merry!" Maia gasped.

The two sprang apart, Merry's face crimson, Sir Bertram as composed as though Maia had caught him perusing a book.

"What are you doing here?" Merry demanded. "I thought you were home!"

"My presence was no longer required, so I came here," Maia said. "What are *you* doing?"

"Merope and I were discussing the working conditions of my factories," Sir Bertram said smoothly. "And then the conversation turned to more personal matters." He smirked at Maia, whose blood rose at the sight.

It was disgusting—the man had to be in his mid-thirties at least. Merry was only seventeen! This was no longer the era of Miss Austen, when a man of Colonel Brandon's age could marry someone like Marianne without anyone thinking it improper. This was 1921, for heaven's sake. If Merry was too young to know any better, Sir Bertram was surely old enough to do so.

"So I see," Maia said, injecting more than a touch of frost

into her voice.

Merry glared at her, then turned to Sir Bertram.

"Excuse us a moment, Bertram," she said. She grabbed Maia's arm and dragged her behind the next set of shelves. "What on earth are you doing here?" she hissed. "And don't give me any nonsense about not being required at home. Did you come just to ensure Ellie and I were behaving ourselves? Go away! Can't we breathe without you appearing and informing us we're doing it incorrectly?"

Maia ignored most of this. "What are you thinking?" she whispered furiously back, one small part in the back of her mind wondering as she did if it was possible to use a spell to muffle one's voice so that one didn't have to whisper to be private. "He's far too old for you, Merry!"

"It is none of your business who I spend time with and who I don't!" Merry came back. "It's my life, not yours!"

"I only want what's best for you, you know that," Maia began.

"No, you only want what's best for *you*, and you don't care whether or not it's what I want from my life! You're not my mother, Maia, so leave—me—alone!"

With that, Merry turned on her heel and returned to Sir Bertram, leaving Maia stunned.

"I'm sorry about that, Bertram," Merry said, her voice back to normal. "Older sisters, you know. They always think they know better than you about everything. Let's go outside. No one should interfere with us there."

Sir Bertram laughed and agreed, and the two left the library, leaving Maia hurt and angry.

How dare Merry accuse her of only wanting what was best for her own self? Maia would have left Stanbury ages ago if that was the case. She was the only person in their entire family who didn't put herself first! And of course she wasn't Merry's mother—but their mother was too obsessed with gossip, the local Drama Club, and her own grievances against the world to raise her daughters properly, so who else was left but Maia to look out for her sisters?

Merry was clearly behaving irrationally—but Maia's feet still dragged as she left the library to track down Ellie.

If Merry had responded poorly to her intervention, Electra would be worse.

Maia was right—Ellie took one look at Maia entering the billiard room and shrieked,

"May! What on earth are you doing here? Why aren't you at home?"

Maia nodded a weary greeting to Freddie and Mr. Davies, who had been playing billiards while Ellie, presumably, watched. "Aunt Amelia is all settled in and I'm not needed there any longer, so when I heard about the tumult here, I had to come give Julia a hand."

Ellie's pretty face twisted in a sneer. "Of course you did. Nobody can ever do anything unless Maia is there to help!" She laughed shrilly, but there was no humor in it.

"The more the merrier here, I say," Freddie interposed gallantly. "Besides, what else is one to do when a corpse appears practically on one's doorstep, eh? I mean, I wouldn't want to be left out of the fun, either."

Ellie changed her tune, looking up at Freddie soulfully, her artfully darkened eyelashes fluttering as she clasped her hands together at her throat. "Oh, but you're so brave! I would be terrified if you and Mr. Davies weren't here to protect us all. That clodhopper Ray Andrews would arrest me simply out of spite if you weren't here to see fair play, and that's assuming the murderer didn't come try to kill us all in our sleep first!"

Freddie's face flushed, and he tugged at his collar.

"Come now, Miss Electra, that's not entirely fair," Mr. Davies said. "Sergeant Andrews strikes me as quite a bright chap. I'm sure you've no need to fear that he won't arrest the right person for the murder, and we all know that won't be you, so why worry yourself?"

"He's ambitious, you know," Ellie explained with the appearance of candor. "He wanted to marry me once to improve his social standing so that he could rise higher in his career, and he's resented me ever since I turned him down. I don't trust him at all."

Maia had listened to this with mounting irritation, and now she couldn't keep silent any longer. "What nonsense, Ellie. Ray isn't that type at all—and you can't say he wanted to marry you based on his escorting you to one dance. Besides, he doesn't need to marry anyone to further his career—he'll manage that quite nicely all on his own."

Ellie's eyes flashed green fire. "Excuse us, gentlemen," she said. "My sister is clearly distraught over this situation and not thinking clearly."

Once again, Maia found her arm grabbed as a sister dragged her off for a private conversation—or more accurately, a private diatribe.

"How could you come here to spoil all our fun!" Ellie said in the small room next to the billiard room, stamping her foot. "You simply couldn't stand the idea of us enjoying ourselves while you were stuck at home so you had to come to make sure we were as miserable as you?"

"Oh for goodness' sake, get a hold of yourself," Maia snapped back. "That's not why I came at all, but it's a good thing I did if you're going to be going around spreading lies about Ray like that. You should be ashamed to speak so of him!"

"He's a brute who deserves everything I say," Ellie pouted. "Don't change the subject."

"I'm not," Maia said. "Your appalling behavior in public is the subject. Do you know that Julia begged me to speak to you and Merry because you were embarrassing her so as a hostess? And that she will never invite you to another event at Little Oaks if you continue to behave like this? Is that really what you want?"

Tears of rage sprang to Ellie's eyes. "If you didn't act as though we were shaming the family name every time we had a little fun, other people wouldn't be so quick to condemn us! Freddie and Len would have laughed at what I said about Ray if you hadn't been such a prig and lectured me about it in front of them. They had enough sense to see that it was a joke! If other people disapprove of us, it's your fault! I wish you would just go away, May, and let us live our lives the way we see fit! This was one of our few chances for fun without you looming over us like an angry storm cloud, and now you've spoiled that for us as well. I wish it had been *you* who was murdered, not some strange man! Then maybe the rest of us would have a chance at life."

She stamped her foot once more for good measure and whirled out of the room in a storm of green skirt and fluttering scarves, with Maia again left behind to try to control her emotions.

Ellie didn't really wish her dead—she knew that—but that didn't make it any easier to hear such spite-filled words spilling out of her sister's mouth.

If both of her sisters wished her gone so badly, perhaps she should take Aunt Amelia up on her offer and leave now, this moment, regardless of her promises to Mr. Davies and Julia. Mr. Davies hadn't exactly looked happy to see her there in the billiard room, and he clearly had disapproved of her ever since she'd told him she was Amelia Rawlings' niece. Why shouldn't she leave him to solve his own mystery if he was going to turn a cold shoulder to her simply because of her aunt?

As for Julia, well, who was to say that she didn't secretly resent Maia as well, even while insisting Maia was the only person she could rely on? Why was Maia killing herself for others if no one even wanted her to?

Maia did not cry easily, but angry tears burned at the back of her eyes as her breath quickened. Her hands clenched and unclenched, and she was so distracted she didn't hear the door behind her open until a deep voice said,

"Oh, I say—do be careful, Miss Whitney!"

Maia composed herself in an instant, covering all signs of her hurt before she turned to greet Mr. Davies. "Excuse me?"

He motioned to her hands. "I know it's none of my business—frightfully bad form to instruct another person's apprentice—but as your aunt isn't here and she obviously hasn't taught you this yet—"

Maia glanced down and saw with shock that her hands gleamed as though they had been coated with liquid silver. "Good heavens," she said. "What is this?"

"It's common enough in new magicians," Mr. Davies said. "The stronger you are, the more dangerous this time is—and judging by the look of things, you are stronger than most."

Something in Maia's angry heart softened at that compliment, given simply and without adornment.

"The period between learning you have magic and learning

how to control it is the time when you are most likely to, well, have your magic snap out of your control and, er, well … well, consume you," Mr. Davies said.

"Oh," Maia said, fear surging up in her.

"Not to worry," he said hastily, but too late. "It's simply a matter of will, at least at this point. Not too different from learning to control one's temper, in fact. You simply have to be stronger than your magic, so that you control it rather than the other way around. And if that doesn't work, there are a few simple spells one can learn, usually some of the first an apprentice is taught, in fact, that will bleed off some of that power so that it isn't so wild and uncontrollable."

"I see." Maia certainly had had plenty of experience with practicing self-control. She concentrated on feeling her magic and forcing it down into a knot at her core. Slowly, her hands dimmed and at last returned to normal.

Mr. Davies sighed with relief. "Oh, jolly well done. If you like, I can teach you those spells, too. Again, it isn't really done for one magician to train another's apprentice, and your aunt will no doubt be put out with me for doing so, but since you're here to help me it's the least I can do. And I'd rather help you than placate your aunt, anyway," he added in a grimmer tone.

"I'm glad to hear it," Maia said. "I was afraid you had decided I was untrustworthy, after you learned who my aunt is. And I'm not her official apprentice yet," she couldn't help but add. "So you shan't be stepping on her toes. We agreed to let the matter rest until this case is solved."

"Er—yes," Mr. Davies said. He looked around the small room. "You deserve an explanation—but not here. Would you care to join me on a walk, Miss Whitney?"

His words weren't enough to entirely undo all of Maia's pain from her confrontation with her sisters, but they did help her to breathe easier.

"Yes, I rather think I would, Mr. Davies," she answered.

7

Remembering the Past

Len's time since returning to Little Oaks had not been spent pleasantly. He'd had to contact Harrison, who had been furious about how Len had, in his words, "bungled" the entire situation.

"Forty-eight hours, Davies, that's as much time as you have to clean up your mess, or I'm sending Barry out to take over," he'd growled.

Len had had to swallow his protests. Harrison knew how he felt about Agent Barry; sending him in as Len's replacement was clearly designed to spur Len on.

Upon learning that Amelia Rawlings was next door to Little Oaks, and her niece was not only a newly fledged magician but also a co-witness to the murder had also brought about some sharp comments, but in the end, Harrison had to admit that it was more than likely a coincidence.

"The girl, that is. It isn't too surprising that someone with Rawlings blood in her would be a magician, and if she's anything like her aunt she's nosy enough to witness all sorts of murders without there being anything behind it. I'm still suspicious as to what brought the Rawlings woman down at this exact time, though. Find out from the girl, if you can."

As disheartened as he was by his superior's disapproval of his handling of the affair, and as upset as he was at being anywhere near Amelia Rawlings, Len was absurdly pleased by that order, as well as by Harrison's dismissal of the notion of her as a tool—or spy—of her aunt. Not only did it confirm his own judgement about Miss Maia Whitney, it gave him full permission to tell her more of the story than he had thus far. He didn't like having to keep her in the dark. It wasn't fair when she'd been such a dashed good sport over the entire thing so far. Postponing her apprenticeship just to help him! Certainly Amelia Rawlings would never have made that kind of sacrifice.

After seeing the way Miss Ellie treated her elder sister Len was even happier at the chance to spend time with her away from the censorious eyes of others. Sisters presumably always had their squabbles, but he thought Miss Whitney must have been close to a saint to have lived for so many years with Miss Ellie without hitting her over the head with a cricket bat.

He breathed more freely as they left the house, and the further away they walked the better he felt. He took a moment to appreciate Miss Whitney's stride—she wasn't mannish in her walk, like Hermy Winters was, but she didn't mince along like so many young ladies did, either. She walked with a firm, long stride, covering the ground at a pace she could probably maintain for hours without getting exhausted.

Without the need to discuss the matter, they avoided the woods and set out in the opposite direction, toward the rolling green hills that stretched out behind Little Oaks, dotted with sheep and hedgerows and slashed across with paths white from the chalky soil.

Len could have gone on in comfortable silence with Miss Whitney for hours, but once Little Oaks was a safe distance behind them she spoke.

"The explanation, Mr. Davies?"

Tenacious, wasn't she? Ah well, that was the reason for them being here, after all. It wasn't that he didn't want to tell her what was going on, it was more that he didn't know where to start. Not only was he too accustomed to keeping this part of his life secret from everyone, how to explain that magic was involved in the war to someone who had only just learned of the existence of magic altogether?

Dash it, he had to say *something*.

Len cleared his throat. "Right. Well. Er … how much has your aunt explained to you about magic?"

"It is real, it is not of the devil, and it must be kept secret," Miss Whitney said promptly. "Oh, and it is governed by a High Council of magicians, and there are apprentices, journeymen, masters, all that sort of thing. And for some reason cigarette smoke making me nauseous helped to convince my aunt that I was a magician."

"That's it?" Len asked, appalled.

"We haven't exactly had much time for anything else," Miss Whitney pointed out. "I have been attempting to help you with this murder and the recovery of these mystery papers. I assume my aunt will explain more once I am her official apprentice."

"Yes, but …" Len trailed off. It wasn't his place to criticize Amelia Rawlings' methods of introducing magic to a newly-fledged magician when he would never reach mastery level himself or be able to take on his own apprentice, but still! To not even start out by explaining what magic was!

"In order to give you a clearer idea of what is behind the theft of these papers, as well as why your aunt and I are not—exactly—friends, I'm afraid I'm going to have to lecture a bit," he said, looking over at her and flashing an apologetic grin. "I'll try not to be too boring."

Miss Whitney smiled back, her blue eyes warming—or were they green? He still couldn't tell. "Given how new this is, I doubt I could be bored by anything regarding magic."

"Good." Len took a moment to gather his thoughts, gazing after a bird—kestrel, he thought—as it winged across the blue sky overhead. "Magic is, at its heart, a deeper connection with the world around us. I mean that quite literally, by the way—magic only works with the natural world." He scowled to himself, thinking of how that had been twisted and used against them in the case of the papers.

"So that's what Aunt Amelia meant," Miss Whitney said. "She told me that there was no need to think of Faustian bargains when it came to magic, that … how did she put it? 'True magic is merely a twist on the ordinary.'"

Len nodded. "Exactly! Magic uses elements of nature that most people can't see or sense. What magic has your aunt shown you?"

"She created fire out of nothing and it hovered above her hand," Miss Whitney said, eyes glowing in remembrance. "It was a real flame, too—it burned me when I touched it, thinking it was an illusion. And then she did another spell that fixed the burn, though she did say those weren't encouraged for anyone who wasn't a healer."

"I should think not," Len said. "Let's take the fire spell—it wasn't actually created from nothing, y'know. What your aunt did was take the material and the conditions needed to make a fire and bring them together to create a flame, while also ensuring that flame only burned where she wanted it—not her hand." It was a dashed tricky spell to do well; for all his dislike of Miss Rawlings he couldn't deny that she was a brilliant magician.

Miss Whitney's forehead wrinkled. "I think I see."

"You'll understand it better once you start practicing your own spells," Len said. He repressed a sigh. It would have been fun to teach her those basic spells right now, fun to watch her understanding dawn, fun to see the joy that always crossed an apprentice's face when they performed their first deliberate spell successfully. Alas, he was no master, and likely never would be, and this walk was for the purpose of enlightening her about the papers, not teaching her magic.

Although he would teach her some of those spells to bleed off excess magic sooner rather than later if Miss Rawlings didn't, bad form or not.

"This is mostly background to the story I have to tell you," he continued, stopping for a moment to lean against an old, greying wooden fence. Miss Whitney stopped as well, perching on a lower branch of an apple tree near the fence. "Because of the nature of magic, magicians are limited in what they can and cannot do. We are also limited by the prohibitions we've put on ourselves. No magician may use his or her magic to directly harm another, for one. Killing someone through magical means is one of our most heinous crimes, and stripping someone of their magic is merely one half-step below." He flinched, recalling the one and only time he'd seen someone lose their magical abilities. With practiced skill, he shoved the memory away. "Another rule is that magicians may not use our magic to influence political affairs."

"You're speaking of the war," Miss Whitney said at once.

"Leading up to speaking of it, yes."

"Aunt Amelia said that magicians have their own political process for governing themselves—ourselves, I mean."

"Yes, but we don't use magic to interfere in ordinary politics. Not even when we desperately want to, or think it would be for the best. Such as at the start of the war."

"I suppose I can understand that as a principle," Miss Whitney conceded. "When one sees the trouble that can be caused by ordinary politics, one can see how adding magic to the mix would make things even more volatile. Not to mention making it that much harder to keep magic a secret. Though I would expect I would have had a hard time adhering to that if I'd known I was a magician during the war," she added with a rueful smile. "Principles are much easier to keep from an abstract distance."

"Indeed," Len agreed. "This principle is one held by nearly all magicians of all the civilized countries, but from the start of the war in 1914, it became clear to the magicians of this country and a few others that the Kaiser had a magician helping him. Not an untrained witch or wizard, mind, nor even an apprentice or journeyman, but a real master magician. This Kaiser's Advisor—oh I say, that's rather good—was in it, not because she believed in his cause, but for personal power. She wanted to use him to conquer the world, so she could direct everything according to her whims and wishes, without anyone knowing who she was at all."

"How did the other magicians find out about it?"

"Er ..." Len wanted to say that it wasn't relevant, but unfortunately it *was* relevant, as it was the entire reason he was involved in this mess and at the heart of his distrust for her aunt. He cleared his throat. "Yes. Well. Some of us in my line of work suspected there was a magical element to the Kaiser's warfare, so we took it upon ourselves to investigate. Three of us went over, and—and only I returned, due to the other two's sacrifice." He closed his mouth abruptly.

"I see." Miss Whitney's voice was surprisingly gentle. "Is it permitted that I ask what your line of work is?"

"Oh, that," Len said, relieved to have the subject changed, even temporarily. "It's exactly what I told you it was last night, with one difference—I work for the magical government of Britain, not the ordinary one. And not many people know about my role as an agent for Magical Intelligence, so do please keep it under your hat."

She straightened her charming brown felt hat, slightly askew from her climb onto the branch, and smiled at him. "No fear," she said, the boyish slang sounding delightfully absurd coming from her mouth.

Len couldn't help but grin back at her. "When I presented the proof to the Council, they decided desperate measures had to be taken. Against all precedent, they formed an international alliance—a coalition of magicians, if you will. British, French, American, Italian, Greek, and one young lady magician from Japan who had such a different style of practicing magic I'm still not sure I understand it. I wasn't part of the coalition—I'm not powerful or talented enough in my magic—but because of my role in collecting the information I was privy to some of the details." He shook his head, still amazed at what they'd pulled off. "One dozen of the finest magicians in the world."

"What happened?" Miss Whitney asked.

"They stopped her. I'm still not exactly sure how—Harrison

never said." Len remembered the occasion with crystal clarity. His mentor had knocked on the door of the dingy hotel room Len was staying in while he waited to hear the results of the spell. Len nearly wrenched the door off the hinges in his nervous eagerness for information.

Harrison's face was grey and old, but there was a fierce light of satisfaction in his eyes. "It's done," he said. "They did it."

"She's dead?" Len asked, gripping the sides of the doorframe.

"She'll never use her magic to hurt anyone ever again," Harrison confirmed. "They stopped her in time."

Len blinked and brought himself back to the present. He cleared his throat and continued his tale. "The spell they created and used was tremendous; nothing like it had ever been done before. Not that was recorded, anyway. Think of it, Maia—I mean, Miss Whitney—all the power behind each magician, each nationality's distinct style of magic, all working together for one purpose. It was remarkable."

"Then what?"

"With the Kaiser's Advisor (whom I shall now refer to as the K.A. so as to save time) stopped, the surviving members of the coalition scattered back to their previous pursuits. I returned to the war as an ordinary soldier." Len paused. Might as well tell her the whole truth. "Well no, actually, I was a spy. But an ordinary spy, not a magical one. The war returned to one fought by ordinary means, not magic. Without the K.A, the Kaiser once again had to rely on his own wits and regular advisors, as did we."

Miss Whitney tilted her head. "I'm afraid I'm not seeing the problem. It sounds like a happy ending, or at least as happy as anything could be from the War."

"Each of the magicians brought his or her apprentice, to help with the basic spell-ingredient-collecting, errand-running, and note-taking," Len said, choosing his words carefully. "The apprentices were supposed to destroy all the notes once the spell was complete and the K.A. was defeated. One did not."

"And that was bad."

"Very," he said emphatically. "For two reasons. One, with those notes, if a person could get twelve powerful and unscrupulous magicians together, they could recreate the spell. And the power that comes with it."

"Very bad," Miss Whitney agreed.

"Two, if said unscrupulous person should decide not to use the spell, or couldn't gather together enough magicians to perform it, he could still make use of it by publishing it. There are details in the notes, names, incontrovertible proof that magic, and magicians, exist. All these centuries of balance between magicians and non-magical folk, gone in a heartbeat."

"And those notes are the papers that were exchanged last night."

"Yes," Len confirmed. He drew in a quick breath and then told her the worst of it. "The man whose servant was shot? The one who gave the papers to the murderer in exchange for thirty silver coins? He was the lone apprentice who didn't destroy his notes. Samuel Corbin. Your aunt's former apprentice."

Miss Whitney was silent for a stretch. Then,

"I see," she said.

"You should feel honored, really," Len hurried on. He didn't quite know what he was saying, but he felt he had to say something to take away that frozen look from her face. "Miss Rawlings swore afterward that she'd never take another apprentice. For her to take you on is a significant step."

Miss Whitney did not respond to that platitude. But after

a few more moments, she faced him again, her shoulders squared and her head high. "Under the circumstances, then, who do you think would be most likely to take the papers and shoot Mr. Corbin's manservant? He would have to be a magician, wouldn't he? No one else would know of their existence."

Len felt a pang of surprise. He'd wanted to distract her from the uncomfortable realization that her aunt had fostered a traitor and that her entrance into the world of magic was unfortunately tainted by that—but he hadn't expected her to turn practical *quite* so quickly. It took him a moment or two longer to switch back into thinking about the case. In the pause, Miss Whitney gracefully let herself down from the apple tree and started walking again. Len hurried to keep up.

"It's not necessarily a magician. There were some people close to the Kaiser and his advisor who were not magicians themselves but were made aware of magic because of her deeds—another reason she had to be stopped. We—that is, Magical Intelligence—believe that some of them are working to try to find proof to reveal the existence of magic to the world in hopes of destabilizing Britain, France, and the rest of Europe enough for Germany and Austria to rise to power again."

"I see. So we are looking for either a German agent or a rogue magician?"

Len wasn't sure why, but he told her his worst fear, the one that even Harrison thought ridiculous. "There is also a small group in England of individuals who have become convinced of the existence of magic, and think that magicians are controlling the government and secretly ruling everything, and who are also determined to reveal what they think is the truth to the world. My fear is that Corbin was working with one of them, and that's who shot his man and now has the papers."

"Why them over any of the others?"

"Corbin is a greedy fool and a traitor to magicians, but I don't think he would deliberately betray England," Len told her, hands in his pockets now as he strode along. This was where he and Harrison disagreed. Harrison believed that a magician who would turn on his own kind wouldn't hesitate to betray his country as well. Len, who had actually interacted with Corbin once or twice while the coalition was working, disagreed. He'd seen the way Miss Rawlings treated Corbin, and thought that anyone might be driven to strike a blow against her without actually thinking of themselves as a traitor. He suspected that Corbin had taken the papers more as an act of defiance against Amelia Rawlings than against magicians in general, and only afterward realized what exactly he had done.

"And the magician?"

"A magician who had turned power-mad enough to take those papers for himself wouldn't have hesitated to use a magic spell against Corbin and Carter. At the very least, he would have used a spell to enhance his vision rather than boast of his excellent night vision. And—I don't know, but something in the way he taunted Corbin for the betrayal of 'your own' made it seem like he was outside the community of magicians, not within it."

"That makes sense," Miss Whitney said, surprising and pleasing him. Len was used to being told his ideas were all rot, even when he knew they weren't.

"We should still treat everyone as a suspect, though," he

added hastily, on the off chance his ideas really *were* rot. "At least, all the men. The silhouette we saw leaving Little Oaks was certainly male, wouldn't you agree?"

"Yes, although unfortunately too far away to tell whether tall, short, old, young, fat, thin, or anything. I only saw the outline of the trousers and tailcoat, and the way he walked." Miss Whitney sighed. "I wish I'd known then of a spell to use on my eyes to improve my vision!"

"I wouldn't recommend it," Len hurried to warn her. "Casting spells on one's own self isn't quite as frowned upon as casting spells on others, but it's still dangerous. And vision spells are some of the hardest to master. Can often end in a person going blind, y'know."

Maia shuddered. "Perhaps it's just as well I didn't know about it, then."

"Now, there is one spell that's perfectly safe to cast on yourself. I call it a chameleon spell, though properly it's known as a blending spell. You can't turn yourself invisible, not really, but you can use magic to help you blend into the background, cause people to not notice you."

Miss Whitney turned an amused look on him. "I can see why you would like that one."

Len frowned. "Why is that?"

"A chameleon—that's who you are, isn't it? You're always shifting your personality to fit into your surroundings. I wasn't sure what to make of you at first, but now I think I see what it is you do. It's because of being a spy—sorry, an agent—isn't it?"

Len found himself walking a little faster, as though trying to avoid the question. It was no good—Miss Whitney simply increased her pace to keep up with him. He didn't answer until they were at the top of the hill, surveying the green and white landscape around them, with the sky seeming so close he could have thought it a blue glass dome arching overhead, impossibly fragile and delicate.

"I suppose I do what the job requires," he said at last.

"Exactly." Miss Whitney nodded, seeming satisfied with that answer.

Len wasn't sure *he* was satisfied. What the dickens did the woman mean, looking into his soul and pulling it out into the light like this? Didn't she know there were some things one simply didn't speak of? Agents weren't supposed to be noticed … people weren't supposed to see through them so easily. Dashed interfering woman, no wonder her sisters were so upset when she arrived. She couldn't leave anyone with their defenses intact, had to go about brutally exposing them to the world.

On the other hand … she'd taken the news that her aunt's prior apprentice was a traitor remarkably well, she'd witnessed a murder without falling to pieces and gone along with his request to keep his involvement secret from the police, and she'd even put off accepting an official apprenticeship with her aunt just to help him find the papers and bring the murderer to justice.

His ire melted away. Even if she was a touch interfering, her good qualities far outweighed the bad, and no one, no matter what, deserved a sister like Miss Electra Whitney.

Miss Whitney breathed deeply of the fresh, cool breeze whipping around the hilltop, teasing the little reddish-brown curls that peeked out from beneath her hat and bringing a sparkle to her eyes, which Len couldn't help but notice now looked much more green than blue.

Peacock feather eyes, he told himself with satisfaction. That's what they were. The same subtle shading of blue shifting into green, the same shine and iridescence … well, not quite the same, but as close as human eyes could get. Stars and peacocks—there was much more to Miss Maia Whitney than first met the eye.

"Thank you for trusting me with this information, Mr. Davies," she said, facing him squarely, with the sun sparkling down on her. "I understand now why you were so suspicious when you learned who my aunt was, and that she was here. I appreciate you taking the time to explain it all to me."

"It wasn't that I suspected you, necessarily, but the situation did look dodgy," Len admitted. "In my line of work it's hard to believe in coincidences, even though that seems to have been what happened here."

"Aunt Amelia certainly seemed genuinely stunned when she learned who was murdered and that you were here," Miss Whitney said. "I don't think she knew any of this was going to happen."

Most likely she'd tried to forget Corbin still existed. It must have been a blow to her to learn that not only was he still around, he'd gone and gotten his servant killed in the middle of an underhanded deal with the papers, and all in front of her niece. But no—Miss Whitney wouldn't have told her all that, of course. Len had asked her to keep quiet about the details, and he had no doubt whatsoever she would have done so. Still, whatever snippets Miss Rawlings had learned would have been enough to shake her complacency for once.

If anything could. It wasn't only her ill treatment of her apprentice leading to him revolting that made Len dislike her. His feud with Miss Rawlings went far deeper than that.

Before he could sink into gloom, he was pulled from his dark thoughts by Miss Whitney speaking again.

"Do you have a plan for recovering the papers and catching the murderer? What do you want me to do? I can't say I've noticed anything terribly suspicious yet, unless you count the odious Sir Bertram Grimes making love to a woman half his age." She scowled fiercely.

Len wasn't sure what she was talking about there, and decided it was safer not to ask. "Sir Bertram is on the suspect list," he said. "As are Mr. Saunders, Robert and Paul Danvers, Timothy Spencer, and Freddie Winters. Foy is clear—he was seen by too many people passing out drinks and being a good host for him to have slipped off to the woods to meet with Corbin. Not to mention that his limp would have been noticeable even from a distance."

"Good heavens," Maia said. "I can't imagine either of the Danvers lads being guilty of any crime, much less Tim. And I don't know Mr. Winters well, but he doesn't strike me as the type to want to destroy everything. Mr. Saunders, now ... I barely even remember him. His wife was the complaining one at dinner, yes?"

Len didn't think the Danvers lads or young Spencer were murderers, either, but who knew how the war had affected them. Even the mildest and kindest of men had come home broken from it. The younger of the vicar's sons—Paul, that was it—was too young for the war, but both Spencer and the older Danvers boy, Robert, had fought. And even young Paul could have caught some political fervor that made him believe the world would be a better place if magicians were revealed to all.

Still, he couldn't help but admit he hoped it was Grimes or

Saunders. "Yes, that's right. But we can't narrow it down too much—those were just the men who were at the house party. It could have been any of the chaps who were there only for the dance, though I'm hoping not. Harrison—my superior—thought that the buyer would be at the house party, so that's where my focus mostly is. My man Becket is looking into the servants."

"The man didn't speak like a servant," Miss Whitney said doubtfully.

"No, but the servants might have a better idea of who is likely to be our guilty party."

Her brow cleared. "Oh, I see. Your manservant works with you, then?"

"Oh yes, I'd be lost without Becket," Len said airily. "Bit of a nervous chap, but jolly good backup."

"It must be nice," she said, and the irony was strong enough in her voice for Len to wonder just what her family's servant situation was like.

"I suppose the plan right now is to poke away at people and hope that something turns up," Len said.

By her frown, it seemed Miss Whitney wasn't fond of something so indefinite. "What about the papers?" she said. "If they were used for such a powerful spell, they must have a great deal of, I don't know, magical residue or something of that sort about them, mustn't they? Can't you cast a spell to find them?"

"I could, except that Corbin has kept them in a Bakelite case ever since he stole them," Len said. At her puzzled look, he elaborated. "Magic only works with natural materials, remember? Bakelite is made entirely of synthetic components. We can't use any sort of a spell to find it."

"I see." She paused, then asked, "Magic is attuned to the natural world, yes?"

"Yes," Len said with patience, reminding himself this was still quite new to her.

"Then couldn't you use a spell to find the spots where nothing responds to magic? Wouldn't that give you at least a place to start looking?" As Len stared at her, she added nervously, "Or is that also something that isn't done? Was that a foolish idea? I'm sorry, perhaps I shouldn't have said anything, I just ..."

"No, no!" he said, his brain beginning to function again. "Don't apologize! That's just—that's *brilliant*, Maia. By Jove! Why didn't that occur to me?"

She flushed, her cheeks darkening to a rosy hue. "Then—it could work?"

"I'd have to think about what spell to use, but yes, by George, I think it very well might. I say, Miss Whitney, you've got quite the knack for this."

"Which—magic or solving puzzles?"

"Both, I should say," Len said. "And by the way, since we're working together now, don't you think we might drop the Mr. Davies and Miss Whitney?"

"It does seem a bit excessive given we witnessed a murder together," she conceded. With an impish grin, she added, "And you already called me Maia just now."

"Did I?" Len hadn't even noticed. In truth, he'd been having a hard time thinking of her as anything but Maia for a little while now. "I am sorry. Didn't mean to be rude."

She shook her head. "Not rude at all. Very well—Lennox. May I help with the spell, once you've decided which one to use?"

"I should say so, Maia," he answered, grinning at her. Generally he didn't care for friends using his full first name, as it made him feel like a small boy in trouble with his mother again, but it sounded oddly nice coming from Miss—Maia. "But first, I think I ought to show you some of the basic spells to use to bleed off excess power."

"Now?" she asked with a little gasp.

He was about to say yes when he caught sight of two figures making their way up the hill toward them. The small blonde one had to be Julia, and the man accompanying her was too burly to be anyone but Sergeant Andrews.

"Dash it all," Len said in annoyance. "Not now. Tonight," he said in a hurry. "We'll meet in the woods after dinner, where we're less likely to be interrupted. I'll teach you one or two spells, and then we can cast the spell to find the spots where magic isn't."

Maia nodded, her eyes still bright despite the disappointment of having to wait until later to do anything with her magic. With her in the lead, they started down the hill to learn whatever it was Julia and Sergeant Andrews had come all this way to tell them.

8

The Wrong Murderer

Maia didn't think she'd had such an exhausting day since she'd been in France, and it wasn't over yet. From discovering that magic was real to learning the story behind the mysterious stolen papers to having her sisters wish her dead to discovering that her aunt's prior apprentice was responsible for all of this … she wasn't sure which was more overwhelmed, her head or her heart. She was almost thankful for the search for the missing papers and the murderer, as it gave her something to focus on until she could sit down quietly and untangle all her other emotions and thoughts.

"Oh good," Julia called, pausing halfway up the hill and waiting for them to come to her. "You're together." Maia tried to ignore the speculation in Julia's gaze and the way she lingered over the word "together."

"Were you looking for us both?" Mr. Davies—Lennox—asked.

"Mostly you at the moment, but I wanted to find Maia next," Julia answered. "Sergeant Andrews has found the murderer, isn't it marvelous? He says we can carry on with the house party."

Maia nearly tripped in her surprise. Goodness, could Ray really have uncovered the murderer while she and Len were talking? And if he had—what had become of the papers?

"I say, jolly good show!" Len said heartily. There was no trace of surprise or concern in his voice. He was a *very* good chameleon. "Who is it, or mustn't I ask?"

They had met up with the other two now. Ray gave Maia a nod of recognition before answering Len.

"No one staying at Little Oaks, I'm happy to say. Not even a guest at the dance. A man named Corbin, who appears to have been the victim's employer."

Maia blinked a few times. "Goodness," she managed to say. "However did you manage to find him?"

"Not a very bright fellow," Ray said. "He'd checked into the Owl's Dance two nights ago and was still there, the silly juggins. We found his footprints all around the body and matched them to the boots he put out to be cleaned late last night. The only thing we haven't found is the gun, but even a fool would know enough to get rid of the murder weapon."

"Strange chap," Lennox mused. "Why come all the way out to the countryside with your valet and then shoot him in the middle of the woods at midnight, and then drag his body to the nearest estate, and then go back and sleep at the same inn? You'd think it would have been simpler just to shoot him wherever it was this Corbin chap was living rather than making such a song-and-dance of it."

Ray shrugged. "Who knows what he was thinking? There's enough evidence to charge him, and that's what the C.C. told me to do, so there's an end to it."

Despite his words, Maia had the notion Ray wasn't entirely

happy about the situation. He had to know as well as she did that the evidence was only circumstantial, and despite his rebuttal of Len's objection, the glint in his eyes showed it had gone home. But what else could he do if the Chief Constable told him to make an arrest?

"Isn't it marvelous?" Julia repeated, seemingly oblivious to these undercurrents. "Now we can relax and enjoy the rest of our time together." She looped one arm through Maia's and the other through Len's, tilting her head to beam up at first one, then the other. "If it weren't for the fact that a man died, I'd almost be glad this happened, as otherwise Maia would never have joined the house party, but now that she's here we certainly won't let her leave again, will we, Len?"

"I should think not," Len agreed amiably.

Maia couldn't keep her shoulders from stiffening instinctively. While she did think it was important to stay in order to help Lennox catch the real murderer and recover the stolen papers, her heart told her she was being patronized. Julia meant well, but her constant attempts to "help" Maia come out of her shell and enjoy society more tended to have the opposite effect than what was intended. Maia enjoyed certain types of society well enough, and while she knew she was reserved, she didn't consider that she had a shell, but Julia's conviction always made her want to build one and retire behind it from society forever. Len's casual falling-in with Julia's tone and mindset grated as well. She was sure it was all a part of his cover, but it was frustrating nonetheless.

She felt that she had been given the occasional glimpse of the true Lennox Davies, but every time she did his mask came back on and the man she felt she could respect and even befriend vanished. How could one trust a man who wore so many faces and adapted so easily to what other people expected him to be?

And in all this, poor Ray was left awkwardly striding down the hill after them, excluded from their cozy group by virtue of his class and his job alike. Maia deftly freed her arm from Julia and dropped back a step to smile up at the tall policeman.

"How's your father, Ray?"

His shoulders loosened a trifle, and he offered her a tentative smile in return. "As cranky as ever, thank you, Miss Whitney."

"Good heavens, Ray, since when have I been Miss Whitney to you? First Alan, and now you. When you consider all the mischief we stirred up as children ..."

He shrugged. "Must follow protocol," he said, then closed his mouth in a stubborn line. Maia recognized that expression. There was no use in coaxing him further. When Ray Andrews wore that expression, his mind was made up and nothing would change it.

Julia glanced over her shoulder at them. "Mischief? What sort of mischief? I can't imagine Maia ever doing anything so improper as mischief, even as a child."

It took all Maia's self-control to neither roll her eyes nor flinch, and she couldn't decide which impulse had been stronger. Ignoring it, she said, "When I was six years old, Mother brought me shopping in the village with her for the first time. She saw a friend and they started talking, and I got more and more bored until I saw a group of boys heading out of town. I promptly abandoned Mother and followed them. They tried to get me to leave once they noticed me, but one boy, about my age, said they should set me a test and if I passed I could stay and fish with them. The first test was whether or not I could put a worm on a fishhook."

She had hated that, but set her teeth and did it despite the way it made her stomach turn flips.

"Ugh," said Julia. "How horrid."

Ray gave a reminiscent smile. "None of us thought you'd do it, but even when your face turned green you stuck with it and finally got the worm on."

"The next test was after one of the boys caught their first fish. They removed the hook and told me I had to hold the fish." That had been almost worse than the worm, holding that wriggling, slippery, slimy fish while it desperately tried to writhe from her grasp.

Now Ray chuckled. "She succeeded in that as well, and we had just decided to give her a rod of her own and let her fish with us when all our mothers came storming down through the trees, furious at us boys for luring the little Miss Whitney away."

"Except my mother, who was furious at me for ruining my frock and behaving in such an unladylike fashion and scaring her half to death by vanishing from the street," Maia picked up the thread. "In the end, we were all in disgrace. None of the other boys ever forgave me for ruining their fishing fun like that, but Ray, who was the one who had first suggested testing me, stuck by me. We used to sneak away together to fish whenever I could escape from my governess."

"I admired her pluck," Ray said. "How could I not?" He grinned outright. "And then after we started fishing together, I realized that I caught twice as much when she was with me than I did on my own, so of course I wanted to keep fishing with her. I guess she chased them all away from her line toward mine."

"I still think it's horribly unfair that I never caught anything and you caught everything," Maia said with a sniff of mock outrage.

"Sneaking away from your governess, fishing with the boys, hiding things from your mother … I never thought you had it in you," Julia said, shaking her head.

"People are always surprising us, even our nearest and dearest," Len murmured, as though to himself. Maia looked carefully at his profile and thought she detected the hint of a smile.

"I learned how to climb trees from Alan—Constable Maddox," Maia said. "His grandfather was our groundskeeper when I was a girl, and Alan spent almost all his free time either helping his grandfather or playing with Ray and me. And," she added with a smug look at Ray, "I am still the only one of the three of us who can whistle through my fingers."

Ray shook his head. "Tried and tried, we did, but it was no good."

"And now both you and Constable Maddox are with the police," Julia said. "Maia, why didn't you join the force as well?" She chuckled. "You'd have made a smashing constable yourself."

Maia felt the pang once again that she had felt the day the boys had told her she could only keep playing with them if she played the role of victim of whatever crime they were investigating as Sherlock Holmes and A.J. Raffles. It had been the beginning of the end of their friendship, and the beginning of the end of her childhood as well.

"Oh well, they were both mad about Sherlock Holmes and Raffles when we were all about twelve," she said lightly, hiding the hurt that still lingered. "So naturally they joined the force. Alas, there were not so many stories about lady detectives, so my path went in a different direction."

"Lady Molly of Scotland Yard," Len said unexpectedly. "Dorcas Dene. Miss Violet Strange. Miss Loveday Brooke." He grinned at the three identical looks of surprise the others showed him. "Detective fiction is a bit of a hobby of mine."

"I wish you'd been around when we were younger," Maia said, once she had her breath back. "Perhaps you could have persuaded the boys to let me join in as a detective in my own right!"

"Not likely," Ray observed. "You would have beaten all of us at detecting. Trying to convince you to be the victim was the only way we could keep our sense of superiority."

Maia laughed, but she couldn't help but wonder if that really was why they had shut her out, and if so, did it change anything in how she viewed the past?

There was no time for introspection now, as they had returned to the grounds and were met by a contingent made up of Ellie, Freddie, Hermione and Rob Danvers. Eyeing the Honorable Hermione's knickerbockers and knitted jumper, Maia couldn't decide if she envied the other woman her insouciance in wearing men's clothes, or disliked the belligerent attitude that accompanied it, which seemed to invite people's disapproval whether they were initially inclined to be scandalized or not.

The knickerbockers did look more comfortable than the tweed skirt Maia was wearing, though, and far more practical for walking, let alone hunting down stolen papers. And wouldn't Ellie be horrified if Maia started wearing such things!

Maia smothered a wicked grin at the idea. She knew she'd never have the courage to wear men's clothing in public, but oh, the idea was tempting, if only to see how her sisters and mother would react.

"There you are!" Ellie called out, rushing up to them and latching onto Len's free arm. She tugged a bit in an attempt to free him from Julia, but either Julia or Len or both held on with unusual tenacity, and Ellie was forced to share him. "Have you heard? The police have finally managed to catch the brute who murdered that servant, and we are all free to go about our business. I was sure *you* would be the one to catch him." She pouted up at him. "I'm ever so disappointed you let the police beat you to it."

"That is their job," Len said mildly.

"We were wondering about a spot of tennis," Rob said, swinging a racket. "Still seems a bit insensitive, given that the poor chap just died, but it isn't as though any of us knew him, and it seems as though the whole thing isn't connected to anyone here in any way ..." He trailed off, his upbringing as a vicar's son fighting against his natural desire to enjoy life.

"Marvelous," Julia said. "Maia, Len, you'll play, won't you?"

Maia thought she might have been the only one to notice Len's nearly imperceptible sigh. "Of course," he said, and again Maia's ears picked up a hint of weariness. No wonder, having to play games and keep up a good face when all he really wanted was to find those missing papers—and the murderer.

She was not so constrained, though she didn't have the magical skill yet to cast the spell to find the papers, or rather, identify where they weren't. She had another task on her mind, however. "I'll pass, Julia. You know how appalling my tennis skills are."

"We certainly do," Ellie put in with a laugh.

"We are none of us professionals," Julia swiftly countered. "But of course you needn't play if you'd rather not." She glared at Ellie, who almost, but not quite, put her tongue out at her in return.

"Merry won't play, I know," Rob put in, sounding gloomy. "She doesn't approve of tennis, and she's busy with that Sir Bertram Grimes, discussing factories or something. But hopefully most of the others will join."

"They've been thick as thieves ever since the dance," Freddie added with a laugh. "Saw them with m'own eyes, dancing every dance together. How our mothers would have been shocked! Wasn't there some rule back in their day about no more than two dances, three at the most? Glad times have changed. Imagine having to try to keep up with all those maths."

Without meaning to, Maia cast a quick glance at Len, only to find his eyes on her. Sir Bertram had an alibi, and it was Maia's own sister! Their best suspect, gone in a flash. What a frightful nuisance.

Not to mention that she still wasn't comfortable with her very young sister getting so closely involved with a man as cold and calculating as Sir Bertram Grimes. Merry might have been seventeen, but she was still mostly a child in her outlook on life, despite thinking she was grown-up. In some ways, Maia had been hoping he would be the villain, as it would forcibly remove him from Merry's presence. Now she'd have to think of something else, along with helping Len find the papers, uncover the murderer's true identity, and ask Aunt Amelia for more information about her former apprentice, Mr. Samuel Corbin, now being held by the police for a murder he didn't commit.

* * *

There was only time for a hurried word with Len as they returned to the house and he made for his room to change into his tennis clothes. When he caught the gist of what Maia wanted, his face lit up with understanding.

"Ah! Jolly good thinking. Right-o—my valet can help with that. He's a dab hand at those sort of simple domestic spells, is Becket. I'll let him know he's to make himself available to you as soon as the rest of us have left to play this wretched tennis."

He twisted his face into a schoolboy grimace, which startled Maia into a laugh, and then vanished into his bedroom. Maia first started to move toward her bedroom, intending to wait there for everyone to leave, but then paused, remembering those tantalizing books she'd seen in the library.

Which reminded her that she hadn't yet had the opportunity to ask Mr. Davies—Len—if Dan was a magician or if it had been one of his now-dead relatives.

If it was Dan, how must it have felt, losing a leg in the war when he knew magic could have healed it if it weren't for the need for secrecy? That must have made him angry. It would have made Maia angry, at least, and she couldn't imagine it being any different for Dan.

Angry enough to steal papers that would force the revelation of magic on the entire world …?

Maia raised a hand as though to physically push the thought away. What rubbish! Dan had been seen for too much of the evening, not to mention that, as Len had pointed out, his limp made his figure too distinctive to have been the individual they saw leaving the house for the meeting in the woods.

Unless, of course, there were spells that could make it look like a person was in one place when in reality he was in another, and to compensate for a missing leg …

The problem was that Maia simply didn't know enough about magic to know whether either of those things were possible. She was speculating wildly at this point, all for lack of enough information. She made up her mind that she would start reading that *Spells and Incantations for Beginners* book and see if she could combat some of this ignorance. If the book wasn't enough, she could always ask Aunt Amelia or Len's valet, but she hated to ask such pointed questions aimed at Dan unless she had no other choice. She didn't want to spread any unwarranted suspicion.

To Maia's relief, the library was empty of all other people, most especially of her sister and Sir Bertram. Maia was able to locate the glowing books, remove the one she wanted, and sit down at the nearest table to read without worrying about anyone seeing her.

She was only a few pages into the introduction when she was interrupted by a diffident cough. She looked up to see a small man with a thin face, sleek brown hair, brown eyes, and nervous hands hovering just inside the doorway.

"Miss, ah, Whitney?" he asked. "Terribly sorry to interrupt, but Mr. Davies said you had a task I could assist with?"

Maia set aside the book. "Mr. Becket, I presume?" At his nod, she continued. "Very pleased to meet you, Mr. Becket. Yes indeed, I would like to contact my aunt to ask her some questions about Mr. Corbin, but I don't want to do it over the telephone, where anyone might hear. Is there a spell that would allow me to contact her instead, and if so, would you be so kind as to set it up for me? I've yet to learn even the simplest incantation," she ended with a sigh, glancing wistfully at the book.

Mr. Becket advanced further into the room. "Certainly,

Miss Whitney. Communication spells are not terribly difficult, though they do require some concentration. I am happy to help. However, I am only a poor magician," he warned. "This spell will not be as good as if Mr. Davies or Miss Rawlings herself cast it."

Maia laughed. "Mr. Becket, I am not even an official apprentice. I can assure you, the simplest spell will impress me."

He smiled. Maia was amazed at the change it made in his face, and she warmed to him.

"From what Mr. Davies says of you, miss, I don't think that will be the case for long."

Maia was surprised to feel herself blush. Perhaps Mr. Becket was even surprised at his daring, for he dropped his eyes and hurried into speech.

"Do you have notepaper and a pen?" he asked.

"There must be some in here," Maia said, opening drawers to check. "Yes, here we are!" She set a sheet of notepaper, an ink bottle, and a pen on the table.

"Excellent," Becket said, sketching an arrow in the air. "*A hac charta illi.*"

Maia stared at the paper. "I don't mean to complain, but … nothing seems to have happened."

Becket patted his forehead with a handkerchief. "You may now write to your aunt as if you were talking to her, miss."

Still skeptical, Maia inked her pen and wrote, *Aunt Amelia?*

As she wrote the final "a," the first had faded from sight, and in a moment the paper was as blank as it had been at first. Maia frowned and checked her pen nib. She jumped when different words began forming on the paper before her very eyes.

Maia? Is that you? Is Mr. Davies with you? What in heaven's name is happening over there?

"Goodness gracious," Maia said weakly. She looked up at the hovering valet. "That's marvelous!"

He beamed and stepped back. "I'm happy to have helped, Miss Whitney." He hesitated, then added, "I will have to remain close by in order to end the spell properly when you are finished, but I will be by the door so as to ensure your privacy."

"You are most kind," Maia said. She turned her attention back to the paper.

The police have arrested Samuel Corbin for the murder of his valet. I have learned the story of the great spell you and the other magicians did during the war, and why it is so important to recover the papers. Can you tell me anything at all about Mr. Corbin, who he might have tried selling the papers to, who his associates might be, anything at all?

There was a pause after the words disappeared. Maia began to think her aunt wouldn't answer at all, when black letters began to appear again.

If the story of the great spell was told you by Mr. Davies, don't believe everything you heard. The man isn't to be trusted. As for Corbin, I have always made it a point not to interfere in my apprentices' personal lives. I know nothing about him beyond the scope of his magical abilities, which are nothing spectacular. If you want to recover the papers so badly, why are you wasting time asking me nonsensical questions? You ought to be out there finding them.

Maia huffed a small sigh. How typical. No help and only criticism. Perhaps her mother and Aunt Amelia weren't so different after all.

I've no intention of wearing myself out running hither and thither after airy nothings if I can instead gain information simply by asking for it, she wrote back, the pen stabbing the paper rather harder than necessary. *It seemed only sensible to go to the person who ought to have known him best before hunting at random for the papers.*

I was never the person who knew him best, the answer came back in big, bold letters. Maia could almost hear her aunt's snappish tone. *He had a lady friend with whom he used to spend all his free time, but I never learned her name. I believe he intended to marry her, as he was always mooning about how wonderful it was to find a woman who cared about raising a family and living a simple life compared to so many modern women, but I paid no attention. It always seemed insensitive to me, though it takes more than that to offend me. I am* proud *of being a modern woman.*

A small snort of laughter escaped Maia, causing Mr. Becket to jump.

"Sorry," she said. He had been so quiet she'd forgotten he was still in the room.

"Not at all, miss," he replied politely.

Is there anyone who would know her name? she wrote.

I am sure somebody would, but no one I can identify, Aunt Amelia answered. *I told you, I didn't bother with his personal life. I don't even know if he had any friends. Mr. Davies spent some time speaking with him—why not ask* him?

Maia frowned. The dislike Mr. Davies and her aunt held for each other seemed to go far beyond what seemed like a reasonable animosity caused by two strong personalities clashing with each other. For all that Len had told her the story of the Kaiser's Advisor—oh good grief, now she was using that absurd title—she couldn't help but feel there was still more he was hiding. As for her aunt, who knew why she disliked Len? It could have been for any number of reasons.

I will, thank you, she wrote. *Any other advice?*

Only that you stop shilly-shallying and finish this quickly. If I have to stay another day with Lettie I won't be held responsible for my actions.

Maia laughed again and looked to the door.

"I believe we are finished, Mr. Becket."

The small man directed a look of intense concentration toward the paper and clenched his hand in a fist. *"Finiatur,"* he said. Maia recognized the Latin imperative that translated to "be finished" in English.

"Are all spells done in Latin, then?"

"Not quite, miss," Becket said. "Latin is not the only language for incantations—and many defensive spells don't even require a spoken incantation, because often when one needs defense, one cannot speak—but when you do need an incantation, it is considered best for English speakers to use Latin for its precision. Most European magicians use Latin in their incantations."

"What of non-European magicians?" Maia asked.

"I believe some of the Russians use Greek. Americans, those who use magic at all, usually use Latin as well. The Japanese work magic in a completely different manner than we do, so I'm afraid I don't know if they even use incantations, or use them in the same way." Becket looked apologetic.

Maia had to close her eyes for a moment.

"Miss Whitney? Are you unwell?"

"It's simply—a bit dizzying," she said. She opened her eyes and attempted a smile. "Learning there's real magic, used by ordinary people. Learning how to use it. Finding that there's conspiracies going on behind even political machinations. We have one way of doing magic, but people in another land have another. And on top of everything else, referring to 'we' at all, because not only is magic real, I apparently have a knack for it!"

Part of her was appalled at speaking so freely to a servant, but hadn't Aunt Amelia said magicians paid little attention to class differences? Besides, if she didn't speak to somebody about all this she would burst.

"It is said that most people have a knack for magic, only they never realize it," Becket said. "Magic is simply another sense, a different way of seeing and interacting with the world around us. I believe that it is the way we live, the choices we make and personalities we develop as we grow from children to young men and women, which determines whether or not we will be able to tap into that innate ability."

It wasn't as flattering as thinking she was born special, but in a way it was even better to think that she, by her own character, had formed herself into a person who could become a magician.

Especially when her personality had always been derided by her sisters, mother, and friends as dull, drab, and boring.

It didn't take away the oddity of everything, but somehow it helped Maia feel less like she was spinning out of control with it.

"Thank you, Mr. Becket," she said softly. "I appreciate your words."

"My pleasure, Miss Whitney," he said, and he gave her another one of his shy but charming smiles.

9

Light in the Darkness

Len finished his set in tennis, then slunk off the court and away from the crowd as stealthily as he could without resorting to his chameleon spell. He was surprised at how reluctant he was to use it after Maia's comment about him *being* a chameleon.

"Oh, Le-en!" trilled Ellie behind him, but Len pretended not to hear and slunk faster, resorting to an outright run as soon as he rounded the corner and couldn't be seen by any of the tennis players or spectators.

Ghastly game, tennis. The only worthwhile part of the exercise had been watching the interactions between the people he still couldn't help but consider his suspects.

The Danvers lads had danced attendance on Mrs. Saunders, who simpered and smirked as she reveled in the young, masculine attention. Mr. Saunders, perspiration gleaming on his balding head as he tried to keep up with Julia on the tennis court, didn't seem to mind or even notice. The husband and wife paid surprisingly little attention to each other.

Tim Spencer had lounged on the side, keeping one eye

on the game and one on his sister. Laura Spencer had spoken earnestly to Foy on some matter or another, while Foy answered her with his eyes on his wife, partnered with Saunders against Ellie and Len himself. Love, or worry? And if the latter, worry about what?

Freddie had mostly watched Ellie and called out encouraging comments, while Hermy stalked around the court with her hands in her pockets, glowering at everybody. Len had found himself wishing more than once that Maia were there, mostly as an antidote to the unpleasantness of Ellie and Hermy. She reminded him of the little stream they had walked alongside for part of their trip up the hill—clear, refreshing, with nothing to hide and only needing a little sunlight to cause her to sparkle, but with unexpected power hidden in her depths, capable of becoming an unstoppable force under the right circumstances.

Not like Ellie, who was all charm and no substance. Nor even Julia, who was sweet and terrifyingly efficient when she put her mind to it, but decidedly uncomplicated. Nor—

Len's thoughts stuttered to a halt as he met the woman in question outside the library. A quick glance around and a whispered spell let him know no one was within eye- or ear-shot at that moment, giving them a brief chance to discuss the situation.

"Aunt Amelia mentioned that Mr. Corbin had a young lady he was hoping to marry before he stole the papers," Maia said quickly, apparently feeling the same rush he did. "She didn't know anything more than that, but suggested that you might have some ideas, as she seemed to recall you spending some time in conversation with him?"

Any conversation had been mostly Corbin whinging about how horrible it was having Amelia Rawlings for a master. Len felt an unexpected rush of anger against Miss Rawlings for insinuating to Maia that he might have information he'd been holding out on her with … until a memory struck him with a force that was staggering.

"By Jove," he said slowly, angry now with himself. "I'd entirely forgotten. What a fool I am!"

"What? You do know something?"

"I don't know how helpful it will be, but … yes, I do recall a conversation we had about women. He'd said something about it being a shame we were at war with Austria as well as Germany, because it seemed to him that Austrian women made far better wives than English women."

"What an appalling stereotype," Maia said. "I'm not sure if that's more insulting to Austrian women or English."

"Both, I should say," Len said. "And I thought so at the time, only common courtesy dictated I not say so to him, so I mumbled something inconclusive and wandered away again. But—Maia, what if he was seeing an Austrian woman? What if between his disgrace and the general prejudice against Austrians in this country following the war, the two of them were separated, and he wanted to win her heart by selling her papers to bring England to its knees?"

"But Len—it was a *man* we followed that night," Maia pointed out. "And there is nobody here at Little Oaks, man or woman, who is Austrian."

Len waved this aside. "Clearly this Austrian woman used somebody else as a go-between," he said. "The man who did the actual killing was her tool."

"Then how does this help us to catch him and recover the papers?" Maia demanded.

Len deflated. He hadn't thought of that. "Er …"

Their conversation was punctured by a cough. Len jumped, then recovered when he saw it was only Becket. Somehow the spell to make sure no one was listening had automatically excluded his valet.

"Excuse me, sir, Miss Whitney," Becket said.

"Yes?" Len snapped, and then was ashamed at his brusqueness. Becket was loyal and faithful and had helped to keep him alive more than once, not to mention was a master at the little household spells that kept a person's life smooth and comfortable, but he'd been tiptoeing on eggshells around Len ever since—since Alec and Jamie... It had got to the point where any more of his careful diffidence and consideration for his employer's feelings was going to push Len into sacking him.

Interestingly enough, this time Becket didn't shrink back into himself. Instead, he said, "It strikes me that perhaps we should be looking for someone expressing a strong anti-Austrian—or German—sentiment. If someone is in fact working with or for an Austrian woman, he might wish to hide the fact by seeming to be opposed to them. People in such situation, especially those without a background in working undercover, often overdo the act."

"That's—jolly good," Len said slowly. That was the sort of suggestion Becket used to make, the sort of help he used to give, back before 1916. Back when they made a much more successful team than they had since.

"The only difficulty is that practically everyone is anti-German since the war," Maia said ruefully. "Even our king, ever since the name changes in 1917. How to distinguish someone overdoing it from someone who has little to no sense of proportion?"

"That's something for Becket and me to look for," Len said. "We have enough experience in these matters—it becomes something of an instinct after a while, not something you can explain or describe."

"I see," Maia said. Her voice was tart. Len realized he had come across as pompous, but dash it, how else was he to put it?

"So then, Becket keeps an eye and ear out for anyone in the servants' hall who comes across as false, while I do the same upstairs. In the meantime, you and I need to put together that spell to find the empty spots where the Bakelite case holding the papers might be found, and we need to introduce you to some basic spells to help keep your magic under control." Len calculated for a moment. "Everyone will be getting ready for dinner now, and then we'll of course have dinner. After dinner, do you think we could slip away and cast the no-magic spell? Then if there's time we can also teach you some magic yourself as well."

"There's likely to be dancing and socializing after dinner," Maia said with a sigh. "Our absence will be noticed."

"Then we'll have to come up with some good excuses." Suddenly, Len didn't want to wait any longer to teach Maia how to use her magical gift—and find the papers, of course, that went without saying. But it was outrageous that she'd had to wait this long to learn how to use her magic.

"I can always claim that most useful excuse for women, a headache," Maia said.

"Excellent," Len said. "Whereas I … will have to write a letter to my steward about some matters on the estate." He was aware that he ought to do that anyway, but Mackenzie was a good man who didn't need Len hanging over his shoulder, and the tenant who had been renting the house and grounds for several years had proven himself a trustworthy manager as well. Despite his mother's hints, Len really wasn't needed at the estate, much to his relief.

Perhaps at some point in his life he'd be happy to retire and take up the role of country gentleman, but at the present time the idea of it was stultifying in the extreme. He enjoyed going back to the Dower House to visit the mater and spending a week or so resting, but he'd go mad if he had to live there.

Still, it made an excellent excuse.

"El—I mean, some of the ladies won't want to let you off that easily," Maia warned.

Len grinned. "Not to fret. I have plenty of experience slithering out of unpleasant social obligations."

To his utter shock, Becket added, "I can confirm that, Miss Whitney," with the slightest of twinkles in his brown eyes.

Well, well. Who would have guessed Maia could bring out Becket's cheeky side?

* * *

Dinner was an odd mix of nerve-wracking and tedious. Len felt the way he usually did on far more dangerous missions— vibrantly alive, aware that the slightest error could spell death and disaster, muscles quivering with suppressed action but forced to be still until the right moment.

It was odd, because he didn't think he was in danger. Nor did he think he was on the verge of uncovering the murderer. No, he was quite certain he had a long way to go before that happened. Too many pieces still didn't fit together. So then why should he feel so on edge?

His eye fell on Maia, sitting on the other side of the table and down a few places from him. She was dressed in a most unbecoming evening frock; Len was no expert in women's fashion, but he did have a sister who had a knack for always combining what was stylish and what was flattering in the best way. So far as Len could tell, Maia's dress was neither. The higher waist, long skirt, and bunchiness around the hips made him think of dresses from the latter years of the war, a far cry from the dropped waist, clean lines, and calf-length skirt that the other ladies (save the Honorable Hermione) wore. The fussiness of it was not attractive, nor did it suit Maia's personality. The color was appalling as well—a candy pink that would have suited Julia quite well but looked babyish and ridiculous on Maia—and to make matters worse it clashed with the red tints in her hair.

The malicious looks Ellie kept darting at her sister suggested that she knew full well how unattractive the dress was, and rather gloated over it. Ellie herself wore a vibrant green frock with the thinnest of straps holding it onto her shoulders and a sheer chiffon scarf providing quite inadequate coverage. Her dark hair was sleeked close to her head, with a beaded headband keeping it in place. Golden snakes twined up both her bare arms, and her jade earrings dangled almost to her uncovered shoulders. Len found the entire look barbaric, but it seemed Freddie, Timothy Spencer, and Rob Danvers were all smitten, judging by the identical dazed look on their faces as they watched her. Ellie's triumphant expression indicated she was well aware of the kind of conquests she was making, but the little glances she kept tossing at Len hinted that she wouldn't be content until he was at her feet as well.

Not that there was a chance of that, even if Maia hadn't been there. But Maia was there, and even in her rubbish frock—Len was suddenly irrationally convinced that Ellie was somehow responsible for Maia owning and wearing it, and hated her for that—he couldn't keep his eyes off her. The *frisson* of excitement running under his skin, he realized, was entirely due to the anticipation of working with her later and showing her how to use her magic.

He would have to pull himself together, or he'd be utterly useless on this task, and then Harrison would have to send Barry to take care of things, and *then* there would be trouble.

He tried to focus on the conversations running around the table, hoping to hear something in them that would indicate someone hiding pro-German sentiment.

Merope Whitney was seated beside him, ignoring both him and young Spencer, on her other side, in favor of conversing solely with Sir Bertram, seated across the table from her.

"But you must agree that eventually turning the factories over to the workers and removing yourself and all overseers and managers entirely is the only thing to do," she was saying, leaning forward in her passion.

"Indeed, but not yet," Sir Bertram said smoothly. "They aren't ready to wholly govern themselves yet. Not until they are will I feel right about stepping away."

"Yes, of course. Too many of the working class have been conditioned by years of abuse to accept things the way they are, to not even feel that they should better themselves. That's why they need education, so that they can learn just what they are capable of."

Sir Bertram caught Len's eye and smirked, unnoticed by Merry. Len's blood boiled up. He had no patience with young Miss Merope's idealistic view of the world, but before he would exploit her idealism and passion in this way …!

"Then what you really ought to be investing in is schoolteachers, wouldn't you think?" he couldn't help but interject into their conversation. Sir Bertram's smirk turned to a scowl as Merry looked at Len with wide eyes. "Rather than wasting your time trying to change things before they are ready to be changed, you ought to be helping prepare the way for that time to come."

"Oh!" said Merry. "I never thought of it like that."

"Schools and schoolteachers are tools of the establishment, my dear," Sir Bertram hastened to say. "There's no point in trying to effect change through them. We have to educate people ourself, in our own way, if we want to make anything happen."

"Oh yes, that's certainly true," Merry agreed, but her eyes still looked troubled.

"Only then you have to be careful you aren't just convincing them to your point of view, which is just as bad as where things are at, only in the opposite direction," Len said. "What you need is to help them think for themselves, even if that means they don't agree with you in the end. Wouldn't you agree, Spencer?"

Timothy Spencer, on Merry's other side, tore his eyes away from Ellie and nobly jumped into the conversation. "I do indeed," he said. "In fact that's something I've been hoping to persuade Laura to help me with on our father's estate, bringing in teachers to the village school who will work with the children to help them think, rather than merely teaching them their ABCs and maths. Though those are important as well," he added.

"Estates and estate owners running the lives of the people

who live there are abominable," Merry said, but she said it mechanically, her eyes looking into the distance.

"Couldn't agree more," Len said cheerfully. "Almost as bad as factory owners trying to run the lives of the people who work for them, eh, Sir Bertram?"

"My dear chap, the situations couldn't be more different," Sir Bertram said.

The conversation was broken then by Merry suddenly turning to Spencer and asking him about his plans for the village school. Before long the two of them were lost to the rest of the table. Glancing around at his fellow diners, Len saw Ellie and Sir Bertram watching the couple with identical expressions of pure spite.

Sir Bertram he could understand—the fellow had clearly been enjoying the wide-eyed calf love of a young lady too innocent to know any better, and now he was going to have to exert himself if he wanted to win her attention back from the younger and more personable Timothy Spencer, who blended idealism with practicality in a way that Len could only hope Miss Merry would eventually emulate.

But why Ellie? She had made it clear she had no interest in Spencer herself, ignoring every attempt of his to gain her attention, so why should she suddenly be so furious at his having a close conversation with her sister?

In any case, it wasn't his business. Len dragged his attention back to the rest of his dinner companions.

Maia was conversing with Mr. Saunders, seated on her right. Len couldn't hear their conversation, but nothing in Maia's expression indicated it was anything more than boring, everyday table talk.

Saunders ...? Len's brain played with the idea of the small, meek man being the one to ruthlessly shoot Carter and come up with the idea of giving Corbin thirty silver coins in exchange for the papers. He couldn't quite reconcile it. Besides, Saunders seemed to have little interest in any of the women here, including his wife. Len couldn't see him being in the thrall of a glamorous German or Austrian female spy.

Rob Danvers had managed to engage Miss Spencer in talk, nothing political for a change. Freddie was attempting to converse with Ellie, who ignored him; Foy was making polite small talk with Mrs. Saunders; and young Paul Danvers, surprisingly enough, was laughing at something Hermy had just said. Even her grim face had cracked a smile in response to his whole-hearted shout of laughter.

None of them gave any indication that they were anything more than they seemed. Len still felt that Sir Bertram was the most likely suspect, by virtue of being odious, if nothing else, but Freddie had given the man a perfect alibi, curse it.

With any luck, Len and Maia would find the papers in the Bakelite case later this evening, their location would prove to be the perfect pointer to the murderer, and they could wrap things up and move on to her magical development.

He highly doubted that would happen, but one could hope.

* * *

Miss Ellie proved as much of a limpet as Maia had warned, but Len was at last able to worm himself away from her clinging grip and escape up to his bedroom. He quickly changed into clothing more suitable for outdoor nighttime excursions than his dinner jacket, cast the chameleon spell, and slunk back downstairs and then outside by way of the servants' stairs and the back door.

He followed a faint silver glow through the garden and was rewarded by seeing Maia standing among the roses. She too had changed into a much more practical tweed skirt and knitted jumper. The silver outlining her entire figure warned him that they had better hurry with the detecting, as it appeared her magic was on the verge of breaking free.

Len had come close to losing control of his magic only once, when Alec died. Even then, the light of his powers hadn't enveloped him quite as significantly as Maia's did now. Magic tended to concentrate in a trained magician's hands. Therefore it had been Len's hands that glowed so fiercely, and the shock of seeing the light travel up his forearms had snapped his control back into place.

Len shuddered to think what might happen to Maia if she was not able to gain that same control, and again cursed the irresponsibility of Amelia Rawlings in awakening her niece to the truth of magic and then leaving her to muddle through on her own. Even if Maia hadn't accepted the role of apprentice yet, the least Miss Rawlings could have done was teach her how to bleed off some of her power.

He pushed his anger aside. They were here to do a task. Several, in fact, and the sooner they got through this first one the more quickly they could move on to helping Maia.

"Lovely evening for a stroll, Miss Whitney," he said in a nearly soundless whisper, despite the fact that they stood far enough from the house that no one ought to be able to hear them. "I understand night air is excellent for headaches."

He heard a muffled laugh in return. "I am not sure that it is the best thing for writing letters, however."

"True. I suppose that means I should get on with hunting

for papers, shouldn't I?"

"I suppose you should."

Len had prepared his spell beforehand, but he wanted to take a moment or two to explain to Maia what he was doing, as this was all so new to her.

"I was originally going to do an inverse of a magic-seeking spell, which lets its caster know where spells have recently been performed, though it doesn't show exactly what spells or who performed them," he said. "But then I realized that wouldn't be quite as helpful, as we aren't looking for spells that *haven't* been cast, so to speak. I'm not even sure that would work at all. What we want is to simply be able to distinguish between places where magic *could* be used, because of the abundance of natural materials there, and places where it couldn't, because it's all synthetic. So I did a little research, and you were right, there is a spell already created for that, I don't even have to adapt anything." Much to his relief. He was a decent magician, but getting creative with magic was not his strong suit. "Most magicians use it to find places that will be strong for magic, but we'll have our focus be on the places where magic isn't at all. For that, I'll simply hold the parameters of the spell firmly in my head, as well as my intent in casting it, while I speak the incantation."

"In Latin, because of its precision," Maia said. "Mr. Becket told me," she added.

Len smiled into the darkness. Good old Becket. "Exactly."

He shook out his hands, closed his eyes, and breathed deeply a few times, relishing the crispness of the September night air. Then, the goal for the spell fixed in his mind, he lifted his hands and said, "*Vidam præcantatio non esse.*"

He felt a tug deep within him, and his energy drained almost at once. In attempting to cover both the ground and the house, he might have extended himself too far. Len set his jaw and forced himself to stand firm, allowing the spell to finish its task. Behind his closed eyes, he saw it as a bronze web, covering both grounds and house, everywhere except—

"There!"

There it was, one blank, empty spot in the midst of everything else teeming with life. Len pinpointed the location in his mind, then ended the spell with a gasped, *"Finiatur."*

"Whew," he said, staggering back with the sudden release. "That was harder than I expected."

He noticed Maia looking in the same direction he had marked as the empty spot. "Beautiful, though," she said dreamily. "Like a spiderweb delicately crafted out of bronze. A few small gaps in the house, where I'm guessing ladies have frocks made of rayon or something similar, but only one rectangle in the size of a dispatch case."

Len felt that jolt again, that sudden tilting of his world. He couldn't quite believe that Maia could still see his magic, any more than he understood how he could see hers. It felt oddly intimate, as though they were each peering into something private in the other's life, even though it was involuntary. He could only speculate that his attempt at using magic in the woods the previous night (good lord, was it really only one night ago?), calling up his power without actually being able to release it into a spell, had somehow mixed in with her blossoming abilities, and they had become intertwined. Not enough for them to draw upon each other's power, thank goodness—the stories about that sort of thing happening never ended well—but enough that they could at least see each other's magic in a way that most could only see their own.

Either that, or it was a sign that their destinies were somehow intertwined with each other. Len found he rather preferred that theory, but even his romantic side had to admit that was unlikely. Destiny, in his experience, was not so kind.

"Come on," Maia said, unaware of his inner turmoil. "Let's go get the papers! Lucky the murderer left them outside."

Lucky—and odd. Len would have laid odds that the fellow would have kept them in his room, but Maia was right—the only blank spot of the correct shape and size was outside near the woods. Shrugging aside his doubts, Len followed her to the spot, wishing he'd thought to bring a spade.

It turned out to be unnecessary. The Bakelite case was merely hidden underneath a thin layer of leaves at the base of the oak.

It was also, when Len had brushed away the leaves and acorns and forced the lock, entirely empty.

Several words passed through Len's mind, none of them appropriate to say in front of a lady, none of them adequate to the situation.

"Well," he said at last.

"Damn," Maia said.

That startled him, from her, and broke his black mood enough to make him laugh.

"Never mind," he said, clambering to his feet. "It's a setback, that's all. We'll still find him—and the papers. Just not tonight. Now," eyeing the angry silver light pulsing around her hands, "now we teach you your first spell."

The pulsing turned into a glorious blaze, and for a moment Len was afraid he'd lost her. When his vision cleared, she was still standing there, thank goodness, eyes lit with a joy that could be seen even in the dim light. "Really? Don't you need to get back into investigating right away?"

"This is more important," Len said firmly.

What he meant was, *you* are more important, but he found he couldn't quite force his mouth to form the word.

Instead, he cleared his throat. "Right," he said. "Let's move a little further into the woods so no one can see what we're doing."

They found the perfect spot a few yards in. A tiny clearing barely big enough for two, away from the path, so no one traveling through would stumble upon them, and with the surrounding trees close together, their tops nearly meeting far overhead, so little light would shine past them.

"Splendid," Len said. "Let's begin."

He closed his eyes and concentrated, touching that part of him inside which was in tune with the intangible parts of nature. "*Lux fiat.*"

He opened his eyes. Even as the glow of his magic appeared and faded at his fingertips, a ball of warm coppery light shone above his palm, hovering in the air. At Maia's intake of breath, the weariness Len felt from working any magic, no matter how small, after he'd just finished with a large spell, faded into pure enjoyment.

"There is light even in the darkest night," he said with a laugh. "That sounds like a proverb, but I mean it literally. I felt where the strands of light were, and pulled a few together to make this—which is, by the way, a very useful sort of spell, as you can imagine."

"So it is both something you sense, and something you direct?"

"In a way. You concentrate on whatever it is you are trying to create with your spell, and at the same time sense the pieces in nature which will help you accomplish that. If you want to build a locomotive, magic isn't going to be much help. But light, or water, or fire, or blending into your surroundings like a chameleon, or hardening the air to prevent bullets from breaking through … all of those are possible with the help of magic." He closed his hand. *"Finiatur."*

The bronze glow winked out.

He nodded, though in the darkness it wasn't likely Maia could see him. "Now, you try. Close your eyes and focus on sensing the light present but unseen all around."

She closed her eyes, and the silver glow rose up around her again—she was accessing her magic. Len watched her blow out a breath, settle her shoulders, and extend her hand.

"Do you sense the light?" he whispered, not wanting to break her concentration.

"No—wait, yes," she answered through her teeth, her jaw clenched with effort. "I think I've got it. Now what?"

"Imagine yourself drawing bits of pieces of that light to yourself, wrapping it up into a small ball you can hold in your hand. When you are ready, focus everything you have on bringing that ball into existence while using the Latin phrase for 'let there be light'."

Maia's face scrunched adorably as, with her eyes still closed, she took one more deep breath and then spoke.

"Lux fiat!"

Lennox laughed in pure astonished joy, and she opened her eyes.

A silver ball larger than her head hovered above them, illuminating the entire grove with its gleam. Hanging like a miniature moon, it showed plainly the wonder and pride on Maia's face.

"A jolly good thing we moved out here, or people might look out and wonder who brought electricity to the forest!"

"I did that?" Maia whispered. Her eyes grew wide. "I did do that!"

"You certainly did," Len said, nearly bursting with pride—which was absurd, as she wasn't his student, and her abilities had nothing to do with him. All the same, he felt as though he wanted to leap and dance with delight over her accomplishment. "By Jove, you'll make the finest magician of the age if this is any indication."

He wasn't sure she even heard him as she continued to look at the light. The expression on her face … Len swallowed and looked away, sensing he was intruding on something more personal than even the ability they had to see each other's magic.

He would have given her more time to enjoy it, but he didn't want to exhaust her too much. The first spell was always draining, no matter how much power had built up ahead of time.

"Terribly sorry to ask to ask it of you, but now can you end the spell and send the light back where it belongs?"

"How?" Maia asked, at last tearing her eyes away from the silver ball to look at him.

"Try to think of it spinning itself out, scattering its pieces back into the night sky, where they came from in the first place."

She sighed a little. "It's my first spell. I rather hate to let it go."

"I understand," Len said sympathetically. "Still, we've a few more to get through tonight. This one is the standard first spell all beginners are taught, but even more important are the subtler spells that let you bleed off your power when you're in a place where you can't use a more noticeable spell."

"Very well." Maia closed her eyes again. *"Finiatur."*

The ball winked out of existence. Len blinked in the sudden darkness. Maia was still outlined with a faint glow, as though she truly had come down to earth from the stars. Len's heart swelled within him, and he took an unconscious step forward. He was struck with the sudden desire to take her in his arms and kiss her mouth, that mouth made for smiling and joy, too often turned down in worry or weariness. He wanted to take her away from her horrible family, who exploited her and scorned her and did their best to make her feel small—small, his magnificent, starry Maia! He wanted to place a crown on her head and jewels on her hands and show the entire world how wonderful she really was—more, show *her* how wonderful she really was. He wanted—

"Shall we begin with the other spells?" Maia asked, opening her eyes.

Len stopped. He swallowed, appalled at the emotions that had surged up in him. How had that happened? He had known her for only twenty-four hours. How could he possibly have fallen in love so fast?

More, what was he going to do about it?

Maia was looking at him, her brow creased in faint puzzlement at the delay.

"Er," Len said. "Yes. Right. Of course! The other spells."

He would have to sort all this out later. Right now, he owed it to Maia to teach her how to keep from being consumed by magic. He couldn't possibly be so selfish as to risk her life merely to satisfy his own emotions.

They would wait. She couldn't.

10

Truth and Consequences

Maia was in a daze as she walked back out of the woods beside Len. It was miraculous enough to witness magic—true magic! It was even more miraculous to be told that she could use magic herself. But nothing, *nothing* compared to actually casting a spell. She had had a tiny fear left in her that something about magic was unnatural, that using it was going to cause her to become an outcast from society, that she was going to have to sacrifice a part of her soul in exchange for this marvelous ability.

Not a bit of it. Using magic felt more natural than anything else she'd ever done. It was right, and good, and proper, that she should be able to interact with the world in this way. She wasn't commanding it, or warping it, or twisting it for her own power. She was connecting with it in a way that made her appreciate its beauty and wonder more than she ever had, giving her an even deeper respect for how everything fit and worked together.

Tonight, Maia felt more properly alive than she ever had.

"Len, how is it you don't have an apprentice of your own?"

she asked, curious. He'd done an excellent job teaching her the basics in a way that was simple to understand without being patronizing.

"I'm not a master, merely an independent magician," her companion answered. "I'll never be strong enough in my magic use to be a master magician. That's one of the reasons I'm so effective in MI—we get into a lot of morally gray areas, and it can be a temptation to more powerful magicians in those situations to start to use their magic in unethical ways. In fact, the only really strong magician I've ever known in MI—well, he's dead now." He closed his mouth abruptly.

Maia stopped walking. "Len, I do realize that this is none of my business, but I would be an idiot if I weren't aware that there is still something eating away at you, something connected to my aunt, and likely even to these papers. I won't pry, but if it will help you to talk about it ..." She let the invitation trail off. He had given her a marvelous gift tonight; the least she could do was offer to share some of his burden.

He was silent for a few more paces. Then he said, "It is only fair that you should know. My opinion of your aunt is ... tainted, and you deserve to know why. And this particular assignment is more personal for me because of it. I'm not necessarily going to be as objective as I should be."

Maia wasn't sure what to say to that, so she waited.

Len continued. "When we first started hearing rumors of a magical advisor to the Kaiser—oh, now that sounds even worse than the Kaiser's Advisor—I volunteered to go investigate, alone. Usually Becket accompanies me on assignments, but for this, I knew I would do better at getting in and out unnoticed if I was alone. The Council overruled me, said they couldn't rely on one person alone for something this important; if something happened to me, they needed somebody else to be able to get the information back to them. Two others volunteered—my mate James, an agent a couple years older than myself, with whom I'd worked before, and a very young agent, barely out of his journeyman years, named Alec. My cousin, in fact."

He fell silent. Maia winced, remembering what he'd said before about him being the only one to make it back. This story would not have a happy ending.

"Our superiors in MI said yes to Jamie, no to Alec. He was too young, had too much promise and not enough experience. The Circle … the Circle overrode them and sent us all. Your aunt was instrumental in that decision. She said it was important for us to have one strong magician on the team in case of trouble, and that Alec's lack of experience was made up for by his magical abilities."

They had made it to the edge of the gardens by this point, and by mutual unspoken agreement stopped so Len could finish his tale.

"Getting the proof about the KA wasn't that hard. She'd been sloppy, and proof was everywhere. Getting that proof out of Berlin and back to England, however …

"Alec accidentally tripped one of the KA's alarms, one that both Jamie and I had seen but neglected to warn him about, thinking he would see it too, except he didn't have the experience to recognize it. The KA threw everything in her considerable arsenal at us as we fled.

"Jamie was caught by a curse—those are illegal and unethical, by the way, not that I can imagine you ever using one, but so you know—as we ran out of the Kaiser's headquarters." Len shuddered, his shoulders twitching. It was one of the nastiest curses he'd ever seen: it first stripped Jamie of his magical abilities, leaving him helpless to try to defend against it. Any magic that Len threw at it was sucked away as well, until Jamie had sworn at him to stop, he was only draining himself to no good use. A proper curse-breaker could have done something, but Len's only training was in defense against curses, not in breaking them, and none of their training had prepared them for something of this sort.

Len forced himself to continue. "He knew he wouldn't make it out in time, so he said he would draw our pursuers off to give Alec and me time to escape. I hated to leave him, but I couldn't—nothing I could do would save him. The only thing to do was make sure his death meant something. So Alec and I went on, while he lured the magicians and soldiers away."

Maia couldn't imagine what a horrible choice that must have been. "A noble sacrifice, but an awful one to be on the other end of," she said softly.

"Yes," Len said briefly. He swallowed hard and continued. "Alec and I made it almost to the border when we ran afoul of a patrol. I know enough German to be able to pass as a citizen, but Alec—well, languages were never his specialty, and after the alarm and losing Jamie his nerves were already in bad shape. Not enough experience, just as I'd been afraid of. If he'd been on a few more smaller assignments, had had the chance to work up to something this big, he would have been the best in the business, but then, it was just too much for him. He panicked, and bolted, and they—they shot him. He was dead before his body hit the ground.

"I went on—I had to. I couldn't let both their deaths mean nothing. If I stayed to avenge Alec, the odds were I would have been killed too, and the proof would have been lost. It was—it was the worst thing I've ever had to do in my life, but I did it. I did my duty."

He puffed out a breath. "Lord, sometimes I wish nicotine weren't so inimical to magicians! What I wouldn't give to be able to puff on a pipe right now."

"Oh!" Maia said, distracted and surprised. "Is that why I get ill around people smoking, and why Aunt Amelia said that gave her a clue that I was a new magician?"

"Yes. It'll get better once your powers settle, but none of us are ever wholly comfortable around it. No one is quite sure why, either, but there is just something about nicotine that reacts poorly with magic-users."

"Fascinating," Maia said, then recalled herself. "I'm sorry, I didn't mean to interrupt your story."

"Not at all. It's just about finished, anyway. I came back and handed the proof over to the Circle and blasted them all for allowing Alec to go, and your aunt came back with some pretty sharp criticisms of my behavior, and we've been enemies of a sort ever since." He gave a bitter bark of laughter. "The end."

Maia gathered her thoughts. What to say in response to a tale as raw and painful as that one? "I'm sorry" was entirely inadequate.

The only thing she could offer in exchange was a story of her own, one that she'd never shared with anyone because it was too painful.

"I had a school chum, Sally Elliot, who joined the VADs the final year of the War. Because of me, because I had done so and in my one year at school she had always imitated me. Who knows why—I was the plainest and dullest of all the girls there. Perhaps because I was kind to her when everyone else made fun of her slowness at lessons and lack of ability at games, I don't know. In any case, I was careless enough to mention that I had joined up in a letter to her, and without telling me she joined as well, and she was killed on her very first day of action. Killed because she didn't pay enough attention to her orders, because she panicked, and because nobody understood that she was a bit stupid, and nobody took the time to make her understand or to help her. I would have, had I been there, but she wasn't part of my unit. I only found out after it was all over, and all I could do was visit her family and extend my condolences." She drew in a deep breath. This was harder even than she'd anticipated.

"And when her parents and younger sister shouted and screamed at me, blaming me for her death, I couldn't say a word in my own defense, because they were right. It wasn't my fault, but it was my responsibility. If it hadn't been for me, she would have stayed safely at home, and because of me, she was killed."

"Oh, but—" Len began to protest, then stopped. "Sorry. You don't want to be told not to blame yourself any more than I do. Always easier to see clearly the other person's situation, eh?"

"I suppose so," Maia agreed. She added, "I do understand better about your conflict with my aunt. Thank you for trusting me with your story."

"Thank you for sharing yours," Len replied. He cleared his throat, then added, "So much for the past," adopting a brisker tone. "I suppose we just have to make sure nothing like that happens in the present."

"Yes," Maia agreed fervently. "So what do we do next?"

"Get a good night's sleep," was his unexpected reply. "We've been doing nothing but discovering murders and magic and missing papers since last night, and neither of us are going to function well without some rest. We'll sleep, and regroup in the morning. With any luck, things will be clearer then."

Maia opened her mouth to protest, then closed it again. He was right—she was weary down to her bones, something that her drive to solve the mystery and her delight in using her magic had hidden until now. "Very well," she said. "But one way or another, we must end this tomorrow."

"I agree entirely," Len said.

* * *

Maia was slightly horrified the next morning to find she had slept until one of Julia's housemaids bustled in with a cup of tea around eight o'clock. Good heavens, when was the last time she had slept past seven? Fashionable though late rising might be, she'd never been able to get into the habit of it. Oftentimes the early mornings were her only hours of peace before her mother and sisters rose, and she'd always made the most of them. Of late, of course, she'd been rising early to try to keep up with the housework, since they couldn't ever keep maids or housekeepers for more than a few weeks at a time.

Sitting in bed with her dressing gown on, sipping a perfectly brewed cup of tea, Maia had to admit there was something rather nice in being pampered for a change.

Not that she intended to waste the entire morning lolling about in bed. No indeed; there was far too much to do today.

She lay back against her propped-up pillow and made a list in her mind.

1. Catch the true murderer of Mr. Carter

2. Find the missing papers

3. Convince Merry that Sir Bertram Grimes is not a good friend

152

4. Convince Ellie to ...

Maia frowned. Convince Ellie to do what? *Stop disgracing the family*, her brain whispered. Maia wriggled uncomfortably, her pillows suddenly feeling full of lumps. What was it Ellie had screeched at her yesterday?

"If you didn't act as though we were shaming the family name every time we had a little fun, other people wouldn't be so quick to condemn us!"

But other people did disapprove of their behavior—Julia was the one who had asked Maia to intervene, for heaven's sake!

Only ... what if there was some measure of truth in Ellie's words? What if there was something in Maia's disapproval, her very attempts to cover her sisters' poor behavior, that made them worse?

Rubbish. Maia set her tea down on the nightstand and shook her pillows out vigorously before leaning back and resuming her list.

4. Avoid Ellie as much as possible

5. Practice magic.

Maia smiled. She had to admit, she was looking forward to the fifth and final item on the list more than all the others, though of course capturing the murderer and recovering the papers had to be her first priorities.

The maid wouldn't return until after Maia had gone downstairs for breakfast, and no one else was likely to come into her room this early. Maia closed her eyes and sought the magic swirling within her veins, then stretched out her senses to gather strands of light into a ball.

"Lux fiat."

She opened her eyes to see a globe of swirling silver light hovering above her bed. A deep sense of satisfaction suffused her entire being.

What did Ellie's tantrums and Merry's folly matter in the face of something as marvelous as this?

Maia remembered Len's warning about not overusing her abilities, but she couldn't bring herself to dismiss the spell so quickly. She kept it going while she quickly dressed in a simple red day frock and sensible shoes, tucking her war souvenir into the top of her stocking as the final touch, and only when she was ready to descend to the dining room for breakfast could she bring herself to say,

"Finiatur."

The light winked out as though it had never existed. Maia sighed, but brightened at the thought that she could bring it back at any time, forever, for the rest of her life—and more spells besides, once she learned them.

Once this case was solved, she had all the time in the world.

She came downstairs determined to see the end of this case today, both for Len's sake and for her own.

Unfortunately, her good intentions and good mood alike were soured as soon as she came off the stairs into the reception space, where she found her sister Merry and Sir Bertram once again tucked into a cozy corner. It seemed that Sir Bertram was no longer content to only kiss Merry's hand, as their lips were only inches away from touching.

"Oh, for heaven's sake," Maia snapped, exasperated beyond her ability to hold her tongue.

Merry jumped and pulled back, but Sir Bertram only turned his head to give Maia an oily smile, leaning casually back against the wall, entirely unconcerned over the fact that he had been caught behaving with gross impropriety. Canoodling with a much-younger woman, both of them guests in another's home, in a public space, and before breakfast, no less! Really, it was one thing for Merry to ignore society's unspoken rules—she was seventeen, and would hopefully outgrow this tedious stage before long. For a man of Sir Bertram's age and experience to flout the rules was far worse, and his encouragement of Merry to behave in a fashion that would, even in today's modern society, soon cause her to be shunned by all respectable folk if she continued in it, was unforgivable.

"Not another lecture, May," Merry said before Maia could say anything else. Her cheeks were red, evidence that she wasn't entirely lost to all propriety, but her eyes sparkled with defiance. "I cannot stomach a lecture before breakfast."

She exited the reception space with her head high, attempting to sweep out with dignity but only managing a pompous strut. Maia sighed and stepped aside to let her pass.

No, a lecture would not be sufficient for this. Merry and Ellie were both so convinced that Maia only wanted to spoil their lives that neither would listen to anything she had to say. Her only hope was to shame Sir Bertram into some sense of his wrongdoing, though looking at his smirk, she highly doubted that would work, either.

She toyed with the idea of using her magic to frighten him away from Merry, or even better, teach him a lesson in how to behave toward younger women in general, but she released that wistfully. That seemed like it would be very high on the list of things magicians were forbidden to do, and for good reasons. Using magic against someone who had none felt very much like bullying, and not even an odious pig like Sir Bertram Grimes deserved that.

Or rather, perhaps *he* deserved it, but *Maia* wouldn't lower herself to behave in such an ugly fashion, regardless of the provocation.

"Really, sir," she said icily instead. "Am I to understand from this that you will be calling on my father shortly to express your intention to marry my sister?"

He laughed. "You may not," he said. "And if you expect Davies to do the same on your account, I warn you that you will be gravely disappointed."

Maia hesitated, taken aback by this seeming non-sequitur. "Excuse—" she began, but Sir Bertram took advantage of her confusion to give her a mocking bow and leave the reception space as well.

What on earth had he meant by that?

Maia gave it up and went to breakfast herself, hoping others were awake so that she wouldn't have to endure the company of the other two all on her own.

There, her luck ran better. Freddie was downstairs, and so was Dan, as well as Tim and Laura Spencer. Glancing at the clock on the mantelpiece, Maia decided that it would be another hour or so before Ellie stirred herself, and that Julia was most likely finishing her toilette, but Rob and Paul had probably already eaten and were now out enjoying the use of the Foy stables with a morning ride. No horsewoman herself, Maia had never understood the Danvers' enthusiasm for riding, but she could sympathize, at least, with their lament that the vicarage had no stables and their father's income was not sufficient to keep even one horse between them, much less two.

As for Hermione, who knew where she was? It wasn't likely that she was still getting dressed, given her choice of a more simple masculine attire, and she had never struck Maia as the type to enjoy a lie-in in the mornings. Maia dismissed the puzzle from her mind in favor of reflecting over the Danvers lads. Was it at all possible that either one of them would have stooped to murder, theft, and treason for the sake of money? Rubbish!

The fact was that Maia couldn't see anyone at this table committing foul deeds—save Sir Bertram, and he had an alibi. Nor could she make sense of it being Mr. Saunders, despite how little she knew of that man. While appearing meek and mild would surely be a good disguise for a spy or traitor, something about him didn't make sense in that role. He seemed content with his quiet lifestyle, whereas someone who was wearing that as a mask would surely chafe beneath it—as Len chafed beneath his "foolish but amiable" mask.

Dan spoke up then, startling her by referring to the very couple she'd been pondering. "I'm afraid we've had to say farewell to the Saunders," he said. "Mr. Saunders informed me last night before they retired that they would have to leave early this morning—something at their estate requiring their attention, terribly sorry and all that. Frankly, I think Mrs. Saunders simply wanted to escape the stigma of being a guest at a house party where something so unpleasant as a murder occurred, even if the murder itself happened off the property and we were only brought into it tangentially." He shrugged. "I suppose I can't blame her."

Maia narrowed her eyes. Maybe she was wrong. Maybe it was Mr. Saunders after all, and now that he had the papers and the police had released all the guests he was going to escape back to his house with them and would send them on their way to Germany from there.

Len ought to be informed of this development, she decided, only to realize that there was no sign of him. Surely he wasn't lolling about in bed. Where was he, then? Already off chasing clues, without her?

Indignation stirred in her veins, subdued only by the stern reminder that she didn't know that was what he was doing, and it wasn't fair to be cross with a man based on a mere suspicion. Much better to wait to be cross until one knew for certain one had been treated shabbily.

"Can't say I'll miss them too much," Freddie admitted. "They didn't seem to add much *go* to the party, what? Not like your sister," he added to Maia. "Miss Ellie certainly livens things up!"

"One could say that," Maia said neutrally. Freddie wasn't the first young man to be smitten by Ellie's charm without seeing the selfishness that lurked beneath. Then again, Maia considered, given the monstrous selfishness of Freddie's father and older brother and the way they had gone through the family's wealth to satisfy their own gambling habits, it was quite likely that Freddie considered Ellie's selfishness to be mild in comparison. And given the way his sister always emulated a man, it was likely that Ellie's exaggerated femininity was also appealing.

Emulating men … Maia nearly jumped. How had she never thought of that before? What if … what if it had been the Honorable Hermione she and Len had seen that night? From a distance, in the moonlight, they had based his identification on the attire, not necessarily the person within the clothes. And while Freddie was far too lazy and amiable to ever become a traitor, spy, thief, and murderer—or any of those individually— Maia could easily see Hermione being ruthless in her desire to regain the family wealth that she was just enough older than Freddie to remember well. Even her gambling—unlike her oldest brother and father, Hermione's gambling seemed less a passion for the sport and more a desire for obtaining money in the only way she knew how.

Not to mention how it had to rankle with her that their mother had tied up her independent fortune into a trust for both Hermione and Freddie, only to be given to them upon their marriages. It protected their futures from being squandered away by their father and brother, but it left them both in relative poverty for now, and given Hermione's lifestyle, left her with little chance she would ever access it. Maia had never been able to decide if Hermione's assumption of masculine garb and attitude was a pose or genuinely whom she felt herself to be, but either way, she would not want to relinquish her role simply to gain her mother's money.

Bother! Now she really needed to speak with Len. Whereas the Saunders leaving early was mildly suspicious, the introduction of Hermione as a suspect was terribly important. Where was the man? And how could she find out without it appearing as though she were taking undue interest in him?

"We seem to be a small crowd this morning overall," she said, hoping she sounded casual enough. "Where are all the others?"

Dan opened his mouth to reply, when Sir Bertram jumped in ahead of him. "If you are wondering about your particular friend, he departed on a walk much earlier this morning. I saw him from my window."

Maia blushed, and hated herself for responding to his baiting. How dare he insinuate that she was fishing for information about Len? Granted, she *was*, but not for the reason he was implying. And how had he discerned that they were becoming good friends anyway? *True* friends, not "friends," as Sir Bertram was hinting.

She was thankful Ellie was not at the table, because no one else responded to Sir Bertram's jibe. Even Merry looked embarrassed rather than amused or triumphant.

"Walking this early in the morning is nothing," Freddie said casually, bless him. "Rob and Paul are out riding, like the horse-mad fellows they are. It's we lazy chaps, Grimes, who are the bad example! Except for you, of course, Foy, because you're here playing host."

"I'm one of the lazy ones," Tim said cheerfully. "Since I'm up early most days during the harvest, I enjoy the chance to have a leisurely breakfast when it's all done."

"You actually work during the harvest?" Marry asked him incredulously.

"Of course," Tim said. "I never felt it was fair to enjoy the fruit of the labor of the men and women working on our estate if I didn't share in the work. Besides, I like farming. Father used to want me to enter the Law, follow in his footsteps, but I've always preferred working the land, and lately he's agreed that it's foolish to try to force me into a career I so clearly am not fit for. He's thinking of turning over running of the farm at Langely to my care next season, and if I make a proper go of it he'll give me the property outright. Says that I'm a throwback to our yeoman heritage, and if I want to farm then I might as well do it well."

"Oh," said Merry, and just like at dinner the previous evening, lapsed into serious thought.

Sir Bertram looked annoyed, though whether it was at Tim's ease in once again gaining Merry's attention or the dismissal of his insinuations by the gentlemen at the table, Maia wasn't sure. She felt a spark of hope—perhaps it wouldn't be necessary for her to say anything to either Merry or Sir Bertram about their behavior, perhaps Merry would see for herself what a cad he was, and the matter would end there.

"A walk does sound delightful," she said briskly, rising from the table. "I don't suppose any of you would care to join me in one? Merry, Laura?"

"What? Oh—no, thank you, May," Merry said vaguely. "I—Tim, don't you worry that by being given a farm you won't value it as much as if you'd worked for it and bought it yourself? Don't you think inherited property is wrong?"

"Under some circumstances, perhaps, but not all," Tim said. "There's a book in the library here that explains it all better than I can—shall I fetch it?"

Merry jumped to her feet. "I'll go with you," she said, then caught Maia's eye and blushed. "I wouldn't want to spoil any of Dan and Julia's books by bringing them to the table," she explained, as though to emphasize to her sister that this trip to the library was caused by attention to propriety rather than an excuse to behave badly.

Maia watched them leave and felt a rush of relief. While Merry might not be safe quite yet, she was well on her way.

"So much for Merry," she said. "Would anyone else care for a walk?"

Laura rolled her eyes. "I would adore a walk, thank you, Maia," she said emphatically. It seemed Laura's idealism would always take second place to sisterly annoyance when it came to her friends interacting with her brother.

"As would I," said Sir Bertram unexpectedly.

Maia's heart sank. Laura's company she didn't mind—she had proffered the invitation in hopes of convincing everyone she wasn't seeking out Len especially, and if she and Laura did happen to come across that gentleman Maia was confident she could convey her information about Hermione to him in a way that wouldn't alert Laura to anything odd. Sir Bertram, though … she was not so certain, not to mention he would take any crossing of paths with Len as further proof of a special relationship between him and Maia.

She couldn't retract the invitation now, though. She would simply have to make the best of it.

With walking shoes, coats, and hats on, Maia and Laura met Sir Bertram on the terrace, not far from the small table where Maia and Len had sat two nights ago and discussed stars and the moon until they were interrupted by the need to follow a thief and murderer into the woods. Laura wore riding breeches, and Maia again wished she dared wear something so much easier to walk in than her dress.

"Oh bother!" Laura exclaimed. "I left my stick in the umbrella stand by the front door." She sighed. "I know it's ridiculous, but ever since I broke my ankle last year Mother insists I use the stick when I walk."

"No matter, we'll wait," Maia said politely. Perhaps this would give her a chance to give Sir Bertram a piece of her mind regarding his behavior toward her sister—and hopefully make him angry enough he'd forego the walk with them.

Accordingly, as soon as Laura vanished back inside, Maia turned to Sir Bertram.

"Sir Bertram, I am well aware that you are a man of the world and live accordingly, but I must, I really must protest your behavior toward my sister," she began. "Merope is young and naive, and—"

He laughed.

Maia stuttered to a stop.

"Spare me your hypocritical platitudes," Sir Bertram said.

"As though you did not make a play for Davies our very first night here—a successful one at that, allow me to congratulate you, though your taste in men could be better." He leered at her.

"How dare you insinuate—" Maia began, her face hot.

"What?" he asked in mock amazement, "do you mean to tell me you did not sit out here awaiting him at the dance? And that the two of you were in the woods alone together both that night and the next? My dear, don't insult my intelligence."

Maia opened her mouth and then closed it again as Laura rejoined them, walking stick in hand.

"All set now," she said brightly. "Thanks for waiting."

Without another word, the three of them set off, Maia's mind whirling.

Apart from Sir Bertram's perfectly filthy insinuations, how had he even known about the two of them being in the woods? For that matter, how had he known about them being on the terrace? That table couldn't be seen from inside—and according to Freddie, Sir Bertram had been dancing with Merry the entire evening.

So then how could he know?

With that in mind, Maia began to cautiously pump Laura. "How did your ankle hold up at the dance?" she asked the younger girl.

"Well enough, though I had to sit out a number of dances," Laura said. "Not like Ellie and Merry!" She sighed. "Don't you think that dancing, the kind of dancing we did that night, is something Socialists shouldn't be bothered with?" she asked Maia. "It's so pointless, and only serves to increase the differences between classes."

"'Every savage can dance,'" Maia quoted. Laura looked blank;

apparently *Pride and Prejudice* was also something Socialists shouldn't be bothered with. Maia continued: "I sat outside for most of the evening myself, until I went home. You say Merry danced every dance?"

"Yes, mostly with Sir Bertram for the first half of the evening, and then Julia said something to her, I don't know what, but after that she danced with Tim, Rob, Paul, and some of the guests who were there just for the dance, and then after all that she finished off the night by dancing with Sir Bertram again." Laura's young voice was sulky.

"Oh, but—" Maia stopped, staring at Sir Bertram's tweed-covered back in front of her. That was not what Freddie had said!

On the other hand, if Freddie had seen Merry dancing with Sir Bertram for the first half of the dance and then at the end, he might have taken in for granted that they had been dancing the entire night. After all, presumably he would have been dancing most of that time himself and not paying the closest attention to the couples around him, whereas Laura, sitting on the sidelines, bored and jealous of her friend's popularity, would have taken much more careful note of Merry's partners.

That meant that Sir Bertram's alibi was worthless. Combined with the fact that he knew where Maia had been sitting on the terrace when he couldn't have seen her from inside, and his awareness that she and Len had been in the woods that night as well as the following night …

Suspicion of Hermione receded in much the same way as suspicion of Mr. Saunders had faltered before Hermione's apparent motives. Sir Bertram was the murderer. Maia was certain of it. Everything pointed to him.

But what could she do about it? She certainly couldn't accuse him now, not with Laura here, and she couldn't even hint about her suspicions to Len if they crossed his path, not without it being obvious to Sir Bertram, who knew too much about their investigative activities already. She had to do something, but what?

Her distressing train of thought was interrupted by the arrival of Rob and Paul Danvers, both indeed astride very fine horses, though Maia couldn't tell anything more about the animals than that.

"Hallo Maia, Laura!" Paul said, tipping his cap to them, his fair skin glowing with pleasure and exercise. "Out for a walk? You should be riding!"

"Now Paul, you've seen me on a horse," Maia said, forcing herself to speak lightly. "Don't you think it's better for everyone if I walk?"

Paul grinned, and Rob laughed. "You have a point," the older brother said. "But Laura—come, your ankle isn't up for a long walk. Won't you join us?" He stretched a hand down toward her.

Laura hesitated, looking at her two companions. "Oh, I wouldn't want to be rude ..."

Maia blessed the Danvers and their fortuitous arrival. Now she could confront Sir Bertram. She would force him to admit to his perfidy and then—well, she wasn't entirely certain what would happen next, but at the very least, he would not bother Merry any longer.

"Please, don't hold back on my account!" she said.

"Nor on mine," said Sir Bertram, his tone expressing his extreme indifference to it all.

Laura's face broke into a spontaneous and sweet smile, reminding Maia of the child she had been before the war, before she became entranced with a political ideal that had no bearing on reality. "Very well, then," she said, accepting Rob's hand and swinging herself up behind him like the consummate horsewoman she was.

The lads nodded courteously to the other two, and then the three of them moved off.

Maia drew in a deep breath. Now was the moment. She wished Len were there to back her up, but she'd have to do this herself.

"Tell me, Sir Bertram, how does it feel to murder a man because he is an inconvenience to your plan to betray your country?"

To her annoyance, Sir Bertram didn't react. He blinked his eyes lazily, smiled, and said, "It isn't my country that I'm betraying, it's those who are trying to control it from behind the scenes. As for murder ... the person I killed was nothing. If I had my way I'd exterminate every being of his type that exists on the earth. I would have killed them both save that it was far more satisfying to see the other charged with murder."

Maia's stomach tightened. Glancing at her hands, she saw silver starting to flicker between her fingers.

"Tell me, do you know Davies' true nature?" he continued casually. "Are you aware of his filthy talent, his unnatural abilities? Have you been lured into his world yet, or did he lie to you and make you believe that this was all government related?" His smile turned vulpine. "For all your silly little sister likes to burble on about a new world order, she has no idea what life will be like once Davies and his kind are revealed for who they are and we take power back into our own hands. He'll be the first to go, if I have anything to say about it."

Fear, anger, and horror exploded in Maia—for Len, for

Merry, for all magicians. How dare this horrible little man trample on this beautiful new world she had discovered, try to turn it into something ugly, and threaten to destroy it all? She would not—could not—allow it!

"Never!" she cried, and without warning her magic burst from her in a cloud of glowing silver and collided with Sir Bertram.

His eyes widened and he collapsed to the ground.

Maia gasped. She hadn't meant to do that! Not to use her magic against him—she wouldn't have done that on purpose! Frantically, she tried to gather the magic back in. "*Finiatur, finiatur,*" she said, but it wasn't a spell, and she couldn't end it so easily. Grimly, she kept trying to reel it in, winding it into herself like a reel of cotton, and at last there was only the faintest shimmer of silver left in the air to show she'd done anything at all.

Maia dropped to her knees beside Sir Bertram and felt for a pulse in his neck. Her breathing steadied when she found it. She hadn't killed him, then.

Sir Bertram stirred, and grabbed her wrist. His eyes opened slowly while his grip tightened. "You're one of them," he growled, his words slurred. "Perhaps you shall be the first to die, not Davies."

Maia tried to pull away, and only then realized how exhausted she was. Len's words about the dangers of uncontrolled magic came back to her. She'd expended most of her strength along with the burst of magic, and depleted the rest of it in getting it back under control. She needed to fight back—needed to stop Sir Bertram—but—

Maia's vision blurred and then went black, and she slumped to the ground, caught in a web of darkness from which there was no escape.

11

The Hunt is Up

Len strolled back to the house, pleased with the results of his morning's walk. He far preferred city life to country, but there were times when nothing stimulated the gray matter like a tramp across the fields before breakfast.

He had come to the conclusion that he was being an idiot about this case, chasing his own tail and playing the game the murderer and thief had set up for him. Discovering the empty case last night had shown him that. It was time he stopped trying to be Sherlock Holmes and relied instead on what never let him down: his intuition.

His intuition told him the murderer was one of the guests staying at Little Oaks—logic and facts backed that up, as there was no other reason for Corbin to drag Carter's body to the house except to try to point the finger of guilt at a house guest, and no other easy way for the empty Bakelite case being on the edge of their property.

His intuition also told him the murderer was not one of the Danvers lads, young Spencer, Freddie, or Dan. That left Saunders or Sir Bertram. Freddie's evidence cleared Sir Bertram, which meant it had to be Saunders, however unlikely that seemed. That was logic again.

At this point, his intuition had told him he was going down the wrong path yet again, that this was the way he was supposed to be thinking. Len sighed and sat down beneath an apple tree, closing his eyes as he leaned back against the rough bark of the trunk, letting his thoughts drift as aimlessly as the clouds above.

What if … what if it there was more to this than what met the eye? What if all of it was sleight-of-hand, meant to focus their attention on the impossible so that they missed what was really happening? His mind went back to the conversation outside the library with Maia, where he'd speculated that a German woman was behind all this and was using the murderer as a catspaw. They had dismissed the notion quickly enough, as there was no proof to it, even with Becket's rather clever idea about looking for someone who was over-sincere in their disdain for Germany, but what if … what if that was actually the right path?

What if … Len's eyes snapped open and he sat upright so quickly he startled a blackbird away from the branch above his head.

"Not Mr. Saunders," he said aloud. "*Mrs*. Saunders."

Whether she'd got her husband to do the actual killing or had used someone else, she was at the heart of this case. He was sure of it.

And so, with that decided, he had begun his return to the house, eager to find Maia and tell her what he'd realized, and then decide what to do next to recover the papers from Mrs. Saunders and extract the truth about the murder from her.

Only, upon entering the kitchen, grabbing a roll from the basket on the table with an apologetic smile at the cook, who shook her head at him but pretended not to see when one of the maids poured him a fresh cup of coffee, he was met in the corridor outside by a worried-looking Becket, who said,

"Sir, Miss Whitney has gone missing."

Len nearly dropped his coffee cup. "What?" He stared at his man, hoping he had misheard or that Becket was overreacting.

"She left for a walk with Sir Bertram Grimes and Miss Spencer after breakfast. Miss Spencer returned an hour ago, and Sir Bertram half an hour after her, but there's no sign of Miss Whitney," his valet elaborated.

"After walking alone with Grimes for half an hour I suppose she wanted to restore her peace of mind—and wash her hands," Len observed, trying to calm both his own fears and Becket's.

"Perhaps, but … Miss Merope is worried, and so is Mrs. Foy," Becket said, un-calmed.

Julia was Maia's closest friend, and for all her foolishness Merry was less self-absorbed than Ellie. If both of them thought this was out of character for Maia, there was good cause for worry.

"I'll talk to them both," Len said, drinking his coffee quickly and swallowing the roll in two bites. "And then I'll talk to Grimes," he added.

Mrs. Saunders would have to wait. There was potentially a damsel in distress who needed rescuing.

Len handed his empty cup to Becket and set off for the main part of the house, not noticing the frown that drew down Becket's eyebrows.

He came across Julia without even having to look for her, as she rushed down the hall toward him, wringing her hands together.

"Len! Is Maia with you?" she demanded.

"No, I've been out alone," Len answered.

"Oh, drat!" Julia said.

Len raised an eyebrow at her.

"I was hoping that she might have come across you on her walk and the two of you would come back together, but if you haven't seen her, she truly is missing." Julia sounded close to tears. "And no one will believe me that something is wrong, so none of the men will go out and look for her. Merry and I were about to go out ourselves when we heard you were back, and we hoped you would have better news for us."

"Now look here, I promise I will take this seriously," Len said, already taking it very seriously indeed. "But I do need to know just why you think it so unlikely that Maia would be out walking alone after leaving Sir Bertram."

"Maia is not a great walker," Julia said. "She has never been one of those to enjoy tramping across the hills alone, communing with the sky and the sheep and what-have-you. It isn't that she dislikes walking or does it poorly—well, you know, she went for a long tramp with you yesterday—but it isn't something she would choose to do for her own enjoyment. It was odd enough that she suggested a walk this morning at all, especially after having been walking with you yesterday. It simply doesn't make sense that she would stay out even longer after the others returned."

"I see." It wasn't conclusive—sometimes people did act out of character—but it was concerning. Unless she had come across a clue and was pursuing it, but even then Len would have expected her to consult with him first.

Of course, he hadn't been here for her to consult with. Surely in that case she would have consulted with Becket?

Unless Len's own dismissal of Becket as a useful ally had persuaded her he had nothing of value to offer.

By now, both Ellie and Merry had joined them, Merry looking worried and Ellie pouting.

"Honestly, you're both being ridiculous," Ellie was saying as the sisters approached. She saw Len and threw her hands up into the air. "And now you've dragged poor Len into it as well! Len, they're fretting over nothing. I am certain that May is fine. No doubt she's sulking because people aren't falling all over themselves to do what she tells them and admire her for managing their lives for them, and so she's decided to punish us all by staying away until we're worried and then graciously deciding to return and forgive us."

If Len hadn't been worried about Maia before this, he would be now. The person Ellie had just described was nothing like the Maia he knew, and if that's what Ellie thought she was doing, most likely the truth was the exact opposite.

"Don't be absurd, Ellie," Merry said. "However irritating May might be to us, she would never be so rude to a hostess as to make her worry like this, especially not Julia. You know as well as I do the only reason she went for the walk with Sir Bertram at all was so she could chide him about nearly kissing me, otherwise she would have decided that looked improper and refused to go with him."

Len thought of their long walk together yesterday, and the midnight excursions in the woods, and decided Merry didn't know her sister as well as she thought, either.

Ellie shook her head in exasperation. "Yes! And last I knew, you were furious at her for trying to run your life. Why are you so worried now?"

Len was wondering the same thing, though he would never have said it.

Merry glared at her sister. "Yes, I am angry, but that doesn't mean I want something bad to happen to her! Once I know she's safe I'll happily tell her off again."

"Oh be quiet, both of you," Julia said. "This is my house, and if I want to make a nuisance of myself by insisting that Len go looking for Maia then I will. Ellie, if you would stop being jealous of Maia for two minutes you'd realize that nothing you say has any relation to reality."

Ellie offered up a brittle laugh. "Jealous! Why should I be jealous of May? Don't mistake me, Len, my elder sister has all the virtues in the world—she is responsible, hard-working, trustworthy, honest, reliable—but frankly, I'd rather be dead than be that boring."

Julia narrowed her eyes. "If you aren't jealous, why do you spend so much of your life trying to make others think of her as boring?"

"Julia my dear, she might be your friend, but even you must admit she is hardly scintillating company."

Len could hold his tongue no longer. "Frankly, Miss Electra, I would much rather spend time with the most boring of individuals—which Maia certainly is not—than with someone so petty and small-minded that she never opens her mouth without trying to hurt someone else."

Ellie and Julia stopped their argument and stared at him wordlessly. It might have been the first time in Ellie's life that someone told her the truth about herself, and Len thought it was more than past time.

"Enough!" Merry cried. "While you all argue over May's qualities, she could be lying in a ditch somewhere, hurt or even dead! We must do something."

"Oh!" Ellie cried, and flung herself around and into the next room. Len didn't think he was the only one who was relieved to see her go.

"Quite right, Miss Merry," Len said briskly. "Now, I assume we don't want to turn out the entire house in a search party, on the off chance that there really is nothing wrong and she is simply enjoying some quiet, contemplative time—something I understand there is very little of in her everyday life, filled as it is with the demands other people place on her. Not that she's said as much to me, but even a thick-headed chap like myself can see through a grindstone when there's a hole in it, you know."

He was severely pleased to see both of them blush and look down at the floor. There, perhaps that would force them to think twice about how they treated Maia, and also meant that if she was out pursuing a clue no well-meaning idiot like Freddie would come along and spoil the trail.

"So I'll take my man Becket and the two of us will go out quietly and see if we can turn her up," he continued. "If we can't find her, then I think it will be time to take more serious steps."

Julia looked as though she was going to protest, but when Len glared at her, she subsided.

"Very well," she said. "I suppose that's sensible. But if she's hurt and we could have got to her sooner except for all this masculine logic and caution, I shall be very cross with all of you!"

"And I will be more than cross if something has happened to May," Merry said, and she also left.

Len looked at Julia. "Why do both of them call their sister

May when everyone else calls her Maia?"

"Because they want to make her feel dull and plain and boring and so they change her lovely, unique name into something common and ordinary," Julia snapped. "There's nothing wrong with the name 'May,' but it isn't *Maia*, and so they use it just to make her uncomfortable." Then she relented. "Or else it's a holdover from when they were children and they all rebelled against their parents' naming choices by shortening each other's names. Only Ellie and Merry like their versions of their names better than the originals, and Maia—well, as you say, the only people who still attempt to use that silly name for her are her sisters, who seem to feel that they'll only ever be able to shine if they can make her small enough to not cast a shadow on them." She rested a hand on Len's arm. "Find her, Len. I don't know how, but somehow I just know that she's in trouble."

"If she's anywhere to be found, Becket and I will find her," Len vowed. He patted Julia's hand and went back to the kitchen to find his manservant.

When he arrived, he found Becket already dressed in his outdoor clothes, a heavy walking stick in one hand and a torch in the other.

"It's broad daylight, old chap," Len said, eyeing the torch and deciding to ignore the fact that Becket had apparently been planning on setting off to search for Maia with or without him.

"If she is in a barn or a cellar, a torch might be useful, sir," Becket answered.

Len could have pointed out that they could use the *lux* spell in that case, but he held his tongue. The important thing now was simply to find her.

Wherever she might be.

* * *

"According to Mrs. Foy, Miss Spencer parted from Miss Whitney and Sir Bertram about there," Becket said, pointing to the place where the path paused at a gate. "Sir Bertram says that after she left them, they turned back from the gate and followed the fence down for a time, at which point Miss Whitney stated that she wished to keep walking, and since he was finding it rather dull, they parted ways and he returned to the house."

Len squinted. Was there—yes, there was! "Becket, old boy, I think we might be on to something," he said, hurrying toward the gate. "Look!" He pointed, forgetting momentarily that no one else would be able to see what he could.

"Sir?"

Len halted by the spot. "Between us, my friend, Miss Whitney and I had something—odd—happen with our magics. It turns out I can see her magic as easily as I can my own, and she can see mine. I've speculated that it's because her magic was stirring to life at the same time as mine was active and we were in close proximity to each other in the woods the night Carter was murdered and Corbin was cheated out of the papers, but that's not important right now. The important thing is that I can see traces of her magic right here."

"Wonderful!" Becket said fervently. He added, "There is precedent for that, sir. It hasn't happened often in our recorded history, but I have read of once or twice where two magicians have interacted in such a way that their magics become attuned to each other." He cast a quick glance at his employer and hurried on. "When it turns up in the stories it is always taken as a sign that the two are fated to have their destinies intertwined with each other, but of course that's only the stories."

"Hm." Len found he didn't mind at all the thought that his destiny and Maia's might be one, not two. Earlier he had feared the thought of destiny—now it was comforting. It was an odd realization for a man so accustomed to working alone he had a difficult time even trusting the man beside him—the man who had never yet failed him, but whom he deeply feared failing.

He pushed the thought away for now.

"This doesn't look like the remnants of a spell," he said, examining the faint silvery cloud. "But it's clearly her magic."

"Does it go anywhere? Did she leave a trail?"

Len scanned the area. "No …" he finally conceded. "I can't see anything more."

Becket's shoulders slumped. "Then we're no better off than we had been. We might as well follow the fence and see if there are any signs of her along that way."

Len held up a hand. "Wait a moment. Think about it, Becket—if Maia used strong enough magic here that there are traces still remaining now, something must have happened to cause that. Who was she here with? Sir Bertram Grimes, a man who is not a magician, nor even a hedge-wizard. What could have happened to cause her to loose so much magic in front of a non-magic user?"

Becket's eyes gleamed. "You believe Sir Bertram to be at fault, sir."

"I think there's enough evidence here to question his word at the very least," Len said grimly. "He can't be the murderer—not unless old Freddie has been lying through his teeth, which I doubt he's even capable of—but he could be connected in some way. Was his valet absent at all during the dance?"

Becket shook his head. "No, sir—the man has a most offensive manner and considers himself quite the ladies' man, which meant we were all subjected to his idea of 'wit' the whole evening. But sir—do I understand that Mr. Winters has said that Sir Bertram was present throughout the entire dance? I think there must have been a mistake. Sir Bertram must have left the dance at some point, because Perkins, the valet, has to excuse himself at one point to fetch his master's overcoat for him, and then again later to take it back."

Len gaped. "Why the blazes didn't you say so before?" he thundered as soon as he'd recovered enough breath.

Becket flinched back, but met his eyes steadily enough. "Because you didn't tell me your reason for eliminating Sir Bertram from your investigation, merely that he had been. Once he was no longer a suspect, there was no reason to tell you this."

Len closed his mouth. Becket was right—it was his own fault. He had been keeping his cards close to his chest, afraid to encourage independent thought in his valet lest danger overtake him the same way it had overtaken Alec. Which wasn't remotely fair, as Becket had just as much experience in this sort of work as Len had, but—Len had been afraid he'd lose him, too.

"Quite right," he said briefly. "My fault entirely, old man. Apologies and all that. Give me a moment, will you? Must rearrange my thoughts. I had someone else pegged as the murderer, y'see, and now this has upset all my calculations."

"Of course, sir," Becket said courteously.

Len leaned on the fence and considered. Back to the beginning. Sir Bertram's alibi was gone. He still couldn't believe that Freddie was capable of deliberately deceiving him, but the chap must have been mistaken. So then, character and opportunity alike pointed to Sir Bertram as the murderer, and Maia's disappearance while on a walk with him indicated that she had come to the same conclusion, confronted him, and was—Len swallowed. He wouldn't allow himself to even think the word "killed." Resolutely pushing aside the memory of the ruthlessness of the individual who had killed Carter, he forced himself to believe she was still alive. After all, she had been able to use magic against him, hadn't she?

Only, if she had used her magic to escape, where was she now?

Len removed his hat and rumpled his hair to help himself think.

"Becket, now we've decided that Sir Bertram is most likely the murderer, and even if not, clearly untrustworthy, correct?"

"Indeed, sir."

"Then we can also assume that he told us the direction he and Maia walked in to deliberately deceive us."

"That would seem a safe guess, sir."

"And that means that we want to look in the other direction," Len said. "He was eager to tell that they didn't go through the gate—so that is exactly where we are going to go."

"Very good, sir. Sir?"

Len halted in the act of opening the gate. "Yes?"

"I hesitate to mention it, but … do you think we ought to inform Miss Rawlings that her niece and apprentice is missing and possibly in danger?"

Len's first impulse was to swear, his second to refuse to consider it. He swallowed both of those.

"It would be good etiquette, sir," Becket said apologetically.

So it would. Normally Len didn't care about etiquette, but in this case, it was just as well to not give the old battle-axe anything to use against him.

"Very well," he said, closing the gate again. "I think I saw a puddle over there we can use for scrying."

Both men moved to the small pool of water and bent over its surface. Len closed his eyes and directed his energy, muttering the words to the spell that would allow him to contact Miss Rawlings through this medium.

He opened his eyes and saw the water ripple violently, as though a rough breeze passed across it, and then settle into a stillness like glass. Only a moment or two passed before Miss Rawlings' figure appeared in the puddle as though seen through a window.

"Davies!" she said, her voice clear but sounding as though it came from a long way off. "What is the meaning of this intrusion into my privacy?"

"Maia is missing," Len said bluntly. "I believe she ran afoul of the murderer. Becket and I are searching for her, but we felt it only proper to inform you of the situation. It appears as though she attempted to use magic—"

Miss Rawlings cut him off. "What? I haven't taught her any spells yet! Good gracious, the child will have been overtaken by her own power—it's too strong for her, I haven't had the chance to teach her control, I never dreamed she'd actually try to use it—"

It was Len's turn to cut her off. "As you saw fit to tell her of her magic and then withhold instruction, I took it upon myself to teach her some of the basic means of controlling her magic so that it would not consume her. I know it is bad form to instruct another magician's apprentice, but I felt it more important to give her the means to protect herself from her own abilities than follow the social niceties in this instance."

There was a pause. Miss Rawlings' face contorted a few times. Len braced himself for a flood of angry abuse. Then—

"I suppose I owe you my thanks for that," Miss Rawlings said at last. "I—made a mistake. I didn't think her powers would go so strong so soon. And—if I must admit it—I was angry that she would rather play detective with you than learn to hone her magical abilities with me. I offered her the world and she said thank you, maybe later!"

Len wasn't sure what to say. He hadn't expected this level of honesty from Amelia Rawlings, of all people.

"I will come help you look for her," she went on to say. "It's the least I can do. She is, after all, my niece and my promised apprentice."

"I'm not sure that will be necessary," Len said. "But if you could put a magical cordon around the county to ensure that Sir Bertram Grimes doesn't leave this area without us knowing and being able to follow him, that would be a tremendous help. That's magic beyond my skill and Becket's combined."

"I see. Grimes, is it? I suppose he's the one who shot Carter?"

"It seems likely."

"Well," she said. "As satisfactory as it is to see Corbin imprisoned, I'd rather see him punished for the wrong he did do, not the one he didn't. I'll see to it Grimes doesn't escape, and in return, you see to it my niece comes through this unscathed."

"I will do everything in my power to see her safe," Len vowed.

Miss Rawlings eyed him oddly. "Yes, you usually do, don't you?" she said cryptically, and cut the connection.

Len breathed out a quick, "*Finiatur*," and wiped the perspiration away from his temple.

"Right," he said, looking across to Becket. "You heard the lady. Our first priority now is recovering Maia."

"Lead the way, sir," Becket said.

* * *

Len led them through the gate and up the hill, driving forward with ruthless intensity and speed. It crossed his mind at one point that he ought to be sure Becket was not struggling to keep up, but he dismissed it. If Becket needed a rest, he would say so. Until then, Len would trust him to follow and be fit for action whenever—and wherever—it was needed.

Len did pause occasionally to cast a seeking spell, hoping to find some trace of Maia's magic. Even though he knew that logically he ought to be able to see it if she had used her magic again, old habits died hard, and he couldn't quite make himself believe that their strange connection that allowed each to see the other's magic had lasted.

Each time he swept the surrounding area, he could get no hint of magic having been used, nor did he see a silver sparkle anywhere. The countryside was vast, and it was maddening to stick to the path when he knew there was every possibility that Maia was behind a tree somewhere off the path, or hidden in dip of the land in the distance, but experience told him that if he tried to search every inch of the countryside he would only wear out himself and Becket to no avail.

If the path did not lead them to Maia, he would return to Little Oaks, collect all the men and any women who were willing to come along, and even get the police involved if he had to. Dash it, both the constable and the sergeant had been friends with Maia when they were young, surely they would come along and bring any able-bodied villagers with them! He would turn the entire county upside down if he had to. For now, he would keep pressing forward.

For all that, it was Becket who found the next clue.

"Sir! Look!"

Len stopped and spun on his heel. Becket held out a bit of torn red ribbon.

"Miss Whitney was wearing a red frock this morning," Becket explained.

Len's heart leaped. "Where was this?" he demanded, snatching the ribbon from Becket's hand and squinting at it. Yes—it wasn't his imagination, he really could see the faintest shimmer of light around it, as though it had absorbed some of Maia's magical energy at some point before being torn from her dress.

Becket indicated a particularly muddy bit of ground. "While you've been looking ahead and around, sir, I've been looking down," he said.

Division of labor—yes, that was how they had always worked. For many years, they hadn't even had to speak of how they were going to split their tasks, they each knew their respective strengths so well. Len had stopped letting Becket do that after '16, though. Now, he was surprised at how good it felt that he could rely on his man in that way again.

"I saw this peeking out of the mud when you crossed the patch," Becket continued.

Len pocketed the ribbon. "We're on the right track," he said exultantly, clapping Becket's shoulder. "Well done! Either Maia tore that off deliberately and dropped it for us to follow her, or there was a struggle and it came off accidentally, but either way, we're on their heels now."

He set off again, up the next hill, wishing this land was more flat so he could spare more breath from climbing as well as have a better view of what was coming, but with renewed energy to find the woman he—

Well, the woman he considered a friend. Further than that he would not go.

Not yet.

He crested the hill and stopped short, nearly causing Becket to bump into his back.

"By Jove," he breathed, staring at the large house in the distance. "Becket, I don't suppose you know who lives there, do you?"

"I believe that is the Saunders residence, sir," the ever-helpful and well-informed valet said.

Len wrenched his gaze away from the house to stare at the other man. "The Saunders?"

"Yes, sir." After a moment, Becket added, "Perhaps you are not aware, sir, but Mr. and Mrs. Saunders left the house party this morning for their own home."

"Did they indeed, by Jove," Len breathed, the wheels turning in his brain. "Becket," he said at last, "I'm starting to believe we're up against a conspiracy here."

"Yes, sir," Becket said. "I was beginning to have similar suspicions myself, sir."

Len considered their options. The simplest, of course, was to walk up to the front door, knock, and ask if Maia was there. If the Saunders were in on the scheme with Sir Bertram, they would lie, of course, but even that might be enough to get Len inside—and once he was in, nothing would make him leave without her. Another option was to attempt to sneak in through the kitchen, but that would only work if the servants weren't particular loyal to their master and mistress, and that was chancy to depend upon. They could always wait until dark and sneak in then, but he was unwilling to leave it that long.

"Sir, if I may," Becket ventured. "I suggest we split forces. While you distract them in the front, I can more easily enter through the back. Even if the servants are part of the plot, it will be less suspicious for them to have another servant knocking at on the kitchen door than it would be for a gentleman to do so. I can claim I was on my half day and out for a walk and got thirsty and was hoping for a glass of water. Meanwhile, you can enter through the front. Once we're both inside, I do not think they will be able to stop us finding Miss Whitney."

Len hesitated. He wasn't surprised at Becket reading his mind, but he was faced with a terrible choice. Becket was right—this made the most sense and gave them the best chance of getting both of them inside. But how could he let Becket risk himself without Len there to protect him should something go wrong? Never mind that Becket had been in countless dangerous situations alongside Len before, and had even helped to pull Len out of a few of them—but not since '16. Not since Alec.

"Sir," Becket said, seeing the hesitation on Len's face, "I am willing to take whatever risk necessary to help Miss Whitney. If I may say so, sir, that is my choice. Not yours."

Len breathed in deeply, and a tension in his shoulders that had been there for the last five years lifted off. He had been carrying too much and never allowed himself to see it. "You'll do it whether I agree or not, is that it?" he asked with a wry smile.

"With all due respect, yes sir," Becket said, the ghost of a smile crossing his face in return.

"I can't think of anyone I'd rather have at my back for this than you," Len told him honestly. "I'll see you inside."

"Very good, sir."

The two men parted, Becket to lose himself in the shadows and hollows of the land until he could work his way unseen to the back premises, and Len to boldly stride down the hill toward the house as though he hadn't a care in the world. He timed his stroll carefully to give Becket enough time to reach the back, and judged that the other man would have reached the back at about the same time as Len himself knocked on the front door of the staring white house.

A long-nosed, supercilious butler opened the door for him. "Yes?" he drawled.

"'Morning, my good man," Len drawled right back him. "Is Mr. Saunders in? I'm here to pay a friendly neighborly call."

"I'm afraid the master isn't—" the butler began, when he blinked, and somehow Len was inside the entryway, smiling affably.

"No need to announce me," he said. "I'll show myself in."

Then he punched the butler in the nose and locked him in the telephone cabinet. Hard lines on the fellow if he weren't part of the plot, but Len wasn't taking any chances—besides, that drawl had irritated him.

"Now," he said under his breath, ignoring the stifled shouts of outrage that came from the cabinet, "hold on, Maia. I'm coming."

12

Wits and Weapons

Maia blinked her eyes slowly. Mercy, her head ached! And *wasn't* she ragingly thirsty? Had she had too much to drink the previous night? She couldn't recall, but it didn't seem likely.

… For heaven's sake, where on earth was she? The room was black as a pit, and she most certainly was not in bed, either her own or the far more luxurious one at Little Oaks. In fact, though she couldn't see, she was certain she was on a hard wooden floor. And—Maia bit back a yelp of panic—she couldn't move her arms or her legs!

For a moment, she was transported back to the Front. Had the last five years been a dream? Had she been injured, and was she now among the wounded rather than tending to them? Perhaps there had been a shell—what if she'd lost her arms and legs?

She forced herself to lie still. Memory began to trickle back. She was not in France, nor had she dreamed the last five years. She was in England, in Stanbury, and she had been staying at Little Oaks, helping to hunt down a murderer.

At that, the rest came back to her in a flash, and Maia abruptly realized she couldn't move her limbs because she was tied hand and foot. Her mouth nearly dropped open, only for her to realize there was cloth tied around that as well, keeping her effectively gagged.

Indignation swept away the last traces of fear. Of all the cheek! Sir Bertram—yes, it must have been he, after she so foolishly lost control of her magic and then used up all her strength bringing it back. He ought to have been grateful that she didn't kill him with it, but instead he'd taken rude advantage of her incapacity by kidnapping her and bringing her to—wherever she was.

Maia took stock of her surroundings as best she could. Wooden boards underneath her. No carpet. A faint outline of light making a square shape in the gloom before her. Of course, that must be a window. She wasn't in a cellar, wherever she was. She sniffed. The air smelled musty and dry, not damp.

An abandoned house? But where? There were no deserted homes anywhere in the county. Besides, as more of her sense engaged, she realized now she could hear the occasional creak of floorboards from elsewhere in the house, along with a murmur of voices, even a giggle once in a while.

An occupied home, then. But an upper floor, perhaps an attic. Though she couldn't see the dimensions of the room, it felt small around her. Servants' quarters, perhaps? A box room would be larger, feel more spacious and airy.

So then, an occupied house, large enough to have servants' quarters upstairs. Surely she wasn't still at Little Oaks!

No, that would be too great a risk. Blackie kept the house in marvelous condition. Not even the attics would be safe to stash a prisoner. Besides, the faint noises from below weren't enough for the size of the house party they had.

Somewhere else. And there her reasoning stalled.

Enough of her location! What could she do?

By shifting a bit, Maia could feel her war souvenir still in her stocking. Sir Bertram hadn't searched her, then. Either he had some trace of gentlemanliness left in him, or—more likely—he hadn't thought it necessary. Not that she could do much while tied up and gagged. Still, it was good to know it was there.

Obviously the next step would be to get free of her bonds. Surely there was some spell she could perform to accomplish that? Rope was made of … well, she wasn't sure, exactly, but it was something natural.

Of course, to do a spell, she had to say the Latin incantation. Which was impossible to do while gagged.

That was probably why Grimes did it. He was no fool, whatever else he was.

She would have to rely on her wits.

Maia grimly smiled against her gag. Sir Bertram would soon find that preventing her from using her magic didn't make her any less dangerous. It only irritated her.

By wriggling around a bit, Maia was able to get a better sense of the room. that it wasn't as dark as she'd assumed. Another square outlined in light opposite the first gave her a sense of the outside walls. That meant that the short streak of light coming in along the bottom of the other wall indicated the door. Even in her circumstances Maia could spare a sniff over a door so poorly fitted that light showed between the bottom of it and the floor. Fortunate for her, though, as that was her first step toward regaining her freedom.

By flexing her heels and scraping her hands along the floor,

Maia was able to inch herself along a few paces. It hurt horribly, and she had to stop every few minutes as her feet would cramp up and she would bite back a yelp inside the gag. Her fingers began to bleed after a while, but finally, she was in front of the door instead of leaning on the wall across from it.

Now, if only there was a guard! She would have to hope for the best, and if there was no guard, she would form another plan.

Lying on her back, Maia swung her bound feet up and thumped them against the door several times. She waited a few moments, then repeated the action.

A squeak and a muttered curse told her someone had inserted a key in the lock and was about to open the door. She swung herself around so that her legs were across the entrance, then closed her eyes so they wouldn't be dazzled by the light.

In a bit of luck, the door opened outward instead of in. As Maia had hoped, the person entering stumbled over her legs, sprawling on the floor with a loud, "oof!" and chin smacking the wooden boards with a satisfying thwack.

The voice that cursed her was not Sir Bertram's. At least one henchman, she noted as she ignored the bruises forming on her legs and tried to roll out the door.

The thug was too quick for her. He sprang after her, grabbed her arm, jerked her back through the doorway, and flung her across the room.

This time it was Maia's turn to hit her head. She lay there, dizzy, while the man continued to swear at her with a disappointing lack of variety and imagination. Sir Bertram must have left orders she was not to be harmed, for he didn't do anything but swear, and eventually ran out of energy and left the room, locking the door firmly behind him.

Maia waited until her ears stopped ringing before struggling to a sitting position.

That had gone even better than she'd hoped.

Between Maia's own roll and the henchman's violent action, the gag had loosened enough that by stretching her jaw and pushing her mouth, Maia was at last able to rid herself of the noxious cloth. As it dropped down around her throat, she gulped in the first full breath of air she'd had since awakening.

It was *glorious*.

Her initial thought had been to rely on the thug losing something useful out of his pockets when she tripped him. That, upon further reflection, seemed leaving too much up to chance. She'd certainly never expected to effect her escape by rolling, still bound and gagged, down who-knew how many flights of stairs and out the front door, while her captors sat tamely by. No, the entire point had been to gain information, information the thug had kindly provided while cursing at her. She now knew where she was—and to whom Sir Bertram was selling the papers.

She had also hoped that the action would do exactly what it had done—loosen her gag enough to free her voice. A sore head seemed a small price to pay to gain that weapon back.

She licked her dry lips, wishing the thug had been kind enough to leave some water behind. What if she was too hoarse to say a spell? What if she wasn't strong enough to perform a spell without using her hands? What if she had drained all of her magic when she had lost control earlier and now it was gone? What if—

Maia forced herself to stop panicking and admit the trouble. She was afraid to use her magic, after what had happened earlier.

She had two choices, as she saw it. She could attempt to use her magic, despite her fears, and suffer whatever consequences might come from her accidental misuse of it before. Or she could use up all her strength trying to free herself from her bonds physically, leaving her with little energy to stand against her captors, not to mention no way of escaping out the door.

Put like that, there was no choice at all. However, she promised herself, this time she would be excruciatingly careful. She would use the smallest spell she could think of—luckily, she remembered one from the *Household Spells* book, a trick for loosening stubborn knots of any sort.

Maia breathed deeply once or twice, building up her nerve. Then—

"*Funes solventur.*"

Like—well, like magic, the ropes unwound themselves and dropped to the floor.

"*Finiatur.*"

The sensation of magic moving through her veins stopped. Maia waited for several beats of her rapidly thudding heart, but nothing else happened. She sagged against the wall, suddenly aware of the fiery prickles of pain running up and down her limbs.

Thankful for something to occupy her mind, she set to rubbing her arms and legs as briskly as possible, biting her lips against crying out as the blood began to move freely again. Her next step was to retie her shoelaces, which had loosened along with her bindings. Maia scowled at that; surely there was a way to be more precise, so that only the knots one wished would come loose, not all of them. Still, a small price to pay, and she was only thankful that her undergarments were all held with straps, elastic, and buttons, rather than ties.

Finally, she was able to stand up and walk around.

One step closer to freedom. Now, she believed, it was time to shed a little—a very little—light on the matter. She hadn't learned a specific spell for a small light, but she remembered enough Latin to be able to adapt the spell Len had taught her.

"*Lux parva fiat,*" she said.

A tiny ball of silver light sprang to life above her open palm.

The relief at being able to see was indescribable.

It was an empty room, with dusty velvet drapes covering the windows and no furniture or anything useful that she could use in escaping. Maia patted the lump in her stocking top to reassure herself that with or without magic, she was not helpless now.

A pity she hadn't remembered it when confronting Sir Bertram earlier!

She moved to open the drapes, but hesitated. What if Sir Bertram or one of his henchmen were outside? The open drapes would show that she had freed herself. No, since she had her magic light, she would use that, and leave the windows be.

The next step was to unlock the door. She directed her light to illumine the lock. No doubt she could simply whisper the Latin word for "open," but she didn't think she even needed to do that much.

It was a very simple lock, and the keyhole was empty, thanks to the thug taking the key with him when he left. Despite the events of the day, Maia still had a few hairpins left. This would not be difficult.

Maia flexed her sore fingers, drew a pin out of her hair, ignoring the curl that promptly swept across her cheek, and went to work.

It had been a long time since she and Ray had taught themselves to pick locks during his Raffles craze, but she had never lost the skill. Indeed, it had come in handy once or twice even in recent years, but never in such dire circumstances as this.

A few final twitches, and the lock gave way. Maia eased the door open onto an empty hallway. Apparently her guard had decided he could do his job just as well from the bottom of the stairs as at her door. Daylight shone through the windows here, causing her to blink and making her little light redundant.

"Finiatur," she whispered, and with a small pang she watched it wink out.

She was free—from her prison room, at least. As for the rest, she'd have to take it one step at a time.

She did wonder if her absence had been noticed yet at Little Oaks, or if they'd all forgotten about her the moment she was out of sight. Was anybody looking for her?

Even if anyone was, there was only a slight possibility they'd think to look here. No, a rescue was not likely to happen. She was on her own.

Maia told herself she preferred it that way, being independent and strong, but she still felt a twinge. It would be nice to have someone to rely on, instead of always being the relied-upon. She didn't want to languish away waiting for someone to save her, but knowing there was even one person out there to help would have been lovely. Someone more than a friend to call on her when in need, but a partner of sorts, someone to help and be helped in equal measure.

Maia pursed her lips wryly. This was hardly the place for romantic dreams. She bent down and took off her shoes and, holding them in one hand, crept in her stocking feet down the bare floor, stepping as lightly as she could to avoid creaking floorboards, hoping against hope she would find the stairs and at least make it down one more story before anyone saw her.

Oh, what she wouldn't give for Len's chameleon spell!

* * *

Maia's luck held until she reached the first floor. There she had the misfortune to bump—quite literally—into a housemaid backing out of one of the bedrooms.

The maid screamed. Maia wasn't sure if it was the unexpectedness of the encounter, or the fact that Maia herself must have looked like something from a horrid gothic novel—bruised and mussed, clothes filthy and torn, fingertips covered with dried blood and unspeakable grime.

Footsteps thundered up the stairs and two footmen burst on the scene. Three more housemaids came running down the hall, their cries of concern jumbling together so no words could be made out. Another door off the landing crashed open, and the thug Maia had tripped stumbled out of the bedroom where he'd apparently been taking a nap in his shirtsleeves, his face darkening with suffused blood when he saw her. Finally, following in the wake of the housemaids, strolling without undue concern, came Mrs. Saunders.

Maia put her back to the wall and whipped her pistol out of her stocking. This time all the housemaids screamed, and one of the footmen turned green.

"Despite being abducted, tied up, stuck in a dark attic, and left to rot, I have no desire to shoot anybody," Maia said. "However, I will do so if I am forced, no matter how distasteful the task."

"I don't believe you," the non-green footman said.

"Believe her," the thug answered, never taking his eyes from Maia's face. "She's mad enough to do anything."

"You can't escape," Mrs. Saunders pointed out, as calmly as though they were once again discussing appropriate behavior for young women at the dinner table. "As soon as you turn your back on one of us, we'll have you captured again."

"And you can't think you can keep me here forever," Maia countered. "Already the police are looking for me." Oh, how she wished that were true! "They will find me, and you, and arrest you. Prison is not, I believe, a very comfortable place for a lady."

"What do you suggest?" the other asked, her upper lip curling in a sneer. Why had Maia never noticed the slight accent lurking behind her words before?

"I suggest," she said, holding the gun steady, "that you and I retire to a more private room, and discuss the matter there."

Mrs. Saunders smiled coolly, all traces of the mousy, fretful, dull woman she had appeared at Little Oaks now vanished. In her place stood a woman in careful control of herself and her situation, despite Maia aiming a pistol at her.

"Very well," she said. "This entire situation has turned into an utter farce as it is. It only goes to show that one cannot trust the English to do anything well." She sighed. "Hawkins, you may wait outside my sitting room until Miss Whitney and I have finished our conversation. The rest of you, back to work. I did not give you permission to stop and gawk at a street show." She smirked at Maia. "Will that suffice, Miss Whitney?"

Maia considered it. She was uneasy about allowing Mrs.

Saunders too much say in how this went. She didn't like the fact that the other woman seemed so confident even in the face of her prisoner having escaped and confronting her with a gun. On the other hand, unless she was a magician herself, there was very little she could do against Maia, who was armed both physically and magically, and was irritated to boot. She found she was experiencing an intense desire to wipe the smirk off Mrs. Saunders' face.

Suddenly, Maia's shoulders relaxed. This was merely a battle of wits between her and the other woman. Both appearing dull to the world but with a hidden secret that transformed them into something else. In Mrs. Saunders' case, the secret was one of deception, treachery, and hatred. But Maia's—ah, her secret was a beautiful one, and it had transformed her life into something full of wonder and excitement. In this situation, she had every confidence she could outwit her opponent.

"The sitting room will do nicely," she said. "Mr. Hawkins may certainly wait outside if that makes you feel more com-fortable."

For the first time, a shadow crossed Mrs. Saunders' face, as though Maia's own calmness had begun to undo hers. It passed quickly enough, and she walked into the sitting room opposite the bedrooms with her back straight and her head high. Maia kept her own back to the wall as she slid around to follow the other woman through the open doorway, turning sideways as she did so as to keep her attention both on the hallway outside and the room within. Almost to her disappointment, Mrs. Saunders was not waiting to trap her, but had seated herself in a green velvet chair, ankles crossed neatly and hands folded demurely in her lap. Maia took one quick look around the room to ensure it was empty, and then she shut the door in the face of the angry Hawkins. Turning the key in the lock, she felt—if not safe, than safer—for the first time since leaving on a walk with Sir Bertram that morning.

Maia glanced out the window as she crossed the room so as to be able to lean against a wall and still keep her pistol steady on her prisoner. She didn't trust herself not to fall asleep if she sat down, but nor did she trust her legs entirely to hold her during their conversation. Across the rolling green hills out the window, she saw a faint bronze light dancing through the air, as though a heat shimmer had taken on color. Maia's heart lifted at the sight.

"What was it you wished to discuss, Miss Whitney?" Mrs. Saunders asked.

Maia turned her attention back inside the room. She decided not to waste time asking Mrs. Saunders why she was doing this or what she hoped to gain. Instead, she went straight to the point.

"Where are the papers you bought from Sir Bertram Grimes?"

Mrs. Saunders shrugged. "I haven't the faintest idea. He has been so occupied with making a fool of your sister and patting himself on the back for having outsmarted you and your Mr. Davies that we haven't had a moment to effect the exchange. I had thought that by retiring to my own house it might make it simpler for him to hand them over in exchange for the diamonds. Imagine my disappointment this morning when instead of bringing the papers he brought me you, with the insistence that I keep you prisoner here until our business was completed, for fear you would spoil everything." She sighed. "Nonsense, of course—as though a silly chit like you could ever spoil plans that have been laid and working themselves out for years—but he was so distressed there was little I could do to talk him out of it. Men, you know, are so emotional."

Maia matched her cool smile with one of her own. She knew perfectly well that every part of Mrs. Saunders' speech was designed to make her lose her temper and so allow the other woman to get the upper hand. She refused to rise to the bait—not even the "silly chit" part, which was as nonsensical as they came. She hadn't been a silly chit since she was about twelve years old, and quite possibly not even then.

As for Sir Bertram making a fool of Merry—goodness, she was seventeen years old, and surrounded by friends and people who cared for her. She would be embarrassed to look back on this incident, no doubt, but it was not enough to cause her permanent harm. Who knew, it might even do her some good?

"In that case, I would ask when you are expecting Sir Bertram to return," Maia said.

Mrs. Saunders jerked a little, as though she didn't quite know how to respond to someone who didn't react to being poked. "Why, any moment," she said after a tiny pause. "Though I doubt he'll have the papers with him. Now that it comes down to it, I wouldn't be surprised if he's having second thoughts. He hates all you magicians, but even to get rid of you he is hesitating over supporting the rise of Austria."

Maia allowed her eyebrows to rise at that. "Austria, is it? Thank you, I was curious. Not that it matters, but one does like to have all one's facts straight, you know. Along those lines, were you the spy who lured Corbin to betray the magicians in the first place, or have you merely swept in later to take advantage of the situation?"

Mrs. Saunders offered a contemptuous smile. "My dear child, I did tell you this plan has been years in the making.

Haven't you yet realized who I am?"

And then—Maia did realize it, and was horrified it had taken her so long. "You're the—you're the magician who advised the Kaiser." Her next thought was ridiculous in light of everything else, but she couldn't stop herself from blurting, "But you're Austrian. Why were you advising the German Kaiser?"

Mrs. Saunders shrugged. "He was a useful tool. Once he had conquered the rest of the world, I would have destroyed him, and then Austria would have finally risen to her proper glory."

"For that, you betrayed all magic-users by using your magic to help him." Maia couldn't fathom it. She added, "But you were defeated by the coalition of magicians when they came together to stop you."

Mrs. Saunders pursed her mouth. "Their attack managed to strip me of my powers, but it didn't kill me. More fools they! I had already approached that idiot Corbin beforehand, knowing he would be a good source for keeping an eye on what the English magicians were doing. I thought I had more time before they found me out, but Davies and his friends got the best of me then—though I made them pay for that." Her face twisted in genuine anger. "My only regret is not making Davies suffer more."

Remembering the anguish on Len's face as he told her about Jamie and Alec, Maia felt such a strong surge of hatred for the woman seated before her that it nearly took her breath away. She glanced out the window again, and what she saw there distracted her from her unexpected emotion. She stood up straight from where she'd propped herself and began to pace slowly from one side of the room to the other, each turn taking her closer to the door. At the same time, she allowed herself to call up just a hint of her magic—not enough for it to unleash itself in an attack as it had earlier that morning, but enough that she could see silver drifting around her hand. Concentrating, Maia sent a tendril of that silver to coil under the door, where it would be invisible to anyone but those who could see her magical aura—herself and Len.

Mrs. Saunders paid no attention to these maneuvers. "I couldn't stop the magicians from completing and performing the spell that took away my magic, but I knew I could turn that to my advantage as well. Once I persuaded Corbin to bring me the notes from the power-sharing, I could use it to siphon magic from twelve other magicians and make myself even more powerful than before. Then I would use those notes as proof of the existence of magicians in the world, and in the chaos that followed I would bring Austria back to her prior glory—even more glorious than before!"

"And what happened?" Maia said. "It's been five years. Why didn't Corbin bring you the notes?"

Mrs. Saunders—or the Kaiser's Advisor—sniffed. "The fool didn't have the nerve. He must have seen a hint of my true nature under all that slop I fed him. Oh, he stole the notes as I wanted, but then he spent the next five years hiding from me. Without my magic, it was nearly impossible to find him, so that's when I found Sir Bertram Grimes and began feeding him rumors about magicians secretly controlling the world and stealing power from the ordinary man—meaning him, of course. He became so enraged at the thought that it was easy to make him think that he himself had come up with the plan to take the papers proving magic's existence from Corbin and sell them to me, so that I could use them to reveal magic to the world while he stepped up and became a hero in rising to take leadership from those who fell."

"And now that has failed you as well," Maia pointed out, still pacing. "For you still don't have the papers, and I am free, and people are looking for me, and all your plans are about to be exposed, and you will be ruined and imprisoned. Your schemes are at an end."

"I think not," Mrs. Saunders said, smiling again. She fluffed her fingers through her fair hair. "Do you really think this is my only iron in the fire? Should Sir Bertram fail me, as it seems likely he will, I have still more ways and methods of regaining my power. It might take me longer, but you really can't stop me. You aren't even a proper apprentice magician yet!"

"I don't need to be a magician at all right now," Maia said, stopping in front of the door, ears pricked. "I have a gun, and you do not."

"Would you shoot me in cold blood?" Mrs. Saunders enquired, as though she were merely academically interested. She examined her nails as she continued. "I am unarmed, after all, and no immediate threat to you. Could you really bring yourself to murder me, you Englishwoman who believes like the rest of your race so firmly in law and justice and order? I think not. I think the best you can do is to attempt to hold me prisoner, even though as long as I live I will be a threat to you and yours." She laughed. "No matter what, I win. If you shoot me, I've made you abandon your principles and become a murderer, and I shall haunt you forever. But if you let me live, you will carry the burden of all my future deeds on your shoulders, knowing you could have stopped me and didn't. It is perfectly exquisite! I only wish it were Mr. Davies here. This would be the perfect torture for him, a recompense for what he put me through when he foiled my plans to use the Kaiser to raise myself to power."

"You call me silly, but not even I believe that nonsense," Maia said as she sprang to the door, whipped around the key in the lock, and took one long step to the side.

As though they had planned it, Lennox Davies burst through the door on cue, his hair mussed and his collar askew, his knuckles bloodied like a prize fighter, and a wild glow in his eyes. For all Mrs. Saunders' boasting that she wished he was there, when he actually appeared she lost her composure for the first time. She shrieked faintly and cowered in her chair.

Aside from one comprehensive glance covering the room and its contents, Len ignored her.

"Maia! Are you—" He paused, his glance sweeping over her. "Well, I can see that you are safe and in control of the situation." A rueful smile twisted his lips. "I should have known you were no damsel in distress needing to be rescued."

"No, but I am exceedingly glad to see you here," Maia said. "I wasn't sure how much longer I could stall, and a house full of enemies was a bit much for even me to subdue alone. However, Mrs. Saunders filled the time quite nicely by kindly admitting to all her misdeeds, both those she has already committed and those she has yet to attempt. I believe Aunt Amelia will be quite pleased with this catch."

Mrs. Saunders stopped shrieking. Her face turned pale. "You—you're Amelia Rawlings' niece?"

"I am," Maia admitted.

Mrs. Saunders slumped back in the chair. An expression of disgust crossed her face. "Of all the ill luck! I should have known that woman would be my downfall."

Len snorted. "You say that as though Amelia Rawlings had

anything to do with this. No, madam, your downfall is entirely at the hands of the intrepid Miss Whitney." He looked again at Maia, and smiled. "I think one day they will be referring to Miss Rawlings as your aunt, not you as her niece."

Despite everything, Maia couldn't help but smile back.

Which was when Sir Bertram burst through the door, a revolver grasped in his hand and aimed squarely at Maia's head.

13

Masks Dropped

Len aborted his first instinct, which was to hurl himself on Grimes and wrench the revolver out of his hand. From the way the man's eyes burned with fanatical hatred as he glared at Maia, he would pull the trigger before Len had a chance to take it. Which left two options: wait for him to make a mistake, or use a spell. Len's eyes fell on Maia's weapon, which apparently Grimes hadn't noticed or considered a threat yet. Len twitched his fingers and muttered a Latin phrase under his breath. The outline of the pistol wavered and melted into the background of Maia's dress.

The chameleon spell worked on more than one's own self. Maia glanced down, startled, and then looked at Len and gave a tiny nod of understanding.

"Both of you, against that wall," Sir Bertram barked, waving his free hand toward the far wall. "Alicia, my dear, are you unharmed?"

Len stiffened as he obediently moved toward the wall. *Alicia …?* He looked again at Mrs. Saunders, now rising languidly and smirking at Maia as they crossed paths.

He had never met the Kaiser's Advisor face to face, but when he had discovered the proof of her perfidy in using her magic to aid the Kaiser in the war, he had also learned of her background as the daughter of a count in Franz Joseph's court, one Alicia von Teufel.

But she—she was destroyed by the spell! Harrison had been present at the performing of the spell and had promised Len afterward that it had been successful, that the Kaiser's Advisor was no more.

Destroyed did not mean dead, his brain whispered, and it was entirely possible for the Kaiser's Advisor to be no more while the Gräfin Alicia von Teufel was still alive and well. The role was not necessarily the woman. And, Len's treacherous brain continued to insist, it would be just like Harrison to make that sort of word trickery.

He made the mental leap even while his body continued to obey instructions, standing against the wall with Maia by his side. The magicians' coalition must have taken her magic and left her helpless, rather than killing her. It made sense—under normal circumstances stripping magic from a magician was the most heinous of acts, but in this case it would have fit the crime, and would have been considered a safer use of magic than using a spell to kill her. But—

That meant that—that *Mrs. Saunders*, a woman he had broken bread with, was no mere German spy partnering with Sir Bertram she was—she was—

Len's mind flashed back to Jamie, caught by this woman's curse, gasping in pain but valiantly promising to draw their pursuers away, overriding all Len's frantic protests, knowing there was nothing to be done. He saw Alec, his face twisted in eternal surprise as he was shot down by guards, his nerve worn away by the horrors of the chase.

He saw red.

Before he could leap on Mrs. Saunders, a small, firm hand closed around his upper arm. Len started, and turned his head. Maia looked steadily back at him, understanding and compassion clear in her wide eyes—eyes that today had far more green than blue in them, he noted with the small part of his mind that was not focused on the situation at hand.

Len breathed in deeply, the wave of hatred broken. If Mrs. Saunders really was Alicia von Teufel, he would see to it that she received justice for her deeds now as well as in the past. He would not doom both himself and Maia to certain death by Sir Bertram by attempting to throttle her with his bare hands. He would not become a murderer for her, either.

"I am annoyed but unharmed, Sir Bertram," said Mrs. Saunders (Len had to keep calling her that in his mind—he still couldn't entirely reconcile the mousy woman he had met at Little Oaks with the fiendishly clever Kaiser's Advisor). She joined Grimes in the doorway. "Miss Whitney kept me relatively entertained while we waited for your arrival, but her prattle grew tiresome."

Len expected Maia's hand to tighten on his arm in annoyance, but to his surprise her hand dropped free and he saw her smile, apparently genuinely amused. When he raised his eyebrows at her, she whispered,

"Mrs. Saunders is the one who did all the talking. If she found our conversation tiresome, it was her own fault."

"Silence!" Sir Bertram snapped, directing his attention away from Mrs. Saunders toward the two of them. "Tell me, what's to keep me from shooting you both right now? Where are your filthy magic tricks now? Now I have the power, do you hear me? I have won, and you have lost, and soon the rest of your kind will know what it is to suffer while others rise up in their place!"

Maia stifled a yawn with the hand not hiding the disguised pistol in the folds of her skirt. "Apologies, Sir Bertram, but I'm really quite tired after all the unexpected activity today. Freeing oneself from captivity does take a toll on one's energy, you know. What were you saying?"

His eyes burned, and he took a step toward her. Len braced himself, but Mrs. Saunders distracted Grimes.

"Never mind the girl, Sir Bertram! Your payment is here, in the drawer of my desk." She waved at the spindly-legged piece of furniture. "Where are the proofs you took from Corbin? I am tired of waiting!"

Sir Bertram tilted his head to look at Mrs. Saunders. Beside Len, Maia stirred and began to slowly move her arm to bring the pistol to firing position.

"I am keeping the proofs, Alicia. As much as I appreciate you making me aware of them, I never intended to give them over to you. Do you really think I want to trade one set of overlords for another? You wish to use the revelation of magic as a way to bring England to her knees and give Austria a rebirth as a world power. I wish to use it to make England stronger, under a new type of leader, leaders who aren't bound by magicians and who aren't afraid to do what must be done to lead the world into a new day!" He seemed to have forgotten his audience as he ranted. He smirked at Mrs. Saunders, who looked furious at this betrayal.

"I will take the money, though. It will come in quite useful as I build my new empire. Then I shall shoot Davies and Miss Whitney, and leave you to take the blame when the police arrive. I thank you for your assistance, Alicia, this has been a most useful association."

"You—you—" sputtered Mrs. Saunders. She tossed her head back and called, "Hawkins!"

"Is that your thug who I saw unconscious outside this room?" Sir Bertram inquired mildly. "I believe Davies did me the favor of incapacitating him before I ever arrived. Your other servants seemed quite occupied with a second man on the ground floor—one of Davies' associates, I believe. He seemed to be subduing them quite nicely."

A ridiculous thread of pride ran through Len at those words. Good old Becket. Help was on its way—not that he was certain they needed it, not with Maia in the room.

Mrs. Saunders glared. "Then I shall take care of you myself!" She sprang at Sir Bertram, pulling a knife from somewhere within her clothes as she did. He took a step back, genuinely startled for the first time since Len had met him, and swung his revolver around to fire at her in what looked like pure instinct rather than a conscious choice.

In that moment, Maia also fired. The room rang with the sound of two shots fired almost simultaneously.

Len blinked.

Mrs. Saunders, the Gräfin Alicia von Teufel, the former Kaiser's Advisor, lay dead on the floor, shot neatly through the heart. Sir Bertram Grimes was also collapsed on the floor, though in his case blood flowed only from his leg. He was still conscious, and he was staring at Maia with outrage.

"You shot me!"

Maia, Len saw, was pale, with lines of tension around her mouth that showed her to be a little sick at the violence she had been forced to commit, but her hands were quite steady. Len ended the chameleon spell now that it was no longer needed and stood ready to support her in any way she needed. His own mind was whirling too much to think clearly.

"I will shoot you again if you attempt to move," Maia told Sir Bertram. "And the next one won't be your leg. I am only going to ask this once: *where are the papers?*"

Sir Bertram opened his mouth, whether to curse them or to tell them the truth Len would never know, for at that moment, open doorway filled with people in uniform, a magnificent mustache overtopping them all.

"Clear the way, you lot, I am a police sergeant!" Ray Andrews roared, pushing his fellow officers and men dressed in everyday clothes out of the way to enter the room. "Maia— Mr. Davies—are you both all right?"

Maia dropped her arm. "Perfectly, thank you, Ray. A little weary, but in no danger. I am sorry to report that I was not quick enough to prevent Sir Bertram from shooting Mrs. Saunders, however."

"That—that's a lie!" sputtered Sir Bertram from his prone position. "That woman killed Alicia Saunders and then tried to kill me! She's mad, sergeant, and I insist you arrest her and Davies both—he's her accomplice."

Sergeant Andrews looked down at him with contempt. "If Maia Whitney had tried to kill you, you'd be dead now, Grimes. Besides, I see the weapon you used against Mrs. Saunders right here." He bent down and carefully picked up Sir Bertram's revolver from the floor by hooking his little finger through the trigger loop.

Len cleared his throat, his wits finally waking up. "I believe that careful examination will show that is the same gun that was used to murder Mr. Carter," he said.

Sergeant Andrews nodded at him. "I was suspecting something of the sort myself, Mr. Davies, thank you. Sir Bertram Grimes, I am arresting you for the murder of Alicia Saunders, the kidnapping of Maia Whitney, and possibly the murder of one Mr. Carter—"

"Drop the kidnapping charge, please, Ray," Maia said. "I believe the murder charges will be sufficient, and for myself, I'd rather stay out of this as much as possible."

"Not much like your sister," Andrews said, giving her a teasing grin. "Miss Ellie'd be insisting that any offense against her'd take precedence even over murder." Len couldn't help but notice that the class barriers had broken down in this moment of stress. For a moment, he saw the friendship that must have existed between them as children, and he felt a pang for Maia having lost that as they grew older.

"Yes well," Maia said, "I'd rather not talk about my sisters at the moment, if you don't mind. I'm tired enough as it is." She swayed on her feet.

Len sprang into action to support her with an arm around her waist. "Yes, if you don't mind, Sergeant, I'd like to take Miss Whitney someplace where she can rest. I believe my valet is here somewhere, he can get her some water or brandy if she needs it. I'd like to get her back to Little Oaks as soon as possible—can you take our statements later?"

Andrews nodded. "We have enough here to keep us busy for quite some time. I know where to find you both. Glad you're safe, Maia."

Len guided Maia, leaning heavily enough on him that he suspected her tiredness was not just for show, past the two on the floor. She stumbled a bit and averted her eyes, ignoring Sir Bertram's curses. As they passed through the doorway, she paused and said over her shoulder to the sergeant,

"How did you know where to find us?"

Andrews grinned again. "Mrs. Foy and Miss Merry were in a right tizzy when Mr. Davies here didn't return with you right away. They phoned the station and insisted we begin a search for you, and even pressed some of the guests and estate workers in as helpers. My group happened to be the one that came this way, and when we passed the house the butler came staggering out the front door, claiming his lady was in danger from a madman who had accosted him and locked him in the telephone cabinet. Why it didn't occur to him to phone us himself while in there, I'll never know." Andrews' eyes dwelt innocently on Len. "I suppose that madman must have been Sir Bertram, eh, Mr. Davies?"

Len refused to blush. "Undoubtedly," he said firmly.

Andrews' eyes twinkled. "Anyway, when we got in we found an entire battalion of unconscious men, all of whom looked the type to bash you over the head with an iron bar and steal your money as soon as look at you. Your valet—I wouldn't like to come across him when he's angry, Mr. Davies."

"*Becket* did that?"

Andrews nodded. "And then he directed us up the stairs toward this room, saying he was quite certain you both had everything under control but that he believed we would find Mr. Carter's murderer here. And he was right."

Len couldn't quite bury his own grin. Well, well. Seemed he had been right to trust Becket. He should have done it sooner.

Maia's hand tightened on his arm, reminding him of the task before him. "Excellent," he said hastily. "Thank you, sergeant. We'll see you back at Little Oaks, once Miss Whitney has rested and we've been able to return."

They were only a few steps into the hallway when Maia leaned in and hissed,

"We must find those papers before the police confiscate all of Sir Bertram's belongings as evidence!"

"Couldn't agree more," Len murmured. "The only trouble is that I still haven't the foggiest clue where the chap hid them."

"If I may, sir," Becket said, suddenly appearing before them, "I have an idea about that."

Unlike Len, who had come out of his encounters with the butler and the bully-boy guarding the sitting room looking as though he'd been fighting for his life all day, Becket was still perfectly neat and tidy, the only evidence of his having been in a fight at all a slight dishevelment around his collar.

"Dash it all …" Len began.

Maia interrupted. "Mr. Becket, how perfectly marvelous! And I must offer my thanks to both you and Mr. Davies for so nobly coming to my rescue today. When I saw the light of Mr. Davies' magic across the fields earlier, I knew you both must be looking for me, and that all I had to do was keep Mrs. Saunders talking long enough for you to find me."

And send a bit of her magic to show him which door he was behind, Len thought. And escape from her bonds in the first place. And keep her head once Sir Bertram turned the tables on them so as to turn them right back again. Yes, that was "all" she had had to do.

Had Becket not been there, Len would have been hard pressed to not sweep Maia into his arms and kiss her.

She likely would have slapped him across the face for it, so it was a good thing Becket *was* there.

"I am glad to see you looking so well, Miss Whitney," Becket said.

"The papers, Becket?" Len prompted.

"Yes, sir," Becket recalled. "Given his plan to double-cross Mrs. Saunders, I believe Sir Bertram would have taken great care to hide them both physically and magically, by surrounding them with other natural fibers, enough to mute the magical signature the papers themselves would have sent out, and then kept in a place where even Mrs. Saunders could not look."

"A linen chest?" Len hazarded, though he didn't quite see how Mrs. Saunders would be incapable of looking there.

Maia gasped. "No, I know," she said. "Mr. Becket, you are brilliant."

Becket blushed.

"Would someone enlighten me?" Len demanded with some impatience.

Maia did.

* * *

In a neat twist, Grimes had come to the Saunders' estate in his motor car, and Andrews agreed that it would be perfectly acceptable for Len to use that to return Maia to Little Oaks. Len tamped down his irritation at how smoothly the car handled—it made his motor car's quirks seem all the more egregious, somehow—and drove the three of them back post-haste. He pulled into the drive with a rattle of gravel against the car's tires and braked quickly, leaving the car standing in front of the house for the time being. Foy could decide for himself what he wanted done with it after the dust was settled.

For once in his life, Becket did not go in via the back; he entered through the front doors only a pace or two behind

Maia. Julia must have seen their approach through the windows, for she came rushing out of the drawing room.

"Maia darling!" she yelped. "What on earth happened to you? You look *dreadful,* you poor dear!" She attempted to envelop Maia in a hug, but Maia eeled her way out of it.

"I'm afraid I've no time to talk about it now, Julia. Suffice to say that Sir Bertram and Mrs. Saunders conspired together to murder that man Mr. Carter who was left in your garden, and attempted to harm me when I discovered the truth, but luckily Len and Mr. Becket had also discovered the truth and the three of us were able to aid the police in capturing them, thanks in large part to you sending Ray Andrews and the others out after us. But right now we need to recover something that Sir Bertram took from Carter before the police find it. I know it's improper, but Len here made a promise."

Len tried to close his gaping mouth. Julia blinked, took all that in, accepted the news that two of her guests were murderers with remarkable aplomb, and promptly came to the obvious—even though wrong—conclusion. "Oh! He was *blackmailing* a lady?" she gasped. "And Len, you promised to recover it for her? You angel!"

"Merely doing my duty," Len recovered enough to say.

Julia beamed. "Of course you must recover whatever it is—if the police return while you're searching I'll stall them. Go, go!"

"Well done," Len muttered as the trio sped past and entered the servants' quarters. Here, they paused only long enough for them to switch places so that Becket could lead.

Maia's grin was equal parts mischievous and triumphant. Len's heart skipped a beat at the sight. "And not one word of it untrue," she said. "Can I help it if Julia misunderstood?"

"Here, sir," Becket said, stopping in front of an unremarkable door. He stepped aside to let Len enter first, but Len shook his head.

"This is your show, old chap. Maia and I are merely here to witness. Carry on."

Becket nodded and tried the door handle. It was locked, but a simple spell from Becket took care of that. Maia watched with interest.

"So much more efficient than a hairpin," she said.

So that explained why her hair was in less than its usual orderly state, and also how she had gotten herself out of whatever room Grimes and Mrs. Saunders had stashed her in.

"Becket and I both carry picklocks as well, in case we are ever in a situation where we can't use magic, but yes, this is a most useful spell," Len said, immediately vowing to give Maia her own set as soon as possible. The next time she was captured and imprisoned, the villain might not be courteous enough to leave her a hairpin—or she might have bobbed her hair more severely and no longer need such tools. A lady should never be without resources.

Becket opened the door, and the three charged in.

Sir Bertram's valet started up from the bed on which he lounged, reading a paper and smoking a cigarette. "What do you think you're doing?" he cried indignantly. "Can't a body get some privacy in this ruddy house?"

"Sorry," Len said briefly.

Becket did not waste time with words, but went straight to the chest of drawers.

"Here, those are my things!" the valet said, moving as though to obstruct him.

Len put out one hand and stopped the man. "I don't know if you are an accomplice to Sir Bertram's murdering and treachery or not, but either way, I recommend you don't interfere."

The man paled and backed away. "Murdering? Treachery? I don't know nothing about those!"

Becket turned away from the chest of drawers, a bunch of clean collars in one hand, and a sheaf of papers in the other. "Here they are, sir."

Len's legs turned watery from relief. At last.

The valet sank back down on the bed. "Those? He told me they were business papers a rival was trying to steal and he needed me to keep them safe. I don't know nothing more about it than that!"

Len patted his shoulder absently. "I believe you." If for no other reason than if the man had known, he would have put up a much stronger resistance to their search.

"Well done, Mr. Becket," Maia said.

"Yes indeed, old chap," Len said. "What made you think of it?"

"I merely asked myself what you would have done if you had papers you needed to hide without appearing to hide them, sir," Becket said. "I believe you would have given them to me."

"So I would," Len said promptly. Especially now. "And I trust you'd be a safer repository than this fellow."

He patted the valet on the shoulder again. The man looked mildly indignant, but said nothing as they left the room, Becket kindly closing and re-locking the door behind them.

"What now?" Maia said. "Do you return them to your superiors?"

"Now," Len said grimly, "We burn them. I don't trust them to anyone, and I don't want to run the risk of them getting lost again."

Maia nodded, and Becket led them to the kitchen.

"Don't mind us, Blackie," Maia said hurriedly to the house-keeper, who sat at the large wooden table sharing a cup of tea with the cook. "I know we look dreadful, but we need to borrow the stove for a moment."

The cook sniffed but nodded when Mrs. Blackwood nudged her, glaring at the scullery maid who was gawking over her shoulder at the newcomers while washing dishes.

"Mind your work, not the gentry, Maggie," she barked.

Becket handed the papers to Len, who smoothed them out, confirming they were all there and that no spell had been used on them. At this point, he wanted to leave nothing to chance.

They were indeed the stolen notes, all of them, and they were intact. Len nodded and handed them back to Becket.

"Have at it, old chap."

Becket deftly opened the door to the stove and pushed the papers inside. The three of them, plus Mrs. Blackwood, the cook, and Maggie the scullery maid, watched in silence as they burned to ash. Then Becket closed the door and wiped his fingers on a handkerchief.

"Much obliged to you, ma'am," he said.

"Any time, I'm sure," the cook said dryly.

The three of them left the kitchen and paused, irresolute.

The task was done. The murderer was caught, the Kaiser's Advisor dead, and the papers recovered and destroyed. Corbin would soon be free from prison and facing justice from the magical world for his true crimes. Maia was safe. Another job well done.

On top of all that, he had come face to face with the woman responsible for Alec and Jamie's deaths, and he hadn't been consumed by his hatred. She was dead, but not by his hand.

He felt—free, for the first time in five years. His ghosts had been laid to rest, and the burden of anger and guilt he had born for so long was gone.

He didn't quite know what to do with himself.

He shook himself slightly, like a duck coming out of the pond shedding water from its feathers.

"I suppose we'd best put together our statements now—what we're going to tell the police. I rather like your explanation to Julia, Maia, only without the blackmail hints. We tell them that you discovered Sir Bertram murdered Carter, and when you confronted him he captured you and took you to the Saunders' estate, where you escaped and learned that he and Mrs. Saunders had conspired to do the deed. Becket and I tracked you down because Julia and Merry were concerned about your absence, and when Sir Bertram and Mrs. Saunders turned against each other, he shot her and you shot him. As with Julia, it's all entirely truthful—it just leaves out a few unnecessary details."

"Ray will want to know why the two of them were conspiring, and why they killed Carter," Maia pointed out.

Len shrugged. "I am sure we would all like to know that, but you know it's only in stories where the villain conveniently spills every detail of his plan before his demise."

Maia laughed.

"And then," Len said, feeling some life starting to return, "I wouldn't mind hearing your part of the story. Just how you pegged Sir B. as the villain of the piece, and just what happened out in the fields to leave such a strong magical signature behind."

"That part is rather embarrassing," Maia said. "But I will tell you if you tell me your side of things. After I get myself cleaned up, and after we satisfy Ray—and, I suppose, after I contact Aunt Amelia and let her know what has happened."

Len would have to contact Harrison as well. He stifled a sigh. The end of a job was never when the opponent was successfully stymied or the stolen papers recovered or the other nation's papers successfully stolen, or whatever task it was he had been set as an operative for Magical Intelligence. No, the end was all the tedious bits of filing reports and making sure all the loose ends were tied up.

He *hated* this part.

"A cup of tea and toasted crumpets when we've finished all our other chores, and sharing of stories," he said. "I'll commandeer Foy's study and Becket shall stand guard to make sure no one interrupts us."

Maia nodded, then winced as the sound of high-pitched voices echoed down the hall toward them. "Especially sister interruptions," she breathed, and then there was no time for anything else before Merry and Ellie were upon them. Len took one look at the situation, decided he was unnecessary here, and slipped away, Becket on his heels.

Ellie's voice was the last thing he heard as he trotted quickly away toward his room:

"May, you look positively appalling! Whatever happened to you? Never mind that now—you'll never guess, the most marvelous thing! Freddie has proposed! One of his mother's brothers owns a bank in New York City and has offered Freddie a job, and as soon as we're married we'll move to New York. Think of it! Rubbing shoulders with the Vanderbilts and Rockefellers, finally away from this boring old village. It's everything I ever dreamed of!"

Len's shoulders shook with laughter he desperately tried to

keep silent.

"Poor old Freddie," he finally managed to gasp.

"Who knows, sir?" Becket replied. "Perhaps once in a new place, with no one around who has any expectations of her, Miss Electra may at last shed some of her more unpleasant behaviors and become a truly devoted wife to Mr. Winters."

"I suppose stranger things have happened," said Len doubtfully.

Still, the important thing was that Ellie would no longer be around to torment Maia. For that, Len was willing to sacrifice Freddie on any number of altars. Although Maia might not be at home much longer to be tormented, either.

Miss Rawlings kept her main residence in London. Len's flat, where he lived when he wasn't being sent hither and thither on jobs for MI, was also in London. He and Maia would be able to see each other when she was apprenticed to her aunt. He could help her with her magic, she could advise or even help him on his jobs ... she was likely too powerful to want to become an agent for MI herself, but they could consider her a consultant ... their friendship would grow and develop, and then, in time, after her apprenticeship was complete and she was free to choose what magical path she wanted to go down and what she wanted to do with her life, then, maybe, there would be room for more than friendship ...

Len did not usually indulge in dreams of the future. For so long, his work had required him to look no further ahead than the next step. Settling down to raise a family and live a life of leisure had never appealed to him, therefore he'd never been particularly interested in any young lady. But Maia—life with her wouldn't be settling down in the slightest. It would a shared adventure.

Far in the future, perhaps, but a dream he would hold onto all the same.

14

A New Beginning

Maia emerged from her bath feeling reborn. Julia sent her own maid to help with hair and dress, and by the time Maia descended to the main level of Little Oaks to meet with Ray, the only traces of her misadventure that remained were some bruises hidden by her clothes, a bump on the head disguised by the new hairstyle Julia's maid had given her, and a lingering soreness around the ankles and wrists where she'd been tied.

Even the interview with Ray wasn't too bad. He did press her a bit on how she'd come to the conclusion that Sir Bertram was the murderer, but Maia answered truthfully that it had come to her when she realized his alibi was false, and he'd admitted the truth to her when she pressed him. As to how Sir Bertram had overpowered her, and where she had got her pistol (and was it registered), she hedged a bit, and finally Ray accepted her excuse that her memory was a bit hazy after it all, though with an exasperated look that suggested he knew she wasn't telling him everything.

After she was dismissed and Len and Becket went in for

their turn at making a statement, Maia realized she could not contact Aunt Amelia magically, as she had not learned how to perform the spell Becket had used for her before. Sighing, she headed for Julia's sitting room to ask if she could use her telephone to ring home.

Merry caught her before she could enter that haven.

"I am still angry with you for interfering with my life, you know," she said abruptly. "Just because you were right about Sir Bertram doesn't mean you have to poke your nose into everything and always try to control us—Ellie and me, I mean."

Maia sighed. She didn't have the energy for this now. Ellie had temporarily forgotten her pique against Maia in the thrill of her engagement (poor Freddie!), and she had hoped that Merry would have let her irritation pass as well.

She should have known better.

"You may be right," she admitted. "It's difficult for me to not want the best for you, but I should remember that I am not your mother, and even if I were, you are old enough to make your own mistakes and learn from them yourself."

"Want the best for us?" Merry's blue eyes widened. "Is *that* why you're always nagging? I thought it was because you were always embarrassed by us, and wanted us to live up to your standards of perfection!"

Maia couldn't help it: she burst into laughter. "Oh goodness," she finally gasped. "How we've been misunderstanding each other all these years! We need to have a real heart-to-heart sometime soon. Only, can it wait until we are both home?"

Merry scowled at her. "Yes," she said. "But not any later than that."

She stepped back, and Maia was able to enter the sitting room and make her request of Julia, who was lounging on her chaise with a paperback novel, happily ignoring all her guests and responsibilities for a brief period.

"Ring home? But why, darling?" Julia asked, setting the novel aside. "Your mother hasn't been worrying about you—no one even told her you'd gone missing."

Maia hunted around for a reason and plumped on one that—again—was practically if not entirely the truth. "Aunt Amelia has invited me to stay with her in London for a time once this house party is over, and I wanted to let her know that I'll be home soon and ready to leave as soon as she wants to go."

Julia blinked a few times, then squealed and leapt up to throw her arms around Maia. "Oh, that's perfect! Even if your aunt is an old battle-axe, it gets you away from your family and your home and all their demands on you! You'll finally have a chance to live for yourself!"

"That sounds so selfish," Maia objected, wrinkling her nose.

Julia was much wiser than her appearance suggested. She sat back down to wrestle that one out.

"It does sound selfish," she agreed. "But I don't mean it that way. Now, what do I mean?" She tapped one finger against her cheek as she thought it through. "It's one thing to put others ahead of yourself," she said slowly. "The church teaches us we should do that, and even though I'm not particularly pious, I do agree with that. But I don't think it's healthy to live in—in *slavery* to the whims of others. It's not helpful for them, for one thing—you're simply inviting *them* to be selfish and pile all their troubles on your shoulders, and even if they don't get mired in selfishness they don't get a chance to grow and learn what they're capable of, either."

Maia recalled her sisters' anger at her interference in their lives, and how despite her lectures and scoldings, they only ever seemed to get worse in their behavior, not better, and she had to admit the truth in Julia's words.

"But even aside from that, I don't think it's wrong to have interests and desires of your own, even while not being selfish about it," Julia said. "Surely there's a balance between only putting others first and living solely for oneself?"

"I think there must be," Maia admitted. "And maybe that's what I'll have a chance to discover once I'm not here anymore."

"Good!" Julia said. "And then you can tell me what it is, because as you can see, I don't quite have it all clear myself." She laughed, and Maia laughed with her. Then Julia's face crumpled. "But oh dear—that means you won't be here for me anymore, either!"

"That will give you a chance to grow and learn what you are capable of," Maia said wickedly.

Julia threw an embroidered cushion from the chaise at her. "Beast! I know perfectly well what I'm capable of—didn't I get promoted to head of Ward D, two months ahead of any of the rest of you? And didn't I just manage to host a splendid house party, complete with two murderers, without losing any of my guests, thus making me the most desirable hostess of the season? I don't need you here to fix my problems, Maia—I will miss my friend."

"I will miss you as well," Maia said honestly. She was more moved than she cared to admit by Julia's words.

Julia left her then to use the telephone in privacy. Maia sat down at the table and rang her home.

Mr. Whitney loathed and despised the telephone, but Mrs. Whitney refused to answer it at all, as that, to her, was clearly for servants and daughters to do. Since there were currently no daughters at home and no servant other than the loyal Mrs.

Humphrey, who was, in her own words, far too busy to be fretting over the telephone all the time, that left Mr. Whitney to nerve himself to answer when it rang.

"Yes, what? Who is this? Oh—Maia. Whatever are you ringing for, child? Wouldn't it be simpler to walk home and speak with us in person?"

"I need to speak with Aunt Amelia, Father," Maia said patiently.

"Really? Whatever for … oh, never mind, I'll fetch her. Really, Maia, it is most inconvenient having no servants about the house these days. Do you suppose you could do something about that when you get home?"

Maia opened her mouth to say of course, she'd see about hiring new servants before she left for London, recalled her conversation with Julia, and changed her mind. "Actually, no, Father, I don't think I will be able to do that. You and Mother will have to find some yourself. I'll be rather busy."

"Busy doing *what*?" Mr. Whitney complained. "Oh—here's Amelia. She must have overheard me saying I would fetch her and come herself. Very well, Millie, yes, it's Maia and she wants to talk to you, but—oh, well, yes, here. Good-bye, Maia."

"Maia!" Aunt Amelia's voice boomed through the line, causing Maia to wince and hold the receiver a little further away from her ear. "What on earth happened to you? Wait— don't say a word. I'm sure there's a girl at the exchange listening to every word we are saying. Hang up, and find a bowl of water."

A click in Maia's ear told her that her aunt had hung up on her end. A bit bemused, Maia left the sitting room and went to her bedroom, where there was an old-fashioned bowl and pitcher decorating the lower shelf of her nightstand. She filled the bowl with water in the bathroom, carried it back to her bedroom, and set it atop the nightstand.

She nearly jumped out of her skin when the surface of the water rippled and Aunt Amelia's face appeared in the bowl.

"Ha! There you are. Well, no one to eavesdrop on us now. Tell me everything."

Swallowing her amazement at this new form of communication, even more peculiar than the instant letters Becket had helped her achieve, Maia told her aunt the entire story, with no embellishments or need to hedge anything. Aunt Amelia's face grew grimmer and grimmer throughout the story.

"So you see," Maia said at last. "Everything is sorted now, and I can come home this evening if you'd like to leave for London tomorrow—that is," made somewhat uneasy by her aunt's ominous silence and bleak face in the bowl, "so long as I haven't made such a mess of things with my magic that you no longer want me as an apprentice."

"You make a mess of things!" Aunt Amelia barked, finally breaking her silence. "Goodness, girl, don't talk such nonsense. Of course you made rather a mess of it when you lost control around Sir Bertram, but good heavens, it could have been much worse. Do you know what usually happens to new magicians who lose control of their magic? They die, that's what! For you to be able to pull it back in without killing either yourself or that wretch Grimes ... well, I don't know that I could have done it when I was a girl, and I'm one of the strongest magicians I know."

"Oh, well ..." said Maia, both pleased and embarrassed.

"However," Aunt Amelia continued, and Maia's heart plunged. "I don't think I ought to take you on as an apprentice after all."

"Oh," Maia managed, biting back all her questions. "I see."

"No you don't!" said Aunt Amelia. She wagged a finger. "Listen: I made a mistake when I trained Samuel, I see that now, and I made a mistake when I told you about your magic and then let you flit off to Little Oaks with no training. I had high expectations of Samuel, but he needed a master who was kinder and more interested in him as a person. I don't blame myself for his moral failures, but I do blame myself for not seeing them coming."

"Oh," Maia said again.

"As for you, I assumed too much again. Because of your personal self-control—living with my fool of a sister would send most people into screaming fits, but you've endured it for twenty-one years—and, I'll admit it, because I was annoyed at you for wanting to put off your apprenticeship and I thought I would teach you a lesson, I waited to give you the basic instructions in controlling magic that every magic-user is supposed to receive as soon as their powers blossom. As a result, you nearly killed yourself and Sir Bertram Grimes— not that he would have been any great loss—and ended up imprisoned and in danger. Clearly, I should not be taking on apprentices. I may be a master magician, but that does not make me a master teacher."

For just a moment, Maia saw weariness and grief in her aunt's face before her habitual expression of self-satisfaction and disapproval of others closed back over it.

"But if I don't apprentice to you, won't I be in just as much danger of losing control?" Maia said. She would not plead with her aunt to change her mind—but oh, to be offered the world and then have it snatched back—!

"I will of course take the responsibility upon myself to find you a proper master," Aunt Amelia said. "There's bound to be a master magician somewhere in this county who can take you on. You will become a magician, Maia, and most likely an excellent one—but not as my apprentice."

She spoke a Latin phrase, and the water in the bowl rippled and then returned to its normal placid state. Maia stared blankly at her own reflection, her castle in the air crumbling around her. No moving to London and escaping her family responsibilities—no learning magic under Aunt Amelia—no further encounters with Len. Stuck at home still, learning magic but with no chance to use it or do anything with it to make her or anyone else's life better.

Ellie would be delighted.

At that thought, Maia moved away from the nightstand and tossed her head. Was she going to accept defeat so easily? She had faced down a many-times murderess, shot Sir Bertram Grimes in the leg without flinching, rescued herself from imprisonment, and helped Len solve his case. She was not going to slump into apathy and despair, or slide back into old bad habits before she'd even had a chance to establish new ones.

She would give Aunt Amelia just enough time to get comfortable back in London, and then—

Maia smiled.

✳ ✳ ✳

"May!" Ellie's screech echoed throughout the house as she stormed through the open window onto the Stanbury terrace. "Tell Mother it is completely unreasonable to announce my engagement with a tea for all her stuffy old lady friends! I want a party, an engagement dance, with Freddie's and my friends, not a dull old tea that will bore me to tears!"

"Frederick is the son of an Earl," Mrs. Whitney said, sweeping after Ellie. "We must do everything properly."

"Freddie is the second son, not the heir, and nobody cares about those old rules of society anymore, especially not us. We are the future, Mother! We do things differently."

"Maia, tell your sister—"

"Maia, tell Mother—"

Maia smiled at them. "Sorry Mother, Ellie, you'll have to settle this yourselves. I'm leaving in fifteen minutes."

They stared at her with open mouths, looking remarkably alike in their shock. They hadn't even noticed that Maia was wearing traveling clothes, or that she had a packed valise at her feet. In fact, they hadn't noticed anything for several days except their own obsession with Ellie's impending nuptials. Merry had lost patience with it two days ago and gone to stay with Tim and Laura Spencer until it was all over. Tim had asked for her help in finding forward-thinking schoolteachers for the village school and persuading the local parents that keeping their children in school until age fourteen was not a burden but a gift.

The house party at Little Oaks had disbursed a week ago. Sir Bertram Grimes was awaiting trial for the murder of Mrs. Alicia Saunders as well as the manservant Carter. Samuel Corbin had been released from jail and was promptly taken into custody by the magical authorities. Maia didn't know what was going to happen to him, but Len assured her it wouldn't be pretty.

Saying goodbye to Len had been unexpectedly difficult. They had known each other for such a short amount of time, but he had become a good friend, one of the best friends Maia had ever had. He had clasped her hand and cheerily said he would see her soon in London, but there was a hint of something else in his deep blue eyes that made Maia think he didn't want to say goodbye any more than she did.

While waiting for Aunt Amelia to get comfortable in London again, Maia had returned home, made a few plans with Mrs. Humphrey, had a long conversation with her father, and endured the fuss of wedding planning by going for long walks as frequently as possible and staying out of her mother and sister's way when in the house as best she could. This morning she had decided she'd waited long enough.

"Leaving? Nonsense," Mrs. Whitney said finally. "Where would you go?"

"You can't leave in the middle of our plans," Ellie added. "I need you, May!"

Maia smiled. "I'm going to stay with Aunt Amelia for a few months, maybe longer."

"What?" Mrs. Whitney bellowed. "Amelia? Have you gone mad?"

Ellie's response was different, but just as outraged. "London? You're going to *London*? Not," quickly recalling herself, "that London is anything compared to New York. And I wouldn't stay with Aunt Amelia if you paid me!"

"Thankfully no one is asking you to," Maia said, picking up her bag and stepping off the terrace. "I'll return for your wedding, Ellie. You don't really need me, you know. You are more than capable of planning this wedding yourself. I'll only get in the way."

Ellie's face took on a thoughtful look as she began to consider herself in the role of the capable one, organizing everyone and everything in order to have the perfect wedding. Maia decided to leave before she realized just how boring such a role would be.

"But—Amelia?" Mrs. Whitney cried plaintively.

"I rather like Aunt Amelia," Maia said honestly enough—for despite everything, she *did* like her cantankerous aunt. Her plan to go to London wasn't all about the magical training. "I told Father and Mrs. Humphrey about my visit days ago. Merry, too, before she left. She thought it was a marvelous plan, although like you, Ellie, she said she wouldn't stay with Aunt Amelia as a gift. I would have told you two, but neither of you ever gave me a chance." She paused and reached into her coat pocket, handing a stack of papers to Mrs. Whitney. "Here are the references for a number of potential servants. I suggest you look into hiring some as soon as possible."

"But—but—but…" Ellie sputtered, wringing her hands as the reality of life without Maia taking care of the mundane tasks started to sink in.

"How can you do this to me?" wailed Mrs. Whitney. She clutched her chest. "How much sharper than a serpent's tooth is an ungrateful child!"

Mr. Whitney wandered out onto the terrace, examining his watch. "Maia, it appears there is a taxi at the door for you. If you don't leave now, you'll miss the train," he said.

"Thank you, Father, I'm just on my way."

He smiled at her and handed her a pocketbook. "A little something to help you buy some pretty frocks once you're in London. My banker will be paying your monthly allowance, but I thought you might want something extra for starting out."

Maia kissed his cheek by way of thanks.

"Robert!" Mrs. Whitney said. "How can you condone this betrayal?"

Mr. Whitney fixed his wife with a mildly inquisitive gaze. "Surely Maia is free to live her own life, just like the other girls?"

While Mrs. Whitney pondered how to say no to that, Maia nodded to them all.

"I'll write when I've arrived at Aunt Amelia's," she said cheerfully, and escaped before anyone could say anything more.

As the taxi rolled down the long drive, Maia's mother's wails echoing in her ears, her sister's shrill tones beating at her back, Maia couldn't find it in her to regret anything except perhaps not doing this years ago.

On the other hand, if she had left years ago she might still not know about her magic. No, in the end, everything had happened as it was meant to, and for the best.

Now all she had to do was persuade Aunt Amelia to change her mind.

* * *

"Absolutely not," Aunt Amelia said. She looked exhausted and haunted, dark circles under her eyes, but she had a stubborn set to her mouth.

Maia wasn't concerned. When necessary, she could be even more stubborn.

Aunt Amelia had been startled to see her niece arrive at the front door of her stately town house in St. James's Square, and even more startled when said niece had announced she was here to begin her apprenticeship. She ushered Maia into the over-crowded drawing room, dismissed the servants, and immediately began arguing—against herself, mostly.

"It is out of the question," Aunt Amelia continued, when Maia said nothing. "I am not fit to be a teacher."

Maia snorted, but said nothing.

"I have almost reached an agreement with another magician to be your teacher," Aunt Amelia said. "It would be dreadfully bad manners to back out now."

Maia picked up a small china dog sitting and begging on the mantelpiece and studied it.

Aunt Amelia threw her hands up into the air. "If you need a break from my dreadful sister and niece, you may stay here for a few weeks, but no magic lessons, understand?"

Maia set the china dog down and picked up a purple duck.

Aunt Amelia muttered a few choice words under her breath. "A few basic lessons in control, and that's all. Just enough to hold you over until we've come to an agreement with the other magician."

Maia finally broke her silence. "That's very kind of you, Aunt. Only, what if I don't want another teacher? You say you aren't fit for teaching, but surely, that should be my choice, if I'm willing to risk it?"

Aunt Amelia glared at her. "Dratted girl." She began to pace. "We've been over all this before. You know why I said I wouldn't teach you. Even if you want to take the risk, why should I?"

Maia turned from the mantelpiece and gave her aunt her full attention. "I respect your opinion, but I am asking you to consider mine. I am not Samuel Corbin. I will not break under hard work, nor will I expect coddling. I am here not because I want my auntie to help me learn magic—I am here because you are one of the finest magicians in the country, and I am not willing to settle for anything less."

"Flatterer," Aunt Amelia said.

Maia laughed. "Come now! Would you do anything different, if you were in my shoes?"

Aunt Amelia considered this and sighed. "Very well. One month of lessons. If it goes well, we'll discuss a formal apprenticeship. If not, you will go to another teacher."

Maia smiled sweetly. "Thank you, Aunt. Where should I take my bag?"

Aunt Amelia scowled. "All sunshine and roses now that you've gotten your own way! The guest room is this way. Lunch is at one-thirty sharp. Don't be late! Your first official magic lesson will be after the meal."

Up the carpeted stairs, through the long and well-lit hallway, to a small guest room at the end. Aunt Amelia left Maia there, saying something about warning the staff.

It didn't take Maia long to unpack. She hadn't brought much, not wanting to carry anything more than the necessities from her old life. Settled in her new room, she looked around and sighed happily.

It was small, yes, but clean and well-furnished, with a comfortable bed, a small writing table and chair, a wardrobe, a fireplace, and a dressing table. Best of all, it was hers, with no sisters to drop in and pinch her clothing or her hairbrush or whatever else they felt they deserved of her things, no mother to sweep in and bewail the miseries of her life, no endless duties and empty drudgeries waiting for her the instant she set foot outside it.

Finally, she was certain she was where she was supposed to be. Let Mother and Ellie fight things out between them, let them learn what it took to run a household or hire someone to run it for you … she was doing exactly what she was meant to do.

A chance to learn magic! Oh, she could have tried to learn from a master magician back at Stanbury, but she knew she would never have been able to give it her full attention. There would always be something or someone at home that demanded her care, and she wouldn't be able to think of herself as anything but the eldest Whitney girl, always ready to take care of everyone else's needs.

Not that she generally approved of running away. One had to face up to life, after all. But in this case, a change of scenery and of pace was exactly what she needed while she explored this brand-new world opened before her, the world of magic and possibility. Perhaps when she was finished with her apprenticeship she would return to Stanbury, more secure in who she was and what she intended to do with her life.

Or perhaps not. After all, it was natural for people to leave home once they became adults. She had left once, but when the War had ended she had returned home like so many of the other young women who had served, and the shackles of responsibility had closed around her again. This time, the entire world was open before her.

Maia leaned her elbows on the windowsill and looked out across the London skyline.

Her adventure with Len hadn't been only an exciting interlude in an otherwise dull and drab life. It had only been the start of all her adventures. She didn't yet know what they would be, or where they would take her, but she had no doubt they were out there, waiting for her.

Maia was not over-burdened with imagination, but she had

a sudden flash of vision of herself and Len, running hand-in-hand, surrounded by a cloud of intermingled bronze and silver threads, both of them laughing as they chased the wind. She blinked, and it vanished.

She certainly didn't intend to hold Len's hand, but she had to admit, the thought of sharing some, at least, of her magical adventures with him was appealing. She had accused him of being too much of a chameleon, back at Little Oaks, but she had the feeling she had seen the Len Davies few others had—the man inside the disguise, a man who was true-hearted, courageous, impulsive, a little bit reckless, and loyal to the bitter end. She was glad he'd been able to see the end of the Kaiser's Advisor, even if that end had been more grisly than either of them would have preferred. The death of one woman couldn't repay the deaths of his cousin and friend, but at least he had the satisfaction of knowing the job the three of them had set out to do was finished at last. Indeed, she was quite certain some of the shadows had already left his eyes by the time they all left Little Oaks.

"Maia!" Aunt Amelia called. "Didn't you hear the gong, girl? Don't be late for lunch—I can't abide tardiness. Don't forget, your first lesson afterward!"

Maia turned away from the window.

"Coming, Aunt!" she called.

She caught sight of herself in the looking glass above the dressing table and gave her reflection a brisk nod. Today marked a new beginning for her. She couldn't wait to see what this new world of magic held.

Back straight, eyes bright, Maia walked out of her bedroom and took her first steps into her new life.

<h1 style="text-align:center">15</h1>

<h1 style="text-align:center">Coda</h1>

Back in his London flat, Len couldn't understand his feelings of restlessness. He had everything to congratulate himself on: the notes recovered and destroyed, Sir Bertram Grimes incarcerated, the Kaiser's Advisor finished for good, Maia safe, Miss Rawlings humbled, the magical world safe for another day. He had even received a letter of commendation from some of the higher-ups in the Circle, along with the hint of a promotion in his future if he played his cards right.

Not that he wanted a promotion—tied to a desk, overseeing others, stuck filling out paperwork while other agents got to work in the field. No, thank you. That life was not for him. He craved adventure and excitement too much to want that. He was happy doing exactly what he did.

Only ... now that Alec's ghost was finally laid to rest, and Jamie's as well, was he still as absorbed in this work as he had been? He had no one to avenge anymore, no shoes to fill or banners to take up. Not that he had ever considered himself doing this work for that reason, but ...

240

He needed a holiday, Len decided. That was all that was wrong with him. He could go up to Scotland, visit his sister and brother-in-law, rest with them for a fortnight. Pippa and Cam were always happy to see him, and the Cameron stables were famous. He could ride every day, blow away all the ghosts of the past that still wanted to linger.

Or … Len got up from his easy chair and began to pace. Or he could stay in London and pay a casual call on Maia, see how her training was going. She had told him a little of her plans before they'd both left Little Oaks, how Miss Rawlings had initially said she wouldn't train Maia after all but Maia was going to persuade her to change her mind. Len had been in a bit of doubt as to which stubborn woman would win, but a note from Maia a few days ago had let him know she had prevailed. She was in London now, and already learning "heaps."

Although, the note had said, *nothing has yet lived up to the lux spell you taught me that night in the woods. I shall never forget the thrill I felt when I saw that light spring to life above my head! It was magical in more ways than one.*

He smiled. He would never forget that moment either.

He made up his mind. He would tell Harrison he needed some time off, and he would spend a few days taking Maia out in the afternoons, after her lessons were finished, showing her London and introducing her to more of the magical community. Then perhaps a week in Scotland with Pippa and Cam, and then, hopefully, he would be refreshed and ready for whatever new tasks came his way.

"Becket!" he called. "I'm on my way to Eastwood's!"

"One moment, sir," Becket said, entering the study with a telegram on a silver tray. "This arrived just now."

Len groaned. Why Harrison couldn't contact him magically with a new mission was beyond him. Why did it always have to be telegrams? He opened this one with no little dread.

"Russia?" he said blankly, staring at the single word.

"I shall pack our warmest clothes, sir," Becket said, preparing to leave the study.

"Wait!" Len called after him, scowling.

"I need a holiday, and so do you," he said. "Harrison can simply send someone else to Russia in our place."

Becket's eyes widened, but he said nothing.

"I'll go to Eastwood's now and tell him so," Len said.

"Very good, sir."

Len crammed on hat and coat and set off at a rapid pace toward East London—it was a long walk, but he needed the movement.

He had apprenticed to Harrison Eastwood at a young age, and started working for Magical Intelligence not too long after that. He had done everything that was asked of him ever since. Sometimes his missions failed, more often they succeeded. Sometimes he had had to do things his conscience still protested long after they were over and done with. He had given himself whole-heartedly to the work, and never once asked for anything in return except what it gave him naturally— a chance to exchange the stultifying life of a country gentleman for one of adventure and excitement, and a chance to protect England's magicians from outside threats while doing it.

Now, though, he needed a rest. Not for good—he couldn't see himself giving up this work any time soon. It was his life, after all. But a rest all the same. Maia's words about his chameleon spell still rankled. Did even *he* know who he was without the mask anymore?

Maia … Len's steps slowed and his face softened as he thought of her. There was a person who was so wholly herself she couldn't hide it if she tried. A jewel of a woman, shining out like a splendor even in the drab setting of her home and her family burdens. He snorted softly to himself, startling a passing woman, as he thought of Ellie's attempt to make Maia look shabby and herself look glamorous. Maia's true worth only shone the brighter in comparison to Ellie's cheap trinkets and shallow charm.

He would have admired and respected her even if she hadn't been a magician. Finding out he didn't have to hide that part of himself from her had only made him all the more glad to consider her a friend. And perhaps one day even more than a friend …?

By the time he reached the warehouse where Harrison kept his office, Len had worked off much of his temper, but he was still determined not to go to Russia, no matter what Harrison said.

"Ah," Harrison said as Len entered the office. "Sit down, Davies."

The same words as before the last mission, the words that had sent him to Little Oaks and started the chain of events. Or were they only one more link in a chain that stretched back far longer than that? Back as far as Corbin's theft, as Alec and Jamie's death, as Len accepting the mission to gain proof of the Kaiser's Advisor's perfidy, of the rumors of her existence that Harrison had tracked down, of his apprenticeship with Harrison in the first place, of even more events before that? Len shook his head. He had no time for philosophical musings today.

"I can't go to Russia, sir," he said abruptly, without taking a seat. "I need a holiday. And so does Becket," he added as an afterthought.

"I said sit," Harrison said.

Len relented and sat down. Harrison passed a folder across the desk to him.

"Read."

"What is it?" Len asked warily. Why hadn't Harrison responded to his declaration?

"Just read it," Harrison said.

Len relented and read. As he did, a heavy weight settled on his soul.

"I see," he said, handing the folder back.

"I wouldn't ask it of you if I had any other choice," Harrison said.

There was never any other choice. It was always necessity. Len's shoulders bowed a little under the weight of duty, but he consciously squared them. He would not complain over what had to be done.

"Russia in winter … it won't be very jolly," he said with an attempt at airiness.

"Then you'll have to do your best to finish the job before winter sets in," Harrison said, un-airy and unamused.

"You know I'll do my best, sir," Len said, dropping the act.

Harrison eyed him, then nodded. "You always do."

Russia it was. Pippa and Cam, Scotland, horses, the delights of London's magical community, and even Maia, would all have to wait.

He still had a job to do.

The End

About the Author

A storyteller from the time she could talk, as soon as E.L. Bates learned to write she began putting her stories down on paper and inflicting them on the general public. Stories of magic and derring-do have been her favorites from almost as young. She is a firm believer in Lloyd Alexander's maxim that "fantasy is not an escape from reality; it is a way of understanding reality." Also, it's a lot of fun both to write and to read.

When not writing, Bates works as a freelance editor and an office admin, and recently returned to school for Information and Library Science. In her spare time (what's that?) she enjoys knitting, reading, and hiking with her family.

You can find out more about E.L. Bates via her website, or you can sign up for her newsletter for exclusive looks at new books and upcoming sales.

You can connect with me on:

🌐 https://www.stardancepress.com

Subscribe to my newsletter:

✉ https://dashboard.mailerlite.com/forms/57518/610902789387725
share

Also by E.L. Bates

Whitney and Davies
   Magic Most Deadly
   Glamours and Gunshots
   Death by Disguise
   Magic & Mayhem (short story collection)
   While Shepherds Watch (a Christmas novella)

From the Shadows (a cozy space adventure)

Writing as Louise Bates
   Pauline Gray Investigates